Praise for the Novels of Lynn Viehl

The Lords of the Darkyn Novels

Nightborn

"Lynn Viehl is an amazing storyteller. *Nightborn* strikes through the heart with stunning strength, creating an addictive, complex world—and characters who are so alive that turning the last page will make you feel as though you're losing the best friends you wish you could have. Especially in a fight." —*New York Times* bestselling author Marjorie M. Liu

"A clever, rip-roaring adventure from start to finish with more twists and turns than a back road in the French countryside. Loved it, loved it."
—#1 *New York Times* bestselling author Patricia Briggs

The Kyndred Novels

Dreamveil

"The Kyndred story line is fast-paced throughout as the action never stops. Yet the cast is strong, as is the romantic triangle containing a delightful, unexp████d late twist.... This urban fantasy is pure mag██ ████ ██ Best Reviews

"Viehl's imagin█████ ████████ ██ ███ as she once more explo██ █████████ ███████████ netically altered Kyndr██ ████ █████ ███████ ███ rets, treachery, and betr███ ████ ██████████ ██ ████ssing. With multiple stor██ ████ ███████ ██████, the revelations come at a br██ ██ ███ █████ans take note: This new Kyndred nove█ ████ ██ ███████y unusual turn."
—*Romantic Times*

Shadowlight

"Hot enough to keep anyone warm on a cold winter's night." —*Romance Reviews Today*

continued ...

NIGHTBRED

LORDS OF THE DARKYN

Lynn Viehl

A SIGNET BOOK

SIGNET
Published by New American Library, a division of
Penguin Group (USA) Inc., 375 Hudson Street,
New York, New York 10014, USA
Penguin Group (Canada), 90 Eglinton Avenue East, Suite 700, Toronto,
Ontario M4P 2Y3, Canada (a division of Pearson Penguin Canada Inc.)
Penguin Books Ltd., 80 Strand, London WC2R 0RL, England
Penguin Ireland, 25 St. Stephen's Green, Dublin 2,
Ireland (a division of Penguin Books Ltd.)
Penguin Group (Australia), 250 Camberwell Road, Camberwell, Victoria 3124,
Australia (a division of Pearson Australia Group Pty. Ltd.)
Penguin Books India Pvt. Ltd., 11 Community Centre, Panchsheel Park,
New Delhi - 110 017, India
Penguin Group (NZ), 67 Apollo Drive, Rosedale, Auckland 0632,
New Zealand (a division of Pearson New Zealand Ltd.)
Penguin Books (South Africa) (Pty.) Ltd., 24 Sturdee Avenue,
Rosebank, Johannesburg 2196, South Africa

Penguin Books Ltd., Registered Offices:
80 Strand, London WC2R 0RL, England

First published by Signet, an imprint of New American Library,
a division of Penguin Group (USA) Inc.

First Printing, December 2012
10 9 8 7 6 5 4 3 2 1

 REGISTERED TRADEMARK—MARCA REGISTRADA

Printed in the United States of America

PUBLISHER'S NOTE
This is a work of fiction. Names, characters, places, and incidents either are the
product of the author's imagination or are used fictitiously, and any resemblance
to actual persons, living or dead, business establishments, events, or locales is
entirely coincidental.

The publisher does not have any control over and does not assume any responsibility for author or third-party Web sites or their content.

For Dad:
I love you,
I miss you,
I love you.

And in the midst of this wide quietness
A rosy sanctuary will I dress
With the wreath'd trellis of a working brain,
With buds, and bells, and stars without a name,
With all the gardener Fancy e'er could feign,
Who breeding glowers, will never breed the same:
And there shall be for thee all soft delight
That shadowy thought can win,
A bright torch, and a casement ope at night,
To let the warm Love in!

—John Keats, "Ode to Psyche," 1820

Chapter 1

"You're a pretty lad," Etienne Guelard, the swordsman wielding three feet of razor-sharp, copper-clad steel, told Jamys Durand. "One step more and you'll not be."

Murmured wagers swept round the loose circle of half-naked onlookers as their watchful eyes shifted from the massive brute waiting inside the warriors' circle to Jamys, who stood just outside the perimeter.

Beyond the sprawling compound of Baucent, nightfall had drawn its deep amethyst cloak across the mountains; its gilded edges had narrowed the glittering gold of sunset to a silken fringe of tangerine. November had sharpened the wind from crisp to cutting, and turned to diamond density every drop of moisture touched by its wintry breath. Ten thousand acres of evergreens stood guard among the bare, leafless branches and trunks of kin that the long, dark months had already sent to sleep.

Jamys kept his back turned against the modernized

version of a medieval mansion. Tonight he could not retreat to the safety of his father's house.

The mortal architect who had been commissioned to
design the mountain fortress of Baucent had never understood the need for the broad, walled space at the
back of the main house, or why the owner had vetoed
any landscaping for it. The human had not been told that
the space would be called the lists, or that it would serve
as the training area for the stronghold's garrison of warriors. To the architect, it had been merely a football-field-
size rectangle of packed dirt.

"Don't hurt the boy, Tien," one of the guards called
out from his watch post above the lists. "The master will
have your head."

Being goaded about his adolescent appearance never
aggravated Jamys; as an immortal Darkyn he had lived
with his youthful form for more than seven centuries. He
had gone to his mortal grave before he had matured, and
since rising to walk the night, he had never aged another
day. He would forever look like a boy of seventeen.

It did not, however, make him a boy.

He ignored the voices as he measured his opponent's
readiness. Tien's scent, as sharp and clean as lemongrass,
enveloped the air around him. Although he had threatened to spoil Jamys's face, Tien had dug in his heels and
held his wrist ready to turn his weapon to a specific
thrusting angle; he would attack first with a jab to the
upper arm. Jamys had watched all the men practicing,
and knew Tien favored disabling to disarm an opponent.
That practice made him the boldest and most effective
member of the garrison's front line.

That knowledge provided Jamys with a distinct advantage. Because he trained alone or with his father, the men of the garrison had never seen him spar or fight.

"Challenge night is for the warriors of the *jardin*, not coddled whelps. Is this not so, men?" Although he spoke to the crowd, Tien never took his eyes off Jamys. "Did not your sire inform you of this? Or are you as deaf as you are dumb?"

The casual insult effectively rendered silent the men surrounding the circle. All of them knew that torture at the hands of their enemies had deprived Jamys of his ability to speak and, for a time, his mind. He had not realized they still believed him mute, however.

No wonder Tien employed his own tongue so freely; he assumed Jamys couldn't respond in kind—or repeat his insults to their master.

Jamys could speak now, but despite long hours of solitary practice he still could not speak quickly or with any ease. It was simpler to remain silent and use his ability to speak through the mortal servants of the keep to convey his wishes. After tonight he would have to rethink that.

"Lord Jamys," Coyan, the garrison captain, spoke in a gentle tone. "If you will return tomorrow sunset, I will be glad to practice with you."

"Our lord shall never give you leave to breathe hard on him, Coy." Tien made an impatient sound. "Go back to the house, whelp. You have wasted enough of my night."

The scent of sandalwood shed by Jamys's own skin quickly overwhelmed the lemon-scented air inside the ring. For the object of his desires he could bear any amount of insolence or derision. Being reminded of the weight of his father's love, however, was almost enough to provoke him to recklessness.

Almost enough.

Jamys stepped over the line, turning on the toe of his boot and arching away from the dark metal blade that punched through the air his right arm no longer occupied. As Tien swung round to follow through, Jamys switched his grip on his sword from right to left, using the flat of the blade to deliver a heavy blow to the back of the bigger man's broad shoulder.

As the men shouted and Tien staggered, Jamys moved in behind him, forcing him to spin again while still unsteady. That provided Jamys the opportunity to kick the sword from Tien's hand and hook his leg to knock him on his ass. He poised the tip of his own sword against the bigger man's septum.

All the voices, movements, and sounds within the lists went as still as Tien himself.

Jamys regarded him. "Pretty nose."

Some of the men uttered low chuckles. Tien's eyes widened, and he swallowed before he said, "I like it."

"Then concede, you idiot," Coyan advised him, "before you lose that, too."

Jamys held the blade for another long moment before he lowered it and offered his free hand to Tien.

The warrior seized Jamys's slim hand with his huge paw and touched his brow to the knuckles. "The circle is yours, Lord Durand."

"Jamys." He pulled Tien to his feet and returned his blade to him before he scanned the grinning faces around them. "Next."

Clashing steel, shuffling boots, and grunts of effort filled the next several hours, and after the sky had gone black and the final challenger had conceded his bout, Jamys stood alone in the circle.

Coyan stepped up to the line, but he didn't cross it. "My men are drilled every night. They are not permitted leave nor rest until they have satisfied me that they are able and ready to defend our lord and this household. On this I have prided myself. Now you step into our midst, wreak absolute havoc, and defeat my finest. I wager you have been watching us from the house for some time."

Jamys inclined his head.

"You are your father's son, my lord." He offered one of his rare smiles before he performed a deep bow of respect. "And the night is yours. What would you have of us?"

Jamys knew well the garrison's tradition of awarding a boon to the last warrior left standing. It was the primary reason he had come to the circle.

"He doesn't want my nose," Tien joked, and then winced as Coyan cuffed the back of his head. "Well, he doesn't."

"I would train with you," Jamys said, taking care with each word. "For battle, and command."

"Aye, my lord. We can prepare you for battle, aye." Coyan's eyes shifted toward the house. "But command is the realm of the master."

"Glad I am to hear it." A massive form separated from a shadowed corner, and the warriors made way as Thierry Durand walked toward them. Flickering light from the burning torches traced the scowl that made harsh his strong, handsome features, and glittered in the black slits of his eyes. Before he reached the ring, the power he shed, which smelled like a field of gardenias being burned, blotted out every other scent in the air.

Jamys remained in the circle until his father took Coyan's place. Only when Thierry folded his arms did he step outside and bow. "Good evening, Father."

"Is that what it is?" The suzerain inspected the ducked heads of his garrison. "I am of a rather different opinion."

Tien stepped forward. "The boy came to the circle tonight well prepared, Master. His arm is fair magic. He bested me in the space of ten heartbeats."

"I counted five," another brave soul muttered.

Thierry, who towered over all the men of the garrison, divested Tien of his sword in less than a blink. "Copper on steel."

Coyan shuffled his feet. "We fight with only the weapons that can harm us, my lord."

"Indeed." The suzerain eyed Tien. "And if you had thrust careless, Etienne, and cut off my son's magical arm? The boy is not a warrior."

"He fights like one," Tien had the nerve to say.

"Is this so?" Thierry looked ready to kill the swordsman. "Had you prevailed, would you have sought boon from me for mutilating my only child? The Brethren never did."

"No need," Jamys said before Tien could answer. "They had it from my mother."

The pain that replaced the anger in Thierry's eyes proved too much for Jamys to bear; he strode to the armory to return his sword to the weapons master. From there he retreated to the house, avoiding the servants on his way to the curving staircase that led to his chambers in the north tower.

He didn't notice the scent of ripe apples until he encountered the petite brunette sitting on the bottom step.

She stood as he approached, and twisted her hands together.

"I tried to keep him occupied," Jema Shaw told him. "But after three hours he figured it out."

That his stepmother had guessed his intentions and tried to help him didn't surprise Jamys; little escaped Jema's shrewd gaze. She also carried the same unseen scars on her soul, thanks to her own greedy, murderous mother, so she understood what his father could not.

"I could talk to him," she offered.

He shook his head, pausing to kiss her cheek before he climbed the stairs.

The top two floors of the tower had been designed as living space independent of the main house, and provided all the physical comforts as well as a panoramic view of the surrounding countryside. Jamys had gradually rid his rooms of most of the furnishings to create more open space. During the day he took his rest on the low, simple bed that occupied the lower floor, where custom electric shutters lowered to seal sunlight from the room.

The top floor served as his private retreat, the one place in the stronghold where he felt completely at ease. Here he had installed a compact computer array and entertainment center, although lately he had been interested only in researching those areas of America that had not yet been assigned to a lord paramount as official *jardin* territories. With all the refugees fleeing from Europe to the States, the land available had begun to dwindle rapidly. In less than a year there would be only deserts and wastelands left unclaimed.

The rapid dispersal of the territories still open to rule was not the only obstacle Jamys had to overcome.

Michael Cyprien, the seigneur who ruled over North America, decided all matters of suzerainty.

The Durands owed everything to Cyprien, who had provided them with sanctuary after they had been freed from the Brethren's torture chambers. His *sygkenis*, Dr. Alexandra Keller, had used her healing skills to repair their broken bodies. And while both Thierry and Jamys had been out of their minds with grief and rage, Cyprien had not exercised his right to end their misery, but had instead gone to great lengths to bring them both back to sanity.

Throughout their mortal and immortal lives Cyprien and Thierry had been as close as brothers; even during the worst of times that affection had never wavered. If Thierry asked Cyprien to deny Jamys the chance to rule his own *jardin*, Michael would not hesitate to do so.

The south-facing window gave Jamys a direct view of the lists, which were now empty, and the line of mountains that lay against the horizon like great storm clouds fallen to earth.

Beyond the mountains lay seven territories, six occupied by the finest of Cyprien's lords paramount. The seventh and most southern belonged to Lucan, once master assassin to High Lord Richard Tremayne, formerly Cyprien's bitterest adversary, and still one of the deadliest Kyn lords in the world.

Lucan commanded a garrison of highly trained, utterly lethal warriors as well as a small army of clever and resourceful human servants, and lived with his *sygkenis*, Samantha Brown, a homicide detective and one of the handful of modern females who had survived the transition from mortal to Darkyn. Yet each night only one among his household occupied Jamys's thoughts.

Christian.

He closed the shutters as her name resonated through his bones.

It was no mystery to him that he needed a woman, and there were certainly enough at hand to be had. As long as he was careful with them, he could use any mortal female within his father's household for blood or pleasure or both. Nearly every one of the unattached women servants had made it clear they would not object to his attentions.

An ample supply for an impossible demand, for while he appreciated the warmth and generosity offered, none of them were the girl he wanted.

Jamys went to the computer, where he pulled up the file he had begun compiling a year ago.

He knew some facts about Chris Lang. The mortal female had been born in Fort Lauderdale in 1990, and was now twenty-one years old. After her mother's death six years past, she had been made a ward of the state and placed in foster care. She had escaped it four months later and disappeared, resurfacing three years later when she had sublet an apartment next to Samantha Brown's.

A year after that, Chris officially took employ as assistant manager of Infusion, a Goth nightclub that served as the public facade of Lucan's stronghold. Unofficially she served as Samantha Brown's personal assistant. She did not belong to a *tresoran* family, but she was trusted as much as one of the mortal allies who for generations had provided loyal, unwavering service to the Kyn.

After Thierry sent him to Lucan three years ago to recover from his final surgery, Jamys had spent a few precious days in Chris's company. At one point during his stay he had been implicated in the murders of several humans, and from the beginning only Chris had refused to believe him responsible.

You think you don't need help, fine. But I'm the only person who knows for real that you're innocent.

While Samantha and even Lucan had viewed Jamys with suspicion, Chris had instead allied herself with him, following and then rescuing him when he was attacked by one of the real murderer's revenants. To help heal his wounds, she had even fed him her own blood.

No pictures of Christian Lang existed on the Internet; not that Jamys required an image to remind him of her gamine features. Beneath a cap of fine hair she dyed in the most outlandish shades, she had large, bright eyes the color of a midnight sapphire, a pert nose, and a mouth that readily curved into the most dazzling and fetching of smiles.

Jamys remembered everything about her: the touch of her hand, the shimmer of her laugh, the taste of her lips. Every word she had said to him remained in his heart, especially those she had used for a final, mocking warning.

You'll be lucky if I don't turn into a love-starved groupie and start stalking you.

When Jamys had left Lucan's territory, he had been convinced that Chris was falling in love with him. Since returning to his father's house, he had waited patiently for her to make good on her comical threat. When her first e-mail arrived, he had expected her to ask him to come back, or permission for her to visit his father's stronghold, or anything that would assure him that he was not mistaken about her regard for him. Instead she'd relayed an amusing story about accompanying Lucan to a mall for holiday shopping, becoming separated, and then finding him trapped by a crowd in a shop filled with china and lead crystal wares.

Jamys had no gift with words, and had no wish to make a fool of himself, so he had kept his reply brief and reserved. The silence that followed had crushed his hopes for months until Chris sent another note asking for his opinion of a Web site she had created for Lucan's club.

Since then they had corresponded a dozen times by e-mail. Chris wrote in a friendly, casual tone, and her wry wit and shrewd observations always made him smile, but she never once spoke seriously of herself or her feelings.

Even if Jamys knew Chris cared for him, and would welcome his affections in return, love was nearly all he could offer her. His position in his father's household provided him with whatever he needed but afforded him no status or privileges. As Thierry's son he was not required to pledge his oath of loyalty to his father, and since he served no other Kyn lord, he had no rank. As such, he had nothing with which to tempt Chris into leaving Lucan and Samantha to make her life with him.

Jamys couldn't leave Baucent to pledge himself to another Kyn lord and attain the rank of garrison warrior; Thierry would never permit it. The only way he could escape his father's overprotective, smothering love was to become his equal: to be named lord paramount, become a suzerain, and acquire his own territory.

Three gentle taps sounded on his chamber door. "Lord Jamys?"

He went to the door and briefly considered bolting it before discarding the spiteful impulse. If he wished his father to regard him as a man, then it was time he began behaving like one.

The manservant waiting outside had a carefully blank expression and worried eyes. "My lord, the suzerain has taken a mount and ridden out from the stronghold."

Jamys nodded and began to close the door, but the mortal held up his hand.

"A courier from Ireland arrived just after your father left," he said. "He brings a message from the high lord."

Chapter 2

Infusion Nightclub
Alenfar Stronghold
Fort Lauderdale, Florida

Thousands of tiny, bloodred lights glittered from the shadowy corners of the nightclub, shedding their scant demonic light over the crowded dance floor. Enormous wall-mounted speakers wrapped Amy Lee's voice around every other sound, every inch of skin, every drawn breath. Sharp-eyed bartenders dressed in scarlet vests over black muscle tees served up Tanya Huff Highballs, Anne Rice Raspberry Smashes, and the latest dark fantasy authorial cocktail craze, Larissa Ione Imperials, classic martinis sporting two black cherries skewered by a miniature silver caduceus.

The club's patrons, all dressed to depress in the latest Gothwear, milled in affected boredom beneath the big-screen televisions soundlessly projecting an assortment of vampire films. Fake blood streaked across the powdered flesh exposed by deliberately tattered purple satin bustiers; porcelain veneer fangs appeared and disappeared behind black painted lips. Two massively muscled bouncers stood watch at the only entrance, from which a long line of leather-and-lace-clad hopefuls waited for someone inside to leave and give them a chance to be admitted.

Thanks to discreetly mounted security cameras, Christian Lang could watch them all from the quiet confines of her small, soundproofed office at the back of the club. But tonight she barely gave the wall of monitors across from her desk a glance as she dealt with the latest delivery disaster.

"I ordered *forty* boxes of the copper-jacketed rounds and *sixty* of the standard nine," Chris told the receiver tucked between her cheek and shoulder. "You shipped me four and six. Where are the other ninety?"

"We're out of standard nine, so they're on back order," the supplier said. "The copper's a custom job; they'll take three more weeks minimum."

"Wait a minute." Chris stopped shuffling through packing slips. "That isn't what you told me when I placed the order."

"What can I say, lady? Every time Homeland Security elevates the threat potential, my inventory starts flying out the door." The man didn't even try to sound contrite. "You got to be patient."

"No problem." Chris swiveled around to open the middle drawer of her filing cabinet and took out the vendor's order confirmation. "When can I expect the reimbursement check?"

"What are you talking about?"

"Read the terms of the bid," she suggested. "There's a ten percent penalty surcharge for every day the delivery is late. Which means you will be paying us the entire bid amount, plus twenty-one days times ten percent of the order. . . . Do you want me to calculate that total for you?"

"You can't do that." The sound of paper flipping came over the line. "I didn't bid on this job to pay you."

"Page seven paragraph fourteen says you will." Chris glanced at her calendar. "So I'll need either the penalty check or the rest of the ammo by Friday at the latest." As the supplier began to swear, she held the phone away from her ear. Another button lit up. "Have a wonderful evening." She punched the button. "Christian Lang."

"Sorry I am to bother you, lass." Turner, the master of the armory, sounded grim. "But we've a situation brewing with the continentals that wants sorting out. Sooner rather than later."

Chris translated Turner's diplomatic jargon into plain English: There was trouble with visiting Kyn, probably the group Burke had warned her were coming in from Europe. Stronghold protocol required all warriors to be escorted to the armory upon arrival in order to surrender their weapons. "But they just got here."

"Aye," Turner said, "and we'd be much pleased to see them go."

The weapons master, a congenial Irishman who Chris knew got along with everyone, sounded ready to personally show them the door, too. "How bad is this brew, Mr. Turner?"

"Blood's not been shed," he said. "Yet."

This was just getting better and better. "What caused the situation?"

"Someone posted a summons from the high lord for all to read." Turner muttered something under his breath before he added, "Soon as they did, the boasting and insulting commenced."

Lucan and Samantha had not yet come down from the penthouse suite; Rafael, Lucan's second-in-command, was currently in the islands training their newest warriors. Herbert Burke, Lucan's *tresora* and the highest-ranked mortal in the *jardin*, had left an hour ago to pick up a courier from the airport.

That meant she would have to handle this. Her first major *tresoran* intervention. Chris ran her fingers along the chain she wore, shifting the weight of the silver cross hanging under her blouse. "I'll be right there."

To get to the service elevators, Chris had to walk through the club, and braced herself for the blast of music that hit her in the face as soon as she stepped outside. Now that the *Twilight* craze had leveled out, she didn't spot too many wannabe Edwards or Bellas, but there were plenty of *True Blood* groupies doing their best to clone Sookie, Bill, Tara, and Eric. A group of sullen Anne Rice diehards, still clinging to their repro lace-cuff and velvet-jacket decadence, occupied one corner, while here and there the undecided stuck to their slinky noncommittal club wear while eagerly flashing their fake canines at anyone who strayed from their vamp herd of choice.

Chris sometimes wondered how the patrons would react if they ever discovered that the hulking, bland-faced bouncers stationed in and outside the club could show them some very real, very lethal seven-hundred-year-old fang.

At least the mood of the crowd seemed less aggressive tonight, Chris thought. On Friday a couple of Lestats had bumped padded shoulders while getting their Louis red wine coolers, and neither had been satisfied by exchanging sneered insults. As soon as the first drink was hurled, the guards had moved in, but a glass to the skull of the other Lestat had resulted in an ugly gash that un-surprisingly didn't heal spontaneously. The guards had removed the pair before the sight and smell of blood had riled up the crowd too much, but the mess left behind had forced Chris to close down the bar for the night.

She spotted a glitter on the carpet by one of the bar-stools and stopped to pick up a piece of broken glass one of the cleaners had missed. Beside her, a wannabe Elvira stretched out her cheap stack boots under Chris's nose. As Chris looked up, the girl used an arm covered with gleaming tribal ink to elbow her chunky companion. "Look, Heather. I think it's an Avon Lady."

Three years ago no one would have even noticed her, but now Chris looked out of place. She didn't have time to play a round of I'm-Legit-and-You're-Not, especially with someone who thought her tragic home perm, too-small fishnet tights, and pot metal bling made her the Queen of the Damned.

She straightened, pocketing the broken shard as she nodded at the girl's upper arm. "One of your tats is peeling off."

Like most Darkyn strongholds, Alenfar had two sides: public and private. Aboveground Lucan maintained the nightclub, the business offices, the guest quarters, the workout rooms, and the penthouse, all of which appeared as modern and functional as any beachfront property. In the expansive network of tunnels and chambers Lucan had built two levels belowground were the real and very private workings of the *jardin*, which included the gar-rison's quarters, training facilities, the weapons forge and armory, the assembly hall, the infirmary, as well as a dozen passages to and from the suzerain's surrounding properties.

Once inside the elevator Chris opened a panel and entered her pass code into a small keypad, which overrode the lift's normal operating functions and sent the elevator down two floors. When the cab stopped, she keyed in a second code to open the doors, and stepped out into what appeared to be a half-empty storage room.

Two guards in full battle armor stood flanking the reinforced steel door on the other side of the room. Both studied her before they lowered their automatic weapons.

"Good evening, Miss Christian." Aldan, a behemoth with a scarred face, braided silver mane, and laser beam blue eyes, inclined his head.

"Hey, Dan." She smiled at him. "I need to go to the armory and see Mr. Turner."

"Would you be needing an escort, Miss Chris?" That came from the other guard, Glenveagh, who was as tall and slim as Aldan was broad and bulky, and wore his blazing red hair in a fiery skullcap.

"No, thanks, Glen, I'm good." She avoided looking directly into his big green eyes, which was the most polite way to discourage the interest of a Kyn warrior.

Aldan used one hand to open the door, which was too heavy for a mortal to budge, but stopped her with a hand as the distant sound of shouting echoed through the tunnel. "Mayhap I will walk you in myself."

Chris would have liked nothing better than to go into the armory with Aldan at her side; the big warrior had a fearsome rep among the garrison. But if Turner had needed a guard, he would have sent for one, and if she kept hiding behind the guys while doing her job, no one would ever respect her as a *tresora*.

"That's okay, Dan. It's just a minor misunderstanding with the newbies," she told him. "I've got it."

He gave her a long, shrewd look before he nodded slowly. "We shall leave the door open until you return."

She also had a valuable resource that the guards didn't, one she kept on speed dial. As she walked down the hall, she tucked her wireless headset over her ear, covering it with her hair before she pressed 2 on her mobile.

"Realm Management," a cool voice answered the line.

"Good evening, Lady Jayr." She kept her voice to a murmur. "How are things in Orlando?"

"As vexing as ever. Aedan wishes to open another theme park, and does not believe me when I say modern mortals have no desire to attend Medieval Torture World." Jayr mac Byrne, the only female suzeraina in the world, had been one of the first Kyn to befriend Chris. "You are well? Why are you whispering?"

"Lucan and Sam are occupied upstairs, Burke is at the airport, and we've got a visiting-warrior situation." Chris stopped in her tracks as she heard angry voices spilling out into the hall. "Evidently the men are squabbling over a summons the high lord sent. If you're not too busy, I could use some advice."

"Tell me what you know," Jayr said at once.

Chris quickly related what Turner had said before she added, "I'm almost to the armory now."

"You should have Lucan attend to this, Christian," Jayr scolded. "Whether bound by oath or visiting, all warriors within the stronghold answer to the suzerain."

"If they were actually trying to kill each other, I would," she assured her. "But Turner called me, and as a *tresora* I'm supposed to try to handle it myself first. Okay, I'm here. Let me take a peek at what's happening." She tiptoed up to the open door of the armory and darted a glance around the edge.

"Tell me what you see," the suzeraina urged.

Chris swung back, pressing her shoulder blades to the wall. Now she *had* to whisper. "Ten guys, five on each side. There's a torn piece of paper on the floor between them, and everyone's holding copper swords pointed at each other. No blood, and no one's dead."

"Yet. The master of the armory, where is he?"

"I don't know, I didn't see him." Which could mean anything; he might be staying out of sight, or he could already be dead. Chris felt the seep of her worry widen into a stream of panic. "Maybe I should get the guards."

"*Jardin* sentries are under orders to eliminate all threats," Jayr reminded her. "They will kill your visitors first and ask questions second."

"Okay, no guards." She couldn't let the men fight, but they wouldn't be intimidated by a mere mortal female. It took a lot more to scare the Kyn. "Damn. I wish you were the high lord, Suzeraina."

A startled laugh came over the line. "For that, you would have to cut out my heart, force me to drink the blood of small felines for fifty years, and cause me to sprout a furry manhood."

"Thanks for that visual, my lady." The shouts grew louder, and she knew she needed to go in and shut down this rumble now. "How can I stop this without anyone getting hurt?"

"Given that this ridiculous summons Richard sent out is involved, I think it may be beyond your capabilities, Christian." Jayr sighed. "Call for your lord. Lucan would never expect you to manage this by yourself."

"No, he wouldn't." And that gave her an idea. "I'm going to try something first."

Chris quickly buttoned her blouse up to her collar

before fastening her jacket and smoothing every tendril of hair back from her face. She needed to channel her old DCF caseworker, Miss Audrey, a pleasant-faced grandmother who'd had the disposition of a bipolar rattlesnake. Clenching her back teeth together and pursing her lips, she strode into the armory.

"Mr. Turner," she called out, ignoring the men as she stalked between them. "Where are you?" Keeping her back to them, she took the ammunition invoice out of her jacket and slapped it down on the desk that served as Turner's counter. "Lord Alenfar has a serious problem with this order. Come out here, please."

"You're trying to get yourself gutted?" Jayr demanded over the earpiece.

"The order will have to wait, lass." The weapons master emerged from behind the shelves he was using as cover. "Perhaps you could come back another time."

"This can't wait that long, Mr. Turner," she snapped. "The suzerain needs more copper rounds, immediately, and this vendor has put us on hold. Would you care to tell Lord Lucan that he can't use his weapons because the ammunition is on back order?"

"That's good; our men aren't used to demanding females," Jayr said over the earpiece. "Show no fear or hesitation. Imagine them as squabbling little boys. Which in truth is all they are."

An ugly mutter made Chris turn her head and glare in that direction. "Excuse me, did you want something?"

"Do not drop your eyes or twitch a muscle," Jayr warned. "Whoever started this will challenge your authority now."

"From a mortal?" One of the strange Kyn, a bull-necked beast with spiked brassy hair, offered her a sneer. "What can you do, Pearl Girl?"

"*That* sounds like the instigator," Jayr said.

One that thinks he's a poet, too. Chris imagined biting into a lime, and let her expression match its sourness. "My name is Miss Lang, sir, and I *do* whatever Lord Alenfar *wants*. What is that?" Before anyone could answer, she walked between the men, scooped up the tattered paper, and scanned it. "This is an official summons from the high lord. What's it doing on the floor?"

One of the *jardin* warriors nodded at the visitors. "They tore it down before we could see it."

Another visitor said something ugly in another language.

"He says we took it from them," the *jardin* warrior translated for her, "before they were done with it. But they cannot understand the summons." He nodded at the spike-haired visitor. "Only that one speaks English."

"Is that all?" Chris sighed and eyed the summons. "It says, 'From Richard Tremayne by the Grace of God High Lord of the Darkyn, Chosen Ruler of the Realms, Territories, and Jardins, Defender of Truth and Eternity, to Our right trusty and well-beloved seigneurs, lords and lady paramount, and warriors sworn, Greetings.'" She lifted her head and regarded the visitor's only English speaker. "You can tell them that would be the high lord's way of saying 'Hi, everyone.'"

"I told them what it means," the spike-haired warrior said.

"Good—then you should have no problem translating the rest of this for your friends." She skimmed the first page, reading out loud the important parts. "He writes, 'The Scroll of Falkonera, stolen of late by our

enemies, has been recovered by the guardian Helada.'
Sounds like the thieves fell victim to its death curse. Too
bad for them. He mentions the ages, and how he commissioned the smith Cristophe Noir to forge the scroll,
and so on and so forth."

"Go to the end and read, Miss Christian," one of the
jardin warriors urged. "The bit about the jewels."

"Jewels, jewels." Chris skipped ahead to the final paragraph of the summons. "Here's something. 'We therefore
are well pleased to offer, for the elimination of this grievous threat, recompense to any oath-bound warrior of the
Darkyn who should carry out a search to locate and secure the three gems. To he who successfully concludes
this mission and delivers unto Us all three emeralds, We
shall immediately grant the title of suzerain and rule of
the territory of Ireland, including all present rights, properties, weapons, guards, warriors, and servants appor-
tioned to the Irish *jardin*.'" She barely controlled a wince.
"'Given at Ì Àrd this first day of November in the nine
hundred forty-fifth year of Our reign—'"

"Aye, all of Ireland for the jewels," the spike-haired
visitor crowed, interrupting her. "I've told that to my
brothers as well. In but a handful of days it shall be ours."

"This is not your territory," a *jardin* warrior said. "It is
ours to search."

"Excuse me. Excuse me." Chris had to raise her voice
to be heard over the angry mutters from the rest of the
men. "This territory belongs to Lord Alenfar, and he de-
cides what happens here. All requests to search for anything will be made to him." She turned to the visitors. "If
you have a problem with that, you can take it up with the
suzerain, as he prefers to manage any problems involv-
ing visiting Kyn. Although I will warn you, he takes a

very hands-on approach." She described Lucan's ability to shatter bones and rend flesh with a single touch before she said to the spike-haired warrior, "Make sure your friends understand exactly what I just said."

As the spike-haired warrior sullenly translated her words, the visiting Kyn lowered their weapons, and after a moment the *jardin* warriors did the same.

"Now, if you don't mind, I have to take care of the master's business with Mr. Turner." She nodded at their swords. "Lord Alenfar doesn't allow sparring in the tunnels, and besides that, stronghold visitors are required to disarm upon arrival. You may leave your weapons here; Mr. Turner will take very good care of them." When none of them moved, she took out her mobile from her pocket and held a thumb over the keys. "I can call the suzerain and have him come down here to explain his policy to you. Personally."

The spike-haired warrior translated one final time, and the visitors grudgingly moved one by one to place their blades on the counter.

Chris almost said "thank you" before she swiveled around to face Turner and tap the invoice with an impatient finger. "Now, about this ammunition back order. I checked the terms of the bid, and according to paragraph seven on page fourteen, if the supplier can't deliver on schedule, a penalty charge of . . ."

As she complained about the problem she had already solved upstairs, Chris kept her back toward the men and watched Turner's dour expression. A moment before she became convinced that they'd seen through her act, she heard the sounds of heavy footsteps moving into the corridor.

"Are they gone?" she whispered to Turner.

"Aye."

Chris sagged against the counter. "Thank God."

Jayr chuckled over the earpiece. "Nicely done."

One of the *jardin* warriors went over and slammed shut the door. "You're a clever girl, Miss Christian." He nodded toward her jacket. "Your pocket is chiming."

"Damn." Chris took out her locator, which displayed an electronic dimensional map of the stronghold. A blue light flashed in the reception room on the third floor. "Mr. Burke must be back from the airport." To Jayr, she said, "I have to go, my lady. I really appreciate the help."

"Tell Lucan about this skirmish and the summons," Jayr said, and then added, "When he's in a gentle mood."

"I will, my lady, and thank you again." She switched off the mobile and removed her earpiece, and saw that the *jardin* warriors had also left. "Mr. Turner, you might want to talk to Aldan about scheduling our guys with the new guys for some quality time in the warriors' circle. And while you're at it, arrange for some interpreters for them."

He nodded. "I believe I'll close the armory for the rest of the night as well. Lass," he said when she turned to leave, "what you did charging in here was very brave, but very foolish. None but that no-necked blowhard could understand you. One jab or swipe of the blade, and they would have done you in."

"You're right, I'm human, and blades are not our friends." She bent to pick up one of the swords, and carefully placed it on the counter. Only then did she give him a wink. "But it worked."

Chris hurried back to the elevator, apologizing to Aldan when he tried to stop her. "I'm needed in reception, guys, TTYL."

As she pressed the button for the third floor, Chris heard Aldan ask, "Tee-tee-why . . . what?"

"'Tis a modern spoken code," Glenveagh drawled. "It means she will converse with you anon—"

Once the doors closed, Chris used her mobile to text Sam about the new arrival in reception—Burke always personally notified Lucan—and then walked around in a circle as she shook her hands. For the most part she'd outgrown the really horrible panic attacks of her teenage years, but every now and then anxiety would start trying to creep back into her head, a silent rat that wanted only to gnaw at her confidence and composure until her brain turned to Swiss cheese.

Once she'd made enough money, Chris had gone to a therapist and paid three hundred bucks to have herself tested. The shrink had wanted to know why, but she'd lied and said it was for her job. A week later she'd gone in to get the results.

"You're a little depressed," the shrink had told her as she handed over the typed report. "Of course I can work with you on that."

"Of course." As long as she forked over more hundreds, which she didn't have, so that was a nonissue. "But I'm not psychotic, schizophrenic, bipolar, paranoid, or in any way a danger to myself or others."

The older woman smiled. "No, you're not."

"That should make my boss happy." Chris skimmed the first page. "What's this part about anxiety?"

"You're a very confident, polished young woman . . . on the surface." The shrink's eyes dipped to the cross-shaped bulge under her T-shirt. "We all wear masks, Miss Lang, in order to project what we want the world to see about us. Most of the time it's an idealized version of our true selves. In your case, however, I have gotten a very strong impression of a completely artificial persona. One you've been constructing and perfecting for some time now. And it's not a mask; it's a full-body costume. One I believe you wear to cover the fears that threaten your ability to function."

Chris got to her feet and held up the report. "Can I take this?"

The shrink nodded. "You paid for it. Miss Lang—"

"Not interested," Chris told her before she walked out.

She had gone to the library, however, and borrowed every book she could find on anxiety and how to deal with it. Which was why she now imagined herself as the center of a lotus flower, drifting delicately on a pool of still water. As she tried to float, she remembered the mantra of affirmations she was supposed to say out loud along with the visualization.

"My thoughts are quiet; my mind is clear. I am in control of my emotions, my decisions, and my life. I am filled with confidence. I am blessed with friends. I am rich with hope. I am starting to sound like a bad Hallmark card. Or someone who has taken too many happy pills." So much for the mantra. She really needed to get a new meditation book from the library on her next day off.

Once the doors opened, she stepped out and walked toward the reception room, but stopped in her tracks as soon as she saw the teenage boy standing with Burke in the hall.

The Kyn lord standing beside Burke, Chris absently corrected herself. Jamys Durand hadn't been a teenager since the Dark Ages.

She had written at least two hundred private posts on

her LiveJournal with a thousand minute details about Jamys, so she noticed the changes first. His black hair, which she'd envied and adored, was no longer in that devastatingly edgy who-gives-a-shag; he'd let it grow out so long he now wore it tied back in a ponytail. Under the time-burnished brown leather of his jacket his shoulders and upper arms showcased some serious new muscle, as did the white tee he wore under it. As he handed a scroll to Burke, the front of his jacket opened a few inches more, flashing his now beautifully sculpted abs. His hands looked rougher, harder than she remembered, and he'd left off wearing the gorgeous old ring with his family's crest in silver. Her gaze drifted down the long legs, which the fitted cut of his plain black trousers showed to be more powerful than lean now. No, now he looked like he could run a couple of New York City marathons before breakfast.

She saved his face for last, not that she needed to ogle it. The young, handsome features were just as she had kept them in her memory: the black slashes of his eyebrows, the angular symmetry of his cheekbones and jaw, the imperial nose, the full, almost passionate mouth that rarely smiled but always made her think of kissing. When other mortals looked at Jamys, they saw a boy, because he had been a teenager when he'd made the transition from human to Darkyn, and like his body his face would be forever young. But Chris saw more; she saw the shadow of the man he would have been, lurking just beneath the surface. A big, dangerous, definitely scary man, exactly like his father.

Chris saw his head start to turn toward her and darted around the corner out of sight. She covered her mouth with her hands, trying at the same time to take in some air, but her lungs were already full and waiting to exhale. She couldn't remember how to breathe for a full five seconds.

Why is he here? He can't be here. I'm not ready.

She'd expected time to plan and prepare, to buff and polish herself, to show him what he'd been missing for the last three years. She'd never be gorgeous or heart-stopping—Chris had accepted that long ago—but she'd grown past cute and quirky, and had been carefully cultivating an Audrey Hepburn–Winona Ryder look that made the most of what she had. She'd given up on Goth and gone for sleek and chic, and had an entire wardrobe of the right looks, all of which were now sitting at home in her apartment.

I can't let him see me like this. I'll bore him to death at first sight. The silver chain around her neck sawed against her skin, and she looked down to see she was clutching the cross through her blouse so tightly the edges bruised the insides of her fingers. *Or he'll think I'm crazy.*

Like an answer to her prayers, her mobile buzzed in her pocket. She rushed to the end of the hall and stepped inside the freight elevator, closing the doors before she answered it. "Christian Lang."

"Miss Christian? It's Connie." Burke's receptionist sounded nervous. "I have a video call from Italy waiting on hold."

"Then you're costing them a lot of money, Connie." Chris frowned. "Are they calling for Lord Lucan?"

"No, miss. It's for you."

Chapter 3

"Why are you dressed and out of bed?"

"I have to go to work." Samantha Brown smiled as the scent of night-blooming jasmine crept into the bathroom where she stood brushing her hair. "And they don't let me do my job in the nude."

Once the domain of corporate executives, the top two floors of the Alenfar Building had been renovated into luxurious penthouse accommodations. Wraparound panels, made of specially reinforced safety glass, provided stunning views of Fort Lauderdale, from the skyscrapers that soared into the skyline to the west to the wide ribbon of shell-speckled amber sand to the east that bordered the gilded jade edge waters of the Atlantic Ocean.

Three years ago Sam had never imagined living in a high-rise penthouse. The salary she made as a homicide detective had barely covered her living expenses and the rent for a small apartment in a decent neighborhood. It didn't bother her; she hadn't joined the force to get rich.

Sam was still a cop, although everything else had changed. Including her life, which thanks to her bioengineered DNA and a transfusion of vampire blood was now virtually immortal.

She tried not to think too much about that, or the fact that the man who had saved her life was one of the deadliest creatures on the planet.

As Sam gathered up her straight, dark brown hair with an elastic band, a shadow loomed behind her, and huge hands covered by black velvet gloves reached around to unfasten the waistband of her trousers.

"I'm only working a half shift," she said as she straightened her ponytail. "So I'll be home in a few hours. Stop that."

Cool, wickedly talented lips drifted down the side of her throat. "Call in sick."

"My boss is a *tresora*, and he knows I don't get sick." She shrugged into the leather straps of her shoulder holster. Feeling the pointed edges of his *dents acérées* against her skin made her sigh. "No biting. You'll get blood on my collar and I'll have to change."

"No." He nipped the lobe of her ear. "You won't."

"Lucan." She turned around to face six and a half feet of naked, aroused male, and let him gather her against the front of him. Mainly because it helped block the incredible view to the south.

Not that the view to the north was any less impressive. A lion's mane of corn silk hair framed the heartrending, impossibly beautiful face of a fallen angel. The thin, almost cruel line of his mouth balanced the outrageous splendor of his features, while his ghost-gray eyes simmered with sensual knowledge, as if the man could provide every pleasure ever dreamed by a woman.

Which he could, something else she didn't need to dwell on right now.

"I want you, and I love you," she said, putting her hand against the broad muscular vault of his chest, "but if you make me late for work again, I'm going to hurt you."

"Hurt me exactly how?" His golden brows rose. "Your gun is still over on the nightstand. You don't carry a blade. Clouting me on the head will only bruise your knuckles."

"I heal fast."

"So do I." He brushed his lips over her ear, lowering his voice. "I know. You can bite *me*."

It wasn't only the suggestion that sent a shivery thrill through her. Just the whisper of his breath on her skin made her throat tighten and her insides ache. If they had been a human couple, by now they probably would have settled into a comfortable, routine relationship. But even after six years, looking up into Lucan's silver eyes made time rewind, as if this were the very first time he'd touched her.

It delighted her. It worried her. More than anything, it *baffled* her. "Are we always going to be this intense?"

"One can only pray." One velvet-covered fingertip traced the full crescent of her bottom lip. "It's the same for me, love," he murmured. "I can never have enough of you."

A discreet chime from the door in the front foyer effectively broke the spell, and Sam eased out of Lucan's arms. "That's probably Burke." She whisked a kiss against his jawline before she slipped around him and went to retrieve her gun and jacket. "I'll see you later."

"Samantha." He waited for her to look back at him. "If you've not returned by midnight, I will come and get you."

That he would. Lucan didn't make threats; he made promises.

As Sam had suspected, Lucan's *tresora* stood politely waiting in the foyer. "Hello, Herbert. How's it going?"

"Very busy tonight—thank you, my lady." Burke darted a look past her before he asked, "Has the suzerain risen yet?"

"Oh, yeah. He's up." She took hold of his arm. "Why don't you come downstairs with me for a few minutes. He needs some time to . . . settle down."

Burke winced. "Much as I wish I could, my lady, I must relay news. A group of Kyn has just arrived from Europe and they seek an audience with our lord."

"More refugees." Lucan appeared beside Sam, his big frame clad in black trousers and a full-sleeved white shirt he was still fastening. "Does Cyprien intend to send to my doorstep every immortal made homeless by the Brethren?"

"I cannot say, my lord," Burke said. "But I am happy to report that Lord Jamys Durand has just arrived from North Carolina."

"Thierry's son?" Lucan stopped buttoning his shirt. "Why has he come to me? His father made no mention of a visitation when last we spoke."

"He did not provide me with any details, my lord, but he travels alone." Burke glanced at Samantha. "He also asked to see you, my lady."

"I've really got to run." Sam checked her watch. "Tell Jamys I'll catch him later."

As Sam took the elevator down to the first floor, she

wondered how many of the Kyn refugees Lucan would be expected to absorb into their *jardin*. Since the Brethren had stepped up their efforts to drive the Kyn out of Europe, hundreds of the immortals had crossed the Atlantic seeking sanctuary from their American counterparts. Michael Cyprien assigned unoccupied territories to a select few suzerains he trusted, but the majority were sent to existing *jardins*, where nearly all were added to the ranks of the household or the garrison. Now and then old grudges between the American and European Kyn made absorption impossible, which forced Cyprien to send along those who could not be placed to the seigneurs in South America, Asia, or Scandinavia.

From what Burke had told Lucan yesterday, this group of fifteen had come from the same *jardin* on the border of France and Italy, and were the survivors of a Brethren attack that had killed their suzerain, his household, and most of their garrison. Like the others that had come before them, for a time they'd probably be short-tempered, self-defensive, and prone to acts of stupidity. Lucan had been sending the ones he wanted to keep down to the island he owned in the Bahamas, where his seneschal, Rafael, would work with them until they were ready to be integrated with the rest of the stronghold's garrison.

Sam didn't care to get involved in *jardin* business, but this latest group had shown up with little warning. Something seemed off about this, enough to make her reach out and press the button for the third floor.

She'd just have a look at the new guys and then head in to work.

Inside the reception room Sam glanced at Lucan and Burke, who had arrived ahead of her, before she scanned the faces of the visiting Kyn. Collectively they should have resembled a mob of male models waiting for a photo shoot, but centuries of training and working as warriors and guards had developed their musculature to brutal perfection.

"Suzerain Lucan, I am Vander, appointed by Seigneur Cyprien as leader of these men." A man who vaguely resembled a punk-rock bull stepped forward and bent forward, bowing so low his bristle-brush hair nearly touched the floor. "My brothers do not speak English, so they wish me to thank you for granting us an audience. If I may, I will make known to you the names of my companions."

Lucan took his time silently assessing the group before he finally inclined his head, and Vander began the formal introductions.

Burke left Lucan to join Sam. "My lady, Lord Durand awaits in the next room, if you have a moment to greet him."

"Yeah, I do." Sam's mobile beeped, and she unclipped it from her belt and checked the screen, which displayed a homicide call from dispatch. "No, I don't."

She debated whether to tell Lucan, but her lover was in the process of admiring a neck chain with a glittering gold medallion hanging from it. Visiting Kyn always brought expensive gifts as tribute, which Sam considered unnecessary and even a little silly. Lucan, on the other hand, had been universally despised by his kind before he'd become a suzerain. While he always pretended not to care about the show of respect, Sam knew it gave him a lot of satisfaction.

As her phone beeped again, Sam made a face at Burke. "I'll say hi before I go, but would you mind asking

Chris to keep Jamie company until I get back? Last time he was here, they became pretty good friends."

Burke nodded. "I'm sure Miss Christian will be happy to look after Lord Durand."

The *tresora* escorted Sam to one of the smaller meeting rooms, where the scent of warm sandalwood colored the air. It came from Jamys Durand, who was standing at the window and looking down at the sea.

"It's still not too cold if you want to go for a swim," Sam said.

"No bathing costume." Jamys smiled as he came to bow before her.

"Oh, cut that out." Sam pulled him up into a hug before she drew back and took his hands in hers. "You've been working out, kiddo." She patted some of the new muscle bulging under his sleeve. "And I'd love to catch up, but some idiot killed someone downtown and I got stuck with the call. I'm sorry, but would you mind hanging out with my girl Chris until Lucan frees up? You remember Chris, right?"

"Yes." Jamys's dark brown eyes gleamed. "I remember."

"Excellent. Thanks. I'll see you later." She kissed his cheek. To Burke, she said, "Call if you need me." She hurried out to the elevator.

Chris made herself walk, not run, through the club to Burke's office. For three years she'd immersed herself in learning how to be the perfect *tresora*. Burke had taught her everything about protocol, from how to properly greet a visiting lord (with extreme politeness and deference) to getting rid of unwanted human groupies (with a little eucalyptus-based ointment under the nostrils and a quick trip into the outside air). Lucan's men had helped teach her the defense tactics every *tresora* was expected to know, and she had practiced with every weapon she could handle in the armory until she could use it with complete ease and deadly accuracy. She'd even learned how to tolerate blood loss on a regular basis, just in case one of the Kyn needed to use her in an emergency.

From the beginning Burke had warned her that hard work might not be enough. "Being a *tresora* is more than a position of trust and employment. It is a bloodline obligation, handed down to each generation of a *tresoran* family. I am the thirty-eighth Burke to serve the Darkyn."

"Back in the Dark Ages, they had to go out on a limb and trust the first Burke, right?" When he'd nodded, Chris said, "Then I'm going to be the first Lang."

For Chris, being a *tresora* wasn't only about being with Jamys. For all their superpowers and immortality, most Darkyn held on to their medieval mind-set, and as a result often had trouble coping with the modern world's demands. Chris intended to change that. All of the immortals had to stop living like *Lord of the Rings* extras and learn how to drive, operate computers, and use smart phones. The *tresori*—most of whom were trained in Europe—also had to stop worrying so much about protocols and instead pay more attention to practical matters like securing reliable alternative sources of blood, consolidating and improving the business fronts that concealed the *jardins'* existence, and developing more allies among the local businesses, government, and authorities.

Once she was a *tresora* Chris would never again have an ordinary life, but she was willing to trade that to be with Jamys and help protect him and the rest of the Kyn.

Someday in the future she might even earn her own
spot on the *tresoran* council, where she would make decisions that would enhance and safeguard the Darkyn's
future.

For now she'd be happy with simply being named a
tresora, which had turned out to be much more complicated than she'd expected. Burke had helped her prepare her original petition for recognition, and sent it off
to the *tresoran* council, which had sent back a long list of
requirements Chris had to accomplish under Burke's su-
pervision before her petition would be considered. So
for three years she'd studied and practiced and acquired
the skills necessary to satisfy the *padrones* who ruled
over all *tresori*. She hadn't stopped until Burke had
crossed off the last item on the list, and transmitted his
final progress report on her to the council.

Chris had never wanted, or worked so hard for, anything in her life. They *had* to say yes.

There was only one thing she hadn't told Burke, the
council, or even Sam. As soon as she became a *tresora*,
Chris had no intention of giving her oath of loyalty to
Lucan. Instead she'd planned to offer her service to the
only Darkyn she wanted to spend the rest of her life
with: Jamys Durand.

Naturally she wasn't supposed to be in love with the
Darkyn lord she wanted to serve, she thought as she absently fingered the shard of glass. Burke had explained it
to her before he'd agreed to help her train. *You must
understand what our masters desire from us: absolute loyalty, unshakable trustworthiness, and unwavering devotion to their protection and well-being. The Darkyn have
great affection for mortals, and often form close relation-
ships with their* tresori, *but our bodies are too frail and*

*our existence too brief to make us suitable life compan-
ions. They cannot permit themselves to love us.*

So to them we're like dogs, she'd said. *Except we talk,
take care of the house, and balance their checking accounts.*

Her analogy had startled a laugh out of Burke. *Something like that.*

Herbert Burke's office lay tucked in the corner of the
club, and once Chris made her way through the thinning
crowd of patrons, she took out her key card to release
the electronic lock and let herself inside.

Although Lucan had a reputation for being arrogant
and lofty, no doubt reinforced by the languid contempt
with which he treated most people, the suzerain on his
own handled a good deal of the *jardin's* business concerns. Chris knew he had an active interest in the hundred or so businesses he had purchased since taking
charge of Alenfar, and often came up with clever ways to
make them more profitable.

He also invested in the very latest in computer main-
frames, which controlled satellite terminals stretching
from Jupiter to the Keys and constantly monitored his
various investments. Everyone who worked for him in
the stronghold had been networked with the mainframe.
It also served as the central command center for his
stronghold, and his massive wall of surveillance monitors
kept watch over the club's interior as well as every inch
of the properties surrounding the building. Concealed
behind an Alan Pollack painting at the far end of Burke's
office, a vault held enough weapons for the suzerain to
stage a respectable coup.

*Should Castro's brother decide to invade, we must have
the means with which to blow him back to hell,* Lucan

had told her once. *Besides, one can never have too many AK-47s.*

Chris went to the desk, gingerly lowering herself into Burke's chair before she faced his teleconferencing terminal, on which he still had the Darth Vader screen saver she'd installed for his birthday. When Lucan had seen it for the first time, Burke had told him—with a perfectly straight face, no less—what a huge fan of the Star Wars movies he was.

This was no time for joking around now, though. Chris straightened her jacket, smoothed a hand over her hair, and reached out to input the access code on the terminal's keyboard.

Her hand shook as it hovered over the keys. *I can do this,* she told herself. *It's the only way Jamys and I can be together, and I can make something of myself.*

Vader dissolved, re-forming into the deeply lined face of a gray-haired man in a beautiful Italian suit.

"Good evening, Padrone Ramas," Chris said, silently thanking Burke for making her memorize the faces of all the men on the *tresoran* council. "I'm sorry to have kept you waiting." Lord, she was already apologizing. *Be professional. Show him that you're already a* tresora *in attitude if not name.* "How may I be of service?"

"The council has deliberated over your request to be granted official status within Suzerain Lucan's household," Ramas said. "Is it still your desire to attain the rank of *tresora*?"

"Yes, sir." Under the keyboard shelf she crossed her fingers. "I want that more than anything."

"We appreciate your service to the suzerain, Miss Lang. The letters of recommendation you sent from Mr. Burke and Lady Samantha were most persuasive. Burke indicates that you have successfully completed your training in all aspects of protocol and household management." He steepled his fingers in front of his chin. "However, attaining the rank of *tresora* is no small thing. Only a very few humans are trusted with our masters' secrets and livelihood. Your service would be for the duration of your lifetime, and you would be expected to attend to and protect your lord's well-being and safety, even at the cost of your own. Once you embark on this path, Miss Lang, there is no turning back or changing your mind. If you have any uncertainty, now is the time to act on it."

He made it sound as if she was selling herself into slavery, which in a sense she was. "I understand, Padrone, and I don't have any doubt about this decision. The Darkyn are my family. I'd do anything for them."

"I am glad to hear it, for the council has decided to set you one final task with which to prove your loyalty and resourcefulness." He held up a page of parchment filled with calligraphic writing. "The high lord has sent out this summons to every stronghold in the Americas; it will be delivered by private courier to your master within the next several days. In short, it presents a challenge to every Kyn warrior under rule to recover three jewels known as the Emeralds of Eternity. He who delivers the gems to Lord Tremayne is to be given rule of Ireland."

Chris frowned. Should she tell him that the summons had already arrived, and had nearly started a small war between the garrison and the visitors? Burke had always advised her that whatever happened in the stronghold stayed in the stronghold. "That's very generous of the high lord."

"Were these common emeralds, I would agree with

you. But these particular jewels are very rare, and quite lethal." He put down the summons. "While the council appreciates the high lord's . . . enthusiasm for this treasure hunt he commands, he is unaware of the grievous threat these gems present. Were they to fall into the hands of our enemies, I assure you, their enormous power would be used to exterminate mortal kind. That is something we cannot permit, so your task will be to prevent it."

What he was saying made no sense to her. "Sir, how can I stop the Kyn from looking for the gems?"

"You cannot," Ramas agreed. "But you can find the jewels before the Kyn do, and bring them to the council for safekeeping. I am now transmitting all the data we have about the emeralds; we know that they were stolen from Jamaica in the seventeenth century, possibly by pirates."

"Pirates." This was just getting more bizarre by the minute. "Right."

"I suggest you also make use of the extensive research that has been done by Americans on piracy, shipwrecks, and lost treasure troves," Ramas said. "Of course you cannot tell any of the Darkyn about this, as it could strain relations between the high lord and the council. It could also result in unpleasant repercussions for you."

"Unpleasant." Chris loved Lucan, and was pretty sure he liked having her around, but the former master assassin had a very bad temper. He could also make any living thing he touched literally explode. "Yeah." A sudden flood of resentment surged through her. There was no way she could outwit the Kyn, and when she failed, the council would blow off her petition. "With all due respect, Padrone, I'd like to request another task to prove myself. *Any* other task."

"For *tresori*, no sacrifice is too great, and no task impossible." He looked down his nose at her. "Find the emeralds before the Kyn do, Miss Lang, and you will be made one of us. Fail, and you will not."

The monitor went dark.

Chapter 4

Sam borrowed Lucan's Porsche and drove to the address sent by dispatch, at the same time calling the station to check in with her boss.

"Sounds like a robbery that got ugly," Captain Garcia told her. "Do you want me to send Massey down to work the scene with you?"

Jonah Massey was one of the newest detectives assigned to homicide, and unlike her boss, he wasn't one of the Kyn's human allies. "That's okay, I'll use the uniforms for the canvass." She pulled up and parked behind the medical examiner's van. "I'm here. I'll report in as soon as I have something."

Sam showed her ID to the patrolman before she ducked under the tape and entered the brightly lit shop. The coppery, sewer-pipe smell of death washed over her as she approached the slight, balding man crouching next to a body sprawled on the expensive carpeting in front of an empty, smashed display case. "What have you got, Evan?"

"Dead guy, multiple contusions, broken bones, stab wounds, impact wounds, defensive wounds, you name it."

The medical examiner straightened and shook his head. "Your basic fucking mess."

Sam inspected the body. "Any of them cause of death?"

"Pending autopsy, my bet is exsanguination. Throat's been slashed from ear to ear. Liver temp puts time of death around seven p.m." He frowned down at the battered body. "Not as much blood as you'd expect. The perp worked on him somewhere else; maybe sliced him there and then dumped the body here."

Sam pulled on a pair of latex gloves and removed a wallet from the dead man's front trouser pocket. "The ID reads Noel Coburn, sixty-eight." She looked up at the small, chiseled golden letters mounted on the wall behind the trashed, empty display cases that spelled out COBURN FINE JEWELERS. "He's probably the owner."

"Robbery is checking on it," Tenderson said. "The killer cleaned out the place. He even emptied the safe in the office."

"No keys." Sam stood up and gestured for one of the patrolmen standing watch at the entrance. When he came to her, she bagged the wallet and handed it to him. "Ask dispatch to send a unit to the address on the license. This guy may try to hit the victim's house, too."

Sam performed a brief walk-through of the rest of the shop. Coburn's office had been wrecked, and the floor-to-ceiling vault at the far end stood open. Inside she found empty storage racks and ten large wooden shipping crates filled with straw.

Sam spotted a small, strangely shaped plastic knob on the floor and bent to pick it up. "A trigger guard." She bagged it before she went to the crates. Becoming Darkyn had turbocharged her senses; her nose was particularly sensitive to smells most humans couldn't detect. She picked up a few pieces of the straw and sniffed them, instantly detecting very faint odors of oil and burnt gunpowder.

"Detective." Tenderson appeared outside the vault. "You'd better take another look at the body before we remove it."

Sam dropped the straw and walked out of the vault. "Did you find something else?"

The ME grimaced. "No, it's what's missing."

Out in the showroom the body of Noel Coburn had been rolled over, displaying the ragged remains of his jacket, which had been pulled away from his back on either side. Raw muscle and bone, scored by deep, jagged grooves, gleamed from neck to waist.

"Holy shit." Sam walked around the body. "Where's his skin?"

"It's not here. About half the muscle is gone, too." Tenderson came to stand beside her, looking down at the pitiful sight. "It's almost like the perp ran a lawn mower over him. And it gets worse."

Sam stared at him. "How?"

"I'll have to confirm with histamine tests, but from the appearance of these wounds they're antemortem." Tenderson stepped back as two of his techs arrived with a gurney for the body. "He was alive when this was done to him, Sam."

Now Sam spotted the deep scarlet abrasions around the wrists. "Ligature marks. He was restrained for a long time." As the body was moved, something lodged in the shoulder blade caught her eye. "Hang on a second, guys. Evan, you got some tweezers?"

The ME handed her a pair, and she used them to extract a broken piece of barbed, rusty metal from the victim's tissue. She stood and held it up, studying it. "Looks like the end of an old hook." She passed it to Tenderson.

"Too big for fish. Meat hook, maybe." He bagged it. "I'll have the lab run it against the database of weapons for comparison, but this"—he gestured at the victim's mutilated back—"wasn't done with a hook. He was subjected to prolonged torture by something that ground his back into hamburger."

"But what?" Sam murmured. "And why?"

Once Sam left the homicide scene, she drove to headquarters, where she found an enormous bouquet of four dozen roses in a beribboned crystal vase sitting on her desk. At first glance she thought the blooms were black, but on closer inspection she saw they were a deep dark red.

"What's the occasion, Brown?" Jonah Massey called from his desk. "Anniversary, birthday, or smoking-hot first date?"

"None of the above." Sam inspected the fragrant blooms for the card but found none. "They probably aren't even for me."

"You looking for this?" Massey held up a small envelope decorated around the edges with scrolls of gold. "I thought I'd hang on to it for you. You know, so it wouldn't get lost."

Being the only female detective assigned to homicide meant putting up with the usual amount of gender bias and relentless ribbing, and Sam had learned long ago not to make anything an issue unless absolutely necessary.

"So who sent them?"

"No name or sig, just a sweet little message the florist

typed in." Massey grinned and pulled out the card to read it out loud. "'You make my heart burn.'" He chuckled. "Sounds like the guy needs some antacid."

Sam tucked a stack of case files under her arm, walked over, and took the card from him. Lucan generally saved his sweet nothings for when he could deliver them in person, but after the minor standoff earlier maybe he'd thought she needed a reminder.

"Nice." She shoved the card in her jacket. "Thanks for taking care of it. Since you're so interested in being my personal assistant, you can type these up." She dropped the files in front of him.

His smirk disappeared. "Why should I do your grunt work?"

"Because I'm the senior ranking detective in this department, and I just pulled a major case. That makes you my grunt." She smiled. "I'll expect them back by the end of your shift. Tonight."

"Yeah." He eyed the stack. "Thanks. A lot."

"My pleasure." She headed for the captain's office.

Captain Ernesto Garcia was on the phone but gestured for Sam to come in as soon as he saw her. She closed the door and sat down in the visitor's chair.

He ended the call and jotted down some notes before he regarded her. "That was Morales over at ATF. They had Coburn under surveillance for a few months last year, but were never able to put together a case. The man was very careful."

"Not tonight." She related the facts she had so far, and added, "From the tossed office and the excessive torture of the vic, the perp wanted more than diamonds. I don't think he got it, either."

He gave her a narrow look. "You didn't read the blood."

"I wanted to, but the techs weren't finished." She often used her psychic ability to see the last moments of a victim's life through contact with his or her blood, but not in front of others. "I'll stop by the morgue later."

"That's not necessary." Garcia leaned forward. "We already know the last moments of this man's life were horrendous. Don't subject yourself to that."

Her boss had never before balked at using her talent to help solve a case. "I've seen plenty worse, Captain, and I'm not squeamish."

"I never implied that you were." Garcia put on his poker face. "I'm thinking of your welfare."

Suddenly Sam understood why the techs had been dragging their feet collecting evidence. "Lucan told you to keep me from reading the vic, so you had the techs stay until I left." When he said nothing, her temper boiled over. "We agreed that when I'm on the job, I'm a cop, and I work for you. Not him."

"Are you finished?" When she nodded, Garcia said, "You know I have to do what the man says, especially when you're involved. So have this conversation with him, because if you get hurt, he won't fire me or transfer me. He'll splatter me over the nearest flat surface."

Sam sank back down in the chair. "Sorry, Captain."

"For the record, I don't agree with him," Garcia assured her. "Your talent has helped close dozens of cases, and it's never caused you any harm, either. But he was adamant."

"All right. I agree not to use my talent on this vic," she told Garcia, giving him a direct look. "When I go to the morgue, it'll just be to get the autopsy results from Tenderson. And that's exactly what you should tell anyone who asks."

He understood. "Be careful, my lady."

As Sam passed her desk on the way out, she scooped up the vase of roses and dropped it in the big trash can by the coffee machine.

From headquarters Sam drove to the county morgue, where she found Evan Tenderson still working on Coburn's remains. After pulling on a protective shroud, she joined him at the dissection table, and glanced at a particularly vile-smelling collection of fish heads, tails, and innards occupying one of the hanging scales. "I hope that's not your dinner."

"It was his. Two pounds of fish parts." He began suturing together the Y-incision. "Someone force-fed it to him. If he hadn't bled out so quickly, he might have choked to death."

She glanced at the rack of vials next to the table. "Were you able to recover any blood for toxicology?"

"Nothing left in the body. I'll use whatever the techs mopped up from the scene." He nodded at the gaping throat wound. "There's a three-inch section of skin and tissue missing from around the carotid. Whoever did him might have taken it as a trophy."

Or to cover up the first wound, which Sam now guessed had been two puncture marks. "Anything else in the wounds on his back?"

"I found salt residue on his clothing. He was hosed down with seawater, probably to intensify the torture, or maybe revive him when he passed out." He tied off the suture thread between the collarbones.

She released enough of her scent to make his eyes glaze over. "Reserve a vial of the victim's blood for me. Call me when it's ready for pickup."

He nodded and repeated in a monotone an abbreviated echo of her command. "Reserve. Vial. Call."

On her way out of the morgue Sam mentally reviewed what Tenderson had told her. The Brethren liked to torture humans almost as much as they did the Kyn, but they always got rid of the bodies. Coburn's murder, vicious as it was, had been very public, as if the killer wanted to make an example of the victim. If the jeweler had been selling arms, his clientele could be anyone from revolutionaries to cartel bosses.

She smelled Lucan before she saw him leaning against the hood of her car, and glanced at her watch.

"It's one twenty a.m.," he informed her.

"So it is." She noted the scowl on his face, and recalled her promise. "You didn't have to come after me for being late. I've got a case—"

"You forever have a case, Samantha." He sniffed. "Why do you come here? The place reeks of death. I'll have to direct Burke to burn your clothes again. Perhaps I'll have him incinerate the entire contents of your wardrobe."

"The garrison should enjoy that." He sounded seriously annoyed, borderline angry, which posed a direct threat to windows of the morgue, the surrounding buildings, and every car in the parking lot. "If I say that I'm sorry for losing track of time, do I get to keep my clothes?"

His expression thawed a few degrees. "You wouldn't mean it."

She thought of the horror that had been Noel Coburn. "Tonight I would."

Lucan extended a gloved hand. "Come here." When she reached him, he folded her into his arms. "Now I shall have to burn *my* clothes," he grumbled against the top of her head. "And have the Ferrari sterilized."

She glanced past him at his gleaming red sports car, which he loved almost as much as sex. "I'll drive back in the Porsche."

"I think not." He plucked the keys from her hand and pocketed them. "Burke can collect it in the morning."

She drew back a little. "Why are you in such a rush to get me back to the den of iniquity?"

"Why are you reluctant to return?" he countered. "Have I given you cause?" When she didn't answer, he sighed. "Samantha, my patience does have very well-defined limits with which you are intimately acquainted. Now tell me what is the matter before windshields commence exploding."

Confronting him about interfering in her investigation might result in the same, so she tabled that for now. "Nothing is wrong, really. The flowers were beautiful, and very romantic, but having them delivered to the squad room was a bit over-the-top."

"Flowers." He frowned.

"If I were a secretary, I'd love to find four dozen roses in a crystal vase sitting on my desk every day," she assured him as she watched his face. "But I'm a cop, and it's not a cop thing, and you have no idea what I'm talking about."

"Not in the slightest," he agreed. "Someone using my name sent roses to your work?"

"There was no name on the card," she admitted, "just a note."

He nodded. "What color were they?"

"The roses? Red, I guess. Look, it was probably Burke," she lied. "Why don't we head back to the club?"

"We will," he said pleasantly, "as soon as you tell me what the note said."

"It said 'Have a nice day.'" She heard her windshield crack, and winced. "Fine. Whoever sent them thinks I make their heart burn. So I guess I have a new secret admirer."

His eyes turned to chrome. "Not for long." He took out his mobile and pressed one number before lifting it to his ear. "Garcia? Roses were delivered to my *sygkenis* at the station. Contact the florist; I want the name and address of the man who paid for them. Yes. By sunset." He switched off the phone and gazed down at her. "You will leave this to me."

"Dwyer is dead." Saying the name of the man who had harassed her, assaulted her, stalked her, and ultimately ended her human life made her feel sick. But Lucan had endured worse at the hands of a former friend turned Brethren agent. "So is Leigh. Don't let the past play games with your head."

"Such sweet concern." Lucan put his hands on her waist and lifted her up to his eye level. "I daresay you do love me."

"Oh, yeah." She linked her arms around his neck. "Now take me home, my man, and I'll show you how much."

Chapter 5

"So Richard offers rule of Ireland in exchange for some lost baubles. If I'd known that was the sole requirement, I'd never have crossed the pond." Lucan rolled up the summons Jamys Durand had given him and passed it to Burke. "I thank you for delivering it. Shall I have young Chris drive you back to the airport?"

Jamys hesitated. To remain in South Florida long enough to search for the Emeralds of Eternity, he would have to request permission for an extended visit. Lucan would want to know why, and if he told him the truth, it would probably result in a call to Thierry Durand. The moment Jamys's father discovered his son had joined the quest for the lost gems, he would order him back to North Carolina.

A warm hand touched the back of his. "With your permission, Suzerain, Lord Durand would like to stay for a few days," Christian Lang said. "He's been looking forward to spending some time with you and your lady and his friends among the household."

"Has he?" Lucan eyed the girl.

Jamys hid his surprise and inclined his head in agreement.

"Still having trouble getting the words out?" A glimmer of sympathy warmed the suzerain's silvery eyes. "Well, we've plenty of mortals around the place to help you with that. Chris, since you're already acquainted with Jamys, you can look after him while he's here." He rose from his chair. "Now if you'll excuse me, I have to go collect my *sygkenis* before she spends the whole of the night filling out police forms in triplicate."

"My lord, perhaps you should text her first," Burke said as he followed Lucan out of the room.

At last Jamys was alone with Chris, and he turned his hand to catch hers as he projected his thoughts. *What have they done to you?*

"Done? Nothing." She lowered her voice before she added, "I'm sorry, I know I shouldn't have jumped in like that, but I got the feeling you didn't want to play twenty questions."

I don't mean that. He looked at her dark brown hair, which she wore in a sleek twist, and then all over her face, which had been made up with sheer, neutral cosmetics but no longer sported any piercings. The only jewelry she wore, in fact, was two blue pearl studs in her ears and a short, matching strand around her throat. *Why do you look like this?*

She glanced down at the front of her tailored navy blue suit. "This is what I wear to work." Her lips curved in an impersonal smile as she extracted her hand from his. "Would you like a tour of the stronghold? The suzerain has made quite a few changes since your last visit."

Jamys had no interest in going anywhere until Chris gave him some answers. Somehow during the three years they had been apart, Lucan and his *sygkenis* had turned the rebellious, fiercely loyal girl he had known into this polite, cool stranger. If he had not imprinted her features so deeply in his memory, he might not even have recognized her.

"If you'd rather have someone else assigned to you, I can ask Mr. Burke who's available," Chris was saying, this time without the smile. "You just have to let me know what sort of girl you'd like. There's a very pretty woman who runs our property management office downtown. She's a blonde. We also have a redhead who manages the restaurant Lucan just bought over on Las Olas—"

"No." He held up his hand to stop her. "You. I want you."

He had practiced using his voice during his journey from his father's stronghold to Alenfar, so it had improved, but now his emotions made the words sound too rough, like the growl of an animal. He wanted to touch Chris again, and this time channel his thoughts into hers, to make her understand that he had come back in order to win her. Given the force of his emotions, however, doing so would also trigger his talent, which allowed him to enter the mind of any mortals in his presence, and compel them to think, do, or say anything Jamys wished while believing it to be their own desire.

He wanted Chris in every way he could have her, and under the influence of his talent, she would give herself to him completely. For as long as they were together, she would even believe it was her idea.

Nothing had ever tempted him more than the prospect of using his talent to command Chris's passion. Back at his father's stronghold he had often thought on it, and in the dark corners of his heart he knew himself capable of it. He wanted her that much. But to turn this bright and beautiful girl into his personal puppet would be a horrendous transgression, one that would render meaningless everything he felt for her.

If Chris came to him, it had to be without his coercion. He wouldn't have her any other way but willingly.

"You sound tired." Chris reached out to him, but when he stepped aside to prevent the physical contact, she snatched her hand back. "I'm sorry, I . . . I should show you to your rooms now."

Jamys maintained the space between them as he followed her to the elevator. If he had hurt her, she concealed it well; her expression had shifted back to the calm, impersonal mask she wore in front of Lucan and the other Kyn. He wanted to tell her why he had come—to explain to her everything he had planned—but he knew it had to wait until he felt more certain of her feelings and his own self-control.

On the fifth floor Christian led him through a hall interspersed with starkly designed stainless steel block columns to a zebrawood door set between two massive white and gray marble monoliths.

"This is the Winterheart Suite," Chris murmured as she took out a plastic card and swiped it through the electronic locking mechanism. The door slowly retreated inward without a sound on its own. "No one else is staying on this floor, so you'll have plenty of privacy."

Accustomed as Jamys was to the medieval grandeur of Baucent, he preferred the simplicity of open space and clean lines. The design of the suite might have been plucked from his own dreams, effortlessly bringing inside the space, stillness, and stark colors of a moonlit night sky.

He admired the wide swaths of inclusions, in every color of gray, that flowed like smoke across the silver white marble walls. Low-profiled, white-upholstered black lacquer furnishings provided comfort without clutter, while narrow opaque panels shed lustrous blue light to outline the doorways to other spaces.

"I had the contractor install voice-activated lighting controls. Just say what room and the percentage of light that you want, like this: 'living room, one hundred percent.'" As she spoke, lighting panels under the furniture and set inside the ebony wood floor began to glow, as did a frozen glacial shower of small glass spheres suspended on wires from the center of the ceiling.

Jamys appreciated the impressive technology, but he wanted to talk to her, not the room.

"You can whisper if you need to," she told him. "The suite is soundproofed, and the controls are very sensitive." She moved across the room. "This is a gas fireplace. I chose this model because it's cleaner and more efficient than one that burns wood." She demonstrated the device that fed and regulated the flames in the hearth, which occupied a glossy cube of black granite encased in a broad column of brushed steel.

From there Chris led him into a small kitchen. "I thought a refrigerator would be a waste of space, so stores of wine and blood are kept under the counters here." She pulled out a drawer to reveal the refrigerated interior filled with a variety of bottles. "Unless you hang the Do Not Disturb sign on your door, our household staff will come in just before sunset daily to clean and restock. Also, if you're planning to entertain someone who isn't Kyn, just dial nine on the house phone and let our chef know what you'd like prepared for your guest."

She had offered him his pick of females to replace her, and now presumed he would be bringing mortals to his suite, all with such bland indifference he might have been a complete stranger to her. Jamys couldn't understand it. When last they had been together, she had been warm and giving, and—for a time—his only real friend in this place. She had given him her blood and offered him her body. She had more than liked him, he'd been convinced of it.

How could she have stopped caring for him? Was it possible that she had regretted their time together? Had she given him no thought at all in the three years since?

"Is there anything else you need, my lord?" Chris asked politely.

She truly wanted to leave him. He could hear the strain in her voice; he could see the tension in her hands and shoulders. She wouldn't even look at him directly.

A dull anger rose inside him. He would not let her run out of here, no matter how much she wished to escape him. Not until he knew what had changed her feelings for him.

As if she could hear his thoughts, Chris looked up at him, her eyes guarded. "If you don't care for the suite, we have other, more traditional accommodations available."

Suddenly what she had been saying to him took on new meaning. *I had the contractor install . . . I chose this model . . . I thought . . .*

"This is yours." He encompassed the room with a sweep of his hand. "You made this."

"I designed and furnished it, but I don't live here. When Sam moved in with Lucan, she gave me her old apartment." She hugged her waist with her arms and looked away. "Sometimes, when I'm too tired to drive home, I sleep up here."

"Alone?" he couldn't help asking.

Her eyes glittered. "No, I usually invite the entire garrison up to cuddle with me. Unless the guys want to play Strip Scrabble or Naked Twister. Then we go to the rec room down the hall." She stalked out of the kitchen.

She wasn't indifferent to him, Jamys thought; she was furious. Dismay and exhilaration sent him after her, but when he emerged from the kitchen, he found her turned around and walking back to him.

Chris folded her hands in front of her and looked past his shoulder. "I shouldn't have spoken to you that way, my lord," she said in a voice devoid of emotion. "I apologize. It's been a very long night."

Jamys reached out to touch her cheek, but she flinched away. "Christian?"

When she turned around, the face she presented was all distant politeness again. "What more can I do for you, my lord?"

Jamys could think of several thousand replies, but chose the one that would immediately prevent her escape. "Show me the bedchamber."

The heat rising from the collar of Chris's work blouse set her in motion; she would not let him see her all flustered and red-faced. "Of course. I'm sorry I forgot. This way."

Why he wanted to see it when he obviously hated her suite—his suite, she corrected herself—made no difference. He wanted to see the bedroom; she would show it to him. If he wanted her to stand on her head and sing Lady Gaga tunes she'd do that, too. She'd be such a perfect *tresora* that he'd forget about her idiot outburst in the kitchen.

Focus on the task at hand, Mr. Burke would say. *Our*

*masters are not interested in our feelings, only in the effi-
ciency of our performance.*

The master bedroom was the only part of the suite
that could be closed off by a door panel that slid behind
the shoji lighting screen, which Chris demonstrated for
Jamys before she passed over the threshold.

"The bed is an oversize king Savoir, and the sheets
are silk." Black silk, in fact, that she'd ordered because
the sample had reminded her of his hair. "Bedroom
lights, eighty percent."

LED floods set to reflect off the marble walls gradually blended with the glow from the crystalline base of
the center bed installation. Chris had found a Canadian
artist who created large-scale sculptures in Lucite and
steel, and had commissioned him to create the elongated
rectangular platform. He had faithfully captured her vision of disheveled stacks of clear, palm-size cubes encas-
ing polished obsidian spheres inlaid with ribbons of
silver. Larger, identical spheres flanked the low head-
board panel of silver-framed Lucite, although these had
been sheared off at the top to provide the flat surfaces
necessary to hold the house phone and device-recharging
station.

Chris walked over to a rectangle of lights set into the
floor, one of which sent a solid beam of light to a sensor
in the ceiling.

"The master bath is here." She passed her hand
through the beam, breaking the light, and a wide rectangle of onyx stone began to rise from the floor. Water
flooded the interior tub, which she had designed to com-
fortably fit two, and streamed over the sides to fall into
the mesh-bottomed catch channel surrounding the stone.
"The temperature default is one hundred ten degrees,

but you can adjust that and the speed of the whirlpool jets on the control panel." She nodded toward the opaque shoji screens to one side of the bed. "If you or your guests want more privacy, there's another, full bath through there. That's also where all the linens are stored."

Jamys walked over to one of the walls to examine one of the framed manuscript pages. "Poetry."

Chris had personally framed and hung the pages of poetry purchased from the rare-document auctions she followed; she had carefully selected verses penned by such masters as Robert Frost, T. S. Eliot, and e. e. cummings. Knowing how much Samantha loved poetry, Lucan had thought it a charming touch. Chris hadn't bothered to tell him that each poem she'd framed contained some word or phrase that reminded her of Jamys Durand.

Everything in the suite had been chosen for the same reason. She'd designed it for herself, but it was all about him, dreaming of him, waiting for him. The rooms contained everything she couldn't say, every hope locked inside her heart.

He bent to touch the gleaming base of the bed, and then straightened, turning around slowly. "No glass."

"The suite is too close to the penthouse," she said, moving to discreetly straighten a fold of the pleated black chiffon duvet. "It's a safety precaution. When Lord Vader—I mean, the suzerain—loses his temper, all the glass within a hundred yards shatters."

He watched her face. "Why 'Winterheart'?"

"The climate here is tropical, and most visiting Kyn aren't accustomed to the heat," she said, choosing her words carefully so that nothing she said would be an outright lie. "I thought this would provide a sanctuary from the outside world."

Her sanctuary, where she could hide for an hour and vent some of her frustrations without worrying Sam or Burke. In the beginning of her training she had come here almost every day to scream into a pillow until her throat burned, or curl up on the bed and count the sparkling mica flakes embedded in the ceiling's snowy stucco. Over time she'd finally taught herself how to squelch her aggravation and conduct herself with the composure expected of a *tresora*.

Chris still came to the suite occasionally, but only when she was lonely, when her heart ached, and when she didn't think she could bear spending one more night by herself.

Not that she had to, she thought as she watched Jamys disappear into the adjoining bath. The guys in the garrison were big, strong, beautiful men; she'd watched them treat the mortal females they brought to the stronghold with gentleness and respect. Every woman who spent a night in the garrison's quarters left the next morning with a big, dreamy smile on her face.

As protective as Lucan and Sam were of her—and Chris was pretty sure the suzerain had warned his men not to lay one immortal finger on her without her consent—nearly all of the stronghold's warriors had made it clear they found her attractive. All she'd have to do was bat an eyelash in the right direction and she'd never sleep alone again.

Yet as gorgeous as the *jardin*'s warriors were, none of them had big dark eyes, or black hair as fine as a silk fringe, or hands that moved like water flowed. She admired them, she liked them—a couple had become like surrogate big brothers—but no man among the garrison had ever touched her heart.

Jamys emerged and made another circuit of the room, this time inspecting the windows and their black vertical blinds.

Chris had hidden from everyone her feelings for Jamys, but to cope with the loneliness she'd been forced to put her dreams and desires on ice. Now she wanted to throw herself at him, and cling to him, and tell him how hard it had been to train and wait and hope. She wanted him to know it was all for him. Everything.

And the moment she did that, he would gently set her aside, call for Burke, and have the blonde from downtown or the redhead from the restaurant take her place.

She had to get out of the suite and away from him, now, before she made a complete ninny out of herself. What hadn't she told him about the rooms? "The blinds are on a timer, and close automatically thirty minutes before sunrise. They don't open again until thirty minutes after sunset." She squared her shoulders and walked over to show him the manual pulls hidden inside the end panels. "The windows on this floor are sealed, but the transoms open if you want some fresh air. The doors also lock automatically, so you'll need to carry this access card with you."

She reached into her jacket to retrieve the one she'd programmed for him. Pain made her hiss as the shard of broken glass in her pocket sliced across her fingertips.

"Excuse me." She kept her hand in her pocket and hurried into the adjoining bathroom.

Chris held her bleeding hand over the frost-blue bowl of glass that served as the sink, and winced as cold water from the automatic tap washed over the open cuts. Because the Kyn healed spontaneously, she hadn't thought to stock the suite with a first-aid kit; she'd have to wrap some tissue around her hand until she could get back downstairs.

"You're wounded."

The caress of his breath across the bare back of her neck made her close her eyes briefly. Jamys knew she was hurt because he smelled the fresh blood; the Kyn were almost like sharks that way.

"I cut myself on a piece of glass I had in my pocket." She reached for the box of tissues, but Jamys had her bleeding hand in his and was examining the small wounds. "It's nothing."

His eyes shifted to hers, and she saw a thin ring of glowing amber encircling his pupils, which had begun to contract to thin vertical slivers. "Why hide it from me? Do you think I will feed on you?"

"No, I was embarrassed because I was clumsy." From the look he gave her it was clear that he didn't believe her. "I've been assigned to you, my lord, and I'm trained to take care of your needs. If you want the blood, I'll go get a glass."

Jamys kept his eyes on hers as he slowly lifted her injured hand to his mouth. His *dents acérées* flashed for a moment before he sank them into heel of his own hand.

Chris caught her breath as he raised his head. Two drops of blood beaded in the small puncture wounds that were already beginning to close. "What are you doing?"

"Healing you." Jamys guided one of her hurt fingers to his palm, and gently pressed the cut into the blood. Chris caught her breath as she felt the cool mingling of his blood with hers, and then her cut went numb. He repeated the act again with her other finger, and then used a tissue to blot the blood away.

Chris saw both of her cuts had closed, just as fast as the punctures in his palm. "Why did you bother?"

"You are not my food, Christian, or my servant. You are my friend, and I do not want you hurt." He put his hand to the back of her head, holding it as he pressed a kiss to her brow. "Do you understand?"

"Sure. Friendship works for me." No, it didn't, but he wasn't asking for someone else. At least he still liked her. "Your eyes are doing the cat thing, though, and I know that means you haven't fed for a while. Or you want to have wild monkey sex. Or both." Had she actually said that out loud? God, she had. "I'll, um, go make a glass of bloodwine for you."

"I do not want sex with a wild monkey." Jamys removed the long comb holding her hair back and placed it on the counter. As the twist slumped against her nape, he worked his hand through it, releasing the wavy mass. "Your hair was scarlet when I saw you last."

"Mud brown is what I was born with." She knew with it down she looked about sixteen, too. "I stopped dyeing it after you left."

His fingers stilled as he found the one hairpin she wore to keep her silver streak out of sight.

"That's not dyed, either," she admitted. "I started going gray like an old lady back in high school."

"Do not hide it." He spread the strands out. "It does not make you seem older. It is beautiful."

"I don't think any woman under the age of ninety would agree with you." As he brought the silvery lock to his lips, Chris forgot to breathe. "You're kissing my hair."

"It feels like gossamer." He smoothed it back and

looked all over her face. "Your piercings, what happened to them?"

"No one takes you seriously when you wear rings in your eyebrow, so I let them close up." Absently she touched a tiny scar on the curve of her lip, and then she understood why he hadn't recognized her at first. "You were expecting me to look the way I did three years ago?"

"That is how I remember you." He touched each place where she had been pierced, and when he reached her lip he ran his thumb back and forth over the small dimple. "You seem so different now."

"I'm not the same girl I was. I grew up." She ignored the way the cross under her blouse seemed suddenly to weigh as much as an anchor. "Everyone does, even if they're Kyn and they don't age. You've changed, too." She eyed the black hair spilling over his shoulders. She often envied the Kyn their hair, which like their finger-nails sometimes grew several inches longer overnight, usually right after it was cut. The Kyn never had to suffer a bad hair day more than one day. "You've nailed the ponytail look, I think, but how did you get all this new muscle?"

Suddenly he looked tired and unhappy. "I have also been training."

What was wrong with him? Was she being too much of a pest? Was he sick of her already? "Is there anything else I can do for you?"

He turned his head as a three-tone chime sounded. "What is that?"

"Someone's at the door. Probably Burke." Chris sighed. "He worries."

She didn't find Burke waiting in the hall; one of the

visiting Kyn stood outside the suite. As soon as Chris opened the door, the strong scent of almonds wafted over her, and she had to swallow a groan. It was the same spike-haired troublemaker who had started the brawl in the armory.

Why is he on this floor? "May I help you, sir?"

"There ye are, Pearl Girl." His lips peeled back from his white teeth and fully emerged fangs. "The bald one said ye were occupied, but I suspected if I tracked ye, I'd find ye alone." He swiped at her wrist and then frowned when she moved out of reach. "Come, I would have ye before the night wanes away."

Have me? No Darkyn male had ever come after her demanding blood or sex, and for a second she wanted to slap him. But Burke had warned her that European Kyn did things differently; evidently they expected to help themselves to the household humans. Lucan would have no problem with her refusing him, but he would expect her to do so without turning it into an international immortal incident.

"I'm sorry, sir, but I'm not available to serve you tonight." *Or for the rest of eternity, you pretentious ape.* "I'll be happy to call down to Mr. Burke—"

"I want no other." He gave her the once-over and breathed in. "Not been taken tonight, then? Be they blind in this stronghold? Never worry, I'll put ye to good use." He crossed the threshold and, when she backed away, leered at her. "No need to play shy, Pearl Girl. I know how it is with ye household wenches." He stopped advancing and frowned past her. "What is this?"

She glanced over her shoulder to see Jamys just behind her, his eyes glowing, his expression as lethal as the long copper blades in his fists. "This would be the reason

I'm not available, sir." Since they hadn't formally met, it was her duty to introduce them, and now she couldn't remember a single word of the proper protocol. "This is Lord Jamys Durand, son of Suzerain Thierry Durand. And you are . . . ?"

"Vander." He bobbed his head at Jamys and raised his empty hands. "No trespass intended, Durand. I thought the wench dallied alone here." A sly look came into his eyes. "Since ye have no desire to bed the mortal, I'll take her to my chambers."

Jamys stepped around Chris, putting himself between her and Vander.

Chris heard Jamys make a low, fierce sound in his throat and put her hand on his sleeve. Under her fingers she felt his muscles tighten and hoped she could talk faster than he could strike.

"Mr. Vander, my master, Lord Lucan, has given me to Lord Durand for his exclusive use during his stay. Lord Durand is obviously not interested in sharing me, and he would like you to leave." When Vander gave her an incredulous look, she added, "Now, please."

"'Tis unnatural, to draw copper over use of a mere wench." Vander retreated back into the hall, but he gave Chris an ugly look. "I'll be seeing ye again, Pearl Girl."

Not if I see you first, Chris thought as she closed the door and secured it. Only then did she realize she was trembling so hard her knees were wobbling. "I might need to rethink my career strategy."

"Christian." His voice caressed her as if it were rough velvet, as he pulled her around to face him, but he looked ready to kill something. He took his hands off her to pace around the room and utter something lengthy and mangled in French.

"It's all right. The guy made a mistake." So had she, staying here as long as she had. "I'll tell Burke about it before I go home, and he'll have Lucan explain things to him. I'll stop in tomorrow night and check on you." Feeling awkward, she opened the door. "Good night."

Chapter 6

Jamys moved so fast he had her in his arms before she could blink. "Do not go. We have hardly had an hour together. You can stay a little longer."

"I can't. I have to . . ." Something rushed in her ears, and she shook her head, trying to remember what she had to do. All she could think was how much she did want to stay. "You don't need me around."

"I would like some bloodwine." He took her hand and led her to the kitchen. "You can show me how to prepare it for myself."

"Sure. I stocked some of my favorite Spanish red for you. You're going to love it." She started to open the wine drawer but stopped and glanced up at him. "You already know how to mix bloodwine, and five minutes ago you said you didn't want any."

His jaw set. "I changed my mind."

"Okay, fine." She reached into the drawer, took out a bottle, and used the wine opener to uncork it. She took a glass down from the cabinet, filled it, and set it on the counter. "Can I borrow one of your daggers?" she asked as she began rolling up her sleeve.

He drew back a step. "I do not want your blood."

"Bloodwine with no blood. Right." She picked up the glass, sipped from it, and nodded before she filled it to the rim. "Would you like me to run a bubble bath for you? Or I could polish your boots, press your clothes, give you a manicure—"

Jamys took the wineglass out of her hand and set it aside. "Stop talking to me like that. You are not my lackey."

"I'm not supposed to argue with immortals, but I'm afraid that is *exactly* what I am." She took another sip of the wine, which made her lip sting. "So you don't have to waste your talent or fake the friendship thing to make me feel better about it. Serving you is my job."

He put his hand against her cheek. "What have they done to you?"

He didn't know anything about her, Chris realized. Maybe it was time he did. "When I met Sam, I was nothing but trash. A runaway fifteen-year-old kid with twenty-eight cents in my pocket. I'd just gotten fired for punching my boss, who thought the three dollars an hour he paid me under the table also entitled him to treat me like a hospitality wench. When it comes to sexist jerks, humans aren't all that different from the Darkyn."

Jamys moved his hand to her shoulder. "You deserve better."

"I have better." She looked around at the beautiful kitchen that would always, and never, be hers. "Sam and Lucan took me in. Besides trusting me with what has to be the biggest secret of all time, they also care about me. Genuinely care. They gave me this job and, for the first time in my life, a chance to live with some dignity. So that's what they've done, my lord." She smiled blindly for a moment until she tasted blood. "Damn it."

Jamys cradled her face between his palms and tilted her head back. "Vander struck you?"

"It wasn't him. I bit my lip too hard. Old nervous habit." She ran her finger over the tender spot. "With the way this day has gone, tomorrow I'll probably wake up looking like Angelina Jolie."

Jamys's fingers drifted down from her cheeks to trace along the sides of her throat. She half expected him to step away, but his hands kept moving, over the curves of her shoulders and along the outsides of her arms, encircling her wrists for a moment before moving to her waist. At the same time, his thoughts poured into her mind. *You should not be so cruel to something this soft and lovely.* He lowered his head and ran the tip of his tongue over her sore lip.

The tingling heat left by the intimate caress made Chris close her eyes. "Do that again and I'll never leave."

He waited until she was looking at him again before he slowly and deliberately put his mouth on hers. This time he tasted her with a gentle kiss that was as sweet as it was seductive.

Chris curled her hands into fists as she stood perfectly still. She had stopped wishing a long time ago, because she knew dreams didn't come true. Yet here was Jamys, astounding her with a kiss that felt as if it might never end. What did it mean? He didn't want to her to go? He never wanted her to leave him again? That was as crazy as the delight and desire he was pouring into her heart.

Stop behaving like some idiot love-struck mortal. If she messed this up, he'd never want her for his *tresora,* so she'd go by the book. *A Kyn lord has complete dominion over the mind and body of his* tresora, Burke's voice echoed in her mind. *Whatever their wishes may be, we submit to their will entirely, and make no demands of our own. . . .*

The kiss that she wished would last forever ended after four heartbeats. It might have been because she was starting to slither through his arms, Chris thought, astonished now by her legs, which she could no longer feel. The room turned on end, and then righted itself halfway as Jamys lifted her off her feet.

"I haven't fainted since the last time you were here," she murmured to his shirt buttons. "You should carry smelling salts or something."

Jamys put her down on a black cloud, and sat beside her. "Too much." He touched his temple, and then hers.

"Oh, right." She'd forgotten the price tag of being his thought receiver. "Sorry. I have to take a nap now." When he started to stand, she clutched his hand. "Don't tell anyone, please." As he frowned, she closed her eyes. "They'll give you the redhead. I just know it. . . ."

The black cloud shifted, and strong, cool arms came around her. As long silky hair fell across her cheek, Chris smiled.

As soon as the sun set, the Treasure Palace opened its gilded doors to the hordes of patrons clever enough to secure an invitation to the exclusive casino. No one quite knew where the Palace was located; the only way to reach it was by taking a ferry with black-painted windows, on which silent, stone-faced guards prevented any curious passenger from stepping out on deck. Once inside the club, the lure of the free booze and the riches waiting to be won at the high-stakes gaming tables and in the poker rooms made it worth the unsolved mystery.

As one of the Palace's special perks, the casino's staff

was exclusively female. Many of the stunningly beautiful women who were not working the tables or bars mingled with the patrons, their hostess status designated by the demure gowns of satin and silk they wore. These lovely ladies brought drinks, converted cash into chips, fetched snacks, and, for the right price, would escort a patron back to one of the private encounter rooms, where it was rumored they would perform any sex act that the guest desired. The ladies' myriad talents had earned the casino a long-standing nickname as the Pleasure Palace.

Werren made her way across the crowded casino floor, pausing now and then to accept compliments and gently refuse offers from various patrons. She wore a simple winter-blue satin sheath dress that matched her eyes and complemented the upswept coil of her fair hair. The only jewelry she wore was a necklace, which lay out of sight beneath her bodice.

Two of her ladies came to join her, and she took them for a turn around the blackjack tables so they might talk without being overheard by one of the guards standing by the exits. "Has the master returned?"

"Not as of yet, lady." Claudea, a slender waif in a child-size gown of red, returned the appraisal of an older man with an innocent smile. "But two of his bodyguards left before midnight."

"They may have gone for supplies." Werren nodded to a passing socialite carrying a small, bored-looking dog in her enormous designer bag. "Has anyone found out anything from the crew?"

"There has been mention of a nightclub and a police-woman," Claudea said.

"We've only four hours left." Analise, one of her older ladies, touched a plump beringed hand to her silver-streaked black curls. "Or perhaps he won't arrive until after dawn."

Claudea sighed. "If he's wanting sport, he'll not wait. He'll send the guards to drag us from our beds. But could be that he's become infatuated with someone in town. He always takes his time when he is."

"What if he doesn't return?" Analise said, a wistful note in her voice. "What will happen to us? Who will look after us?"

Werren saw one of the guards heading toward them. "I will. See what more you can learn from the crew. Now go and find some business."

She waited for the guard, a spiteful brute named Ralston, who took her arm and marched her to an unoccupied corner. "You have a nice chat with your friends, Duchess?"

"I was suggesting some suitable companions for them." She nodded toward the blackjack table, where her ladies were already engaging the two men with the most chips.

"Looked more like you three were scheming up something." His grip tightened. "Dutch will hear about it, too."

"I've nothing to hide," Werren said, and reached up to center the knot in his tie. "Does your shift end before dawn, Mr. Ralston?"

"You think I'm that stupid? That I don't know what you are?" He shoved her away from him. "Get back to work."

Werren left the hot, smoky confines of the casino and walked out onto the observation deck for some air. She'd hoped that Ralston would not have believed anything said about her and the other women—a few of the guards hadn't, which had proved extremely useful—but lately Dutch wasn't taking any chances. He had recently become wildly obsessed with his search for the treasure that long ago had been stolen from him, pouring much of their profits into hiring investigators and researchers. He'd also begun leaving behind his bodyguards and making trips by himself into the city. Whatever he was doing there made him frustrated and angry, for he always returned to the Palace in a seething, vicious mood. Once Ralston reported to him tonight, Dutch would probably let him watch as he punished her or the women. This time it would probably be her.

She didn't mind the beatings so much anymore. It was the inventive humiliations Dutch inflicted that tore at her soul. One day he would shred what was left of it, and then her ladies would have to look after themselves.

Werren avoided looking at the sea and lifted her eyes to the midnight sky, where the moonlight had silvered the dark clouds. Sometimes, if she stared long enough at the moon, she could remember her mother's face.

It, too, had been round and pale, often ashen with exhaustion from the long days and nights she spent tending the cook pots on the stoves and hanging over the hearths in the duke's kitchens. But when Magda finally came home to their cottage, she had never been too tired to smile on Werren, or brush out her hair, or tell her how lovely she was.

"My little fortune in waiting," Magda would croon. "One day, when you're old enough to marry off, you'll make us so rich, Werry. Then I'll never have to lift another pot again."

How proud would Magda be, to know how many fortunes had been poured into Werren's hands? How aghast, if she knew how Werren had earned them?

The sound of men speaking in low voices drew Werren's gaze across the deck. Dutch stood with two strangers in dark suits, and nodded as one of them gestured to the north. The lights from overhead illuminated a strange design tattooed in a circle around an unsightly scar on the stranger's wrist.

She moved closer.

"You say the one who brought the summons looks like an adolescent," the tattooed man said, speaking in heavily accented English. "He is not a courier or anyone known to us. He could be a spy."

"I will dispose of him soon enough." Dutch didn't seem concerned. "What about the girl?"

"We intercepted a communication between her and the council," the man told him. "They have ordered her to find the emeralds. Alenfar may be having his own men search for them. We will take her, and after we interrogate her–"

Her master grabbed the man by the lapels and jerked him close. "Did I ask you to touch her?"

The other man lifted his hands in a gesture of surrender. "We wish only to assure that your property is returned to you, signore. Once you eliminate Alenfar, you will have the jewels as well as the command of an army of warriors to do your bidding."

"That I will." Dutch dropped the man, who staggered a little. "You will not harm the girl. Follow her, see how much she knows, and report back to me. Now get out of my sight."

Werren slipped back, and waited there until she saw the two strangers disappear. She didn't know whom they served or what they had promised Dutch, and she had never heard of Alenfar, but their conversation troubled her.

"You think I would not know you were watching?"

Werren braced herself before she turned around, and thus was able to accept without a sound the clout of her master's hand. The ferocity of the blow nearly knocked her off her feet, but she caught the railing at the last moment and stayed upright. Her cheek swelled for several moments, and then smoothed out to its usual flawless perfection.

He's still angry.

Werren immediately lifted her satin skirts and lowered herself to her knees. "Forgive me, Master." She stared at the tips of Dutch's boots. Boots she had spent an hour polishing, now caked with damp sand.

He used one to prod her. "Get up."

Werren stood, making sure to hunch over slightly to eliminate a crucial difference in their height. Once, when she had forgotten, Dutch had noticed she stood two inches taller than him, and after beating her bloody had ordered her stripped and whipped in front of the other women.

Dutch lit one of his Cuban cigars and puffed on it. "How much has the house taken in?"

"The count at ten this evening was over two hundred thousand." She tried not to look at the glowing tip of his cigar. "I'm sure we've brought in at least another hundred since."

"What about the whores?" His eyes searched her face, waiting for any flicker of emotion in response. "What have they done for me?"

"The crew kept my ladies occupied for the first several hours." Oh, if she could only cut out her tongue and throw it in his face. "They are now servicing the patrons at a steady pace."

He grunted. "And who have *you* serviced tonight, you idle slut?"

"No one, Master." He had given her strict instructions to touch no man but to wait for him. Had he forgotten? Sometimes he did, and then she would be punished for laziness. "I await your every desire."

"Fucking right you do." His mouth curled around the cigar as he puffed. "You came out here to think about your mother."

She started to reach for her throat before she controlled the impulse. "No, Master. I was waiting for you to return."

"I can smell your tears, you lying bitch."

Werren's gaze went to the cigar; he'd used one just like it to torture her after one of the men had gone missing. "Yes, Master, I lied. I was thinking of her."

"Then we should pay a visit to her hovel."

No argument would sway him, so Werren closed her eyes. When she opened them, the present had become the past, and she and Dutch stood in the tiny, one-room cottage of her childhood. Every detail was absolutely correct, from the crude cross fashioned of twigs and twine hanging over the door to the squat shape of the blackened three-legged pot standing over the cold, dark hearth.

"It baffles me, to see this dung heap from which you sprang." Dutch strode around the room. "Did the duke tup her here, on the rushes, or did he call her up to the main house?"

"I can't say, Master." Werren picked up one of her few playthings, a torn linen napkin that had been mended and knotted into the shape of a hare. The material had been so fine she would sleep with it tucked against her cheek. "I imagine after I was born he stopped using her."

"No, he used her here, in the dirt and the filth." Dutch caught her arm, jerking her over to the rough-hewn table where she and her mother had taken their meals of bread and kitchen scraps. "It's where all you greedy trollops belong." He shoved her down face-first onto the pitted, scarred wood and held her there by the nape of her neck. "Isn't it, Duchess?"

"Yes, Master."

He crouched down to whisper beside her ear, "Admit it. You watched them going at it. That's why you crave it so much."

"Yes." Werren had no memory of seeing Magda with anyone except the undertaker, who had only touched her to search her nightclothes for valuables before removing her corpse from the cottage. "I did watch them."

"What are you waiting for? Hoist your skirts."

Werren reached down and slowly pulled up the voluminous material, baring her buttocks, thighs, and stockings.

Dutch kicked her feet apart with his foot and reached down to release the front of his trousers. "Been thinking about it, haven't you?"

"All night, Master." It was the truth. She'd been dreading this moment for hours. Not for the rough, painful ram of his entry into her body, nor the grunting sound of his pleasure as he pushed in to his root. It was the awful warmth that spread from his hand like a fever, burning down her throat and pooling in her breasts, sucking at her will until it swallowed it whole.

She had never once wanted him, but he forced her to feel whatever he desired. For now it was longing and need; in another moment it might be revulsion and agony.

Dutch's power streamed through Werren, lifting her hips, undulating in time with his thrusts, and moving her hand down between her thighs. One of his favorite ways of humiliating her was to bring her to the very edge before spewing himself inside her and then pulling back his possession of her senses, leaving her without relief.

"You were listening to me and the Italians," Dutch accused, pumping into her harder. "Do you know there is another like me, this Lucan of Alenfar? He is searching for my emeralds, too. What do you think of that?"

Werren had to pant her reply. "Do you wish me to go to him, and find out what he knows?"

"You could never get past his guards." Dutch leaned close. "As if you'd risk your neck for me?"

"I would do anything for you." It sickened her to say such things, but he expected it. "My ladies and I have no way to make a place for ourselves in the world. Without you to care for us, we would die."

Dutch grunted, shuddering and jerking as he had his pleasure.

Werren remained where she was until her master withdrew from her body and shoved her away. Then slowly she stood, rearranging her skirts and ignoring the wetness between her thighs. "Thank you, Master."

Chapter 7

Jamys felt the approaching dawn, and looked down at the girl sleeping in his arms. Chris had barely stirred, but the color had gradually returned to her face, and the tenor of her breathing told him that she was in a deep sleep that would last for several more hours.

Spending much of the last three years training or retiring alone to his tower chambers had sometimes made Jamys wonder if he was fit to share his life with so fragile a creature. He'd meant only to guard his heart, but instead he had retreated from every reminder of the happiness that might someday be his. As much as he cared for his father and stepmother, the effortless manner with which they displayed their love had been a constant, grinding reminder of how alone he was. How many times had he turned away from seeing Thierry weaving a strand of his stepmother's dark hair through his fingers, or Jema sidling against his father, as content as a sleepy cat?

Now he realized it had been more envy than despair. He'd wanted what Thierry and Jema shared for himself, with his own woman, his own wife. Only one would do, and yet would not do, for his dream was Christian, and

Christian was mortal. She could no more share his eternal life than a butterfly could mate with a spider.

Some of the Kyn took human women to wife and loved them as fiercely as they would a Kyn *sygkenis*, but Jamys couldn't even assume Christian would want to be his. The hopelessness of not knowing what she might desire had gnawed at him constantly. Would she prefer a mortal husband, one who could give her children and grow old with her? What if the thought of giving herself and her heart to a Kyn male repelled her?

He was no hulking, muscle-bound warrior; even with the physical changes training had wrought, he'd never look older or more commanding. Without the reward for finding the gems, he wasn't even sure what he could offer Christian, and feared what he might subject her to instead. What if the darkness inside him, with which he had lived since his mother's betrayal, prevented him from ever giving her what she needed?

Now she lay beside him, her soft breaths caressing his skin, her small hand resting against his chest, and he had never felt so right with the world. She fit him as beautifully and naturally as if she had been born a part of his body; like some phantom limb he had lost long ago and forgotten until now.

The scent of her skin and the pulse of her blood beneath it distracted him from his nobler thoughts, and drew his hand to the buttons of her blouse. The garment looked too restricting for comfort, or so he told himself as he released the pearly button over her collarbones. Her thin skin felt as smooth and warm as a brushed kiss against his fingertips, and he slipped free a second button, and then a third. A few inches of silver chain glittered, and he used it to gently tug the old cross free of her garments.

The cross was older than she; older than any he had ever seen in the possession of a mortal. The silver used to fashion it had been hammered, not cast, and the maker's hand had coaxed hair-thin strands into impossibly complicated Celtic knots. In the center of the cross a small cabochon of milky quartz glowed, serene as moonlight save for a single dark green flaw at its heart. The pendant gleamed from the care she had taken to clean and polish it, so it was obviously precious to her, but she wore it hidden beneath her garments, as if it were something secret or shameful.

As Jamys released the pendant, Christian shifted beneath his hand, her blouse falling open another inch to reveal the inner curves of her breasts, flushed now like her throat with a delicate pink.

Jamys rolled onto his back, curling his hands into fists as he stared up at the dark ceiling. Behind his lips his fangs pulsed as they stretched full-length into his mouth, as hot and hard as the shaft swelling beneath the front of his trousers. He could think of nothing but sinking into Christian, his fangs piercing the softness of her throat, his shaft forging deep into the wet heat between her thighs.

The shadows deepened inside him as they attempted to lure him from the strain of resistance. His darkness told him how he could be inside her before she opened her eyes; how simple it would be to bespell her even as he fucked her. Blood and sex always made him stronger; it would be nothing to compel her to give herself to him, to stay with him, to sleep through the day with him. When again the night came, he could wake with her in his arms, warm and eager and willing to see to his every pleasure. This way, he would never hurt her. . . .

Jamys closed his eyes, trying to shut out the images flashing behind them, and once more saw his mother's exquisite face, her lovely mouth curved in a rare, genuine smile. She didn't speak, but he knew what she would say: *After all you have suffered, my poor darling boy, you would deny yourself your heart's desire? If you are careful, you can probably make her last for years.* . . .

Imagining Angelica's approval scalded Jamys, burning away at the lust racking him until nothing remained but ashes of self-disgust. He turned to draw the coverlet over Christian before he rose and went into the front room. He wanted to go down to the lists and challenge the first warrior who looked askance at him, and beat him into the dirt, but that would solve nothing.

Jamys wanted to ask her whether she still had feelings for him, or if he had been completely mistaken in his suspicions. But his fear of her answer was far greater than his desire to know.

He had only one chance to win her, and that was to become a man Christian could admire as well as love. He would do that by finding the gems, delivering them to Richard, and securing rule of Ireland.

Once he retrieved his laptop from his traveling case and set it up on the desk, he switched it on and accessed the Internet. His initial search for information on the *Golden Horde* produced more than eight million references, most of which had nothing to do with seventeenth-century pirates. He recalled the scant information from the high lord's summons, and refined the search to include the keywords *Jamaica, emeralds,* and *lost treasures*.

That narrowed the results to one hundred thousand, among which he found the Web site of Professor Charles Gifford, a salvage specialist turned piracy historian who had spent much of his career searching the waters between Jamaica and Florida for the wreck of the *Golden Horde*. The site, decorated as it was by images of skulls and old coins, offered a surprising amount of information about seventeenth-century piracy around the Caribbean, including an entire section on the island of Jamaica.

Jamys skimmed through it until he found the first mention of the *Golden Horde*:

Port Royal authorities, dockworkers, and islanders recorded sightings of the infamous pirate ship, which all accounts describe as sporting black sails, a skeletal-looking crew dressed in rags, and strange red lights glowing on deck. According to the final entry in the port master's log, the ship circled the island several times but never came into port, nor did the crew ever come ashore.

This record is contradicted by the journal of Father Bernard Bartley, whose mission in Runaway Bay provided sanctuary for reformed pirates, most of whom had been sailors captured during raids and forced into the life. At the time the Horde was sighted on the north side of the island, Bartley wrote this after finding a half-dead man washed ashore near his mission:

"He had been brutally treated, and expecting his demise, I offered him absolution, so that he might go before God with the grace of his sins forgiven. The castaway refused, insisting that Hell would be nothing to his life. He claimed he had brought ashore his master, the captain of his ship, who had him steal the jewels from a relic buried in the sand; jewels that had been used by the first mate to transform his captain into a monster. As the fever took the castaway's wits, he began to rave about this transformation, during which his master had died and then come alive again to drink the blood of the crew. That night, an hour before he died, the castaway cursed his master, this Captain Hollander, that he might never know port again."

Few facts are known about the captain of the Golden Horde, whom some records name as Frederick Hollander. The most popular myth associated with this captain was a bargain he struck with the devil to trade his soul for eternal life. As you might expect, there was a catch, as the legend claims that Satan (or perhaps the curse of the much-abused castaway) doomed Hollander and his crew to sail the seas in darkness forever. Several eyewitnesses supported the myth, and insisted that as soon as the sun rose above the horizon, the Horde would simply vanish into thin air. . . .

Jamys copied the information and stored it in a file before he returned to the Web site's front page. One of the coin images, a Spanish gold piece sporting a cross similar to the Templars' martyrdom cross, looked vaguely familiar to him. When he couldn't place it, he returned to the search results.

Another Web site devoted to salvage diving and recovery maintained an archive of mapped voyages. He checked the index for the *Golden Horde*, and found an antique map that showed several routes around the island as well as one leading up to the American mainland before it ended in a series of dashes. When he checked the legend, he saw that the dashes indicated the last known position of the ship.

Jamys imagined any mortal reading the accounts of Hollander and his ship would dismiss them as myths or superstitions, as the historian had. But details involved with the curse and the castaway's claims made him suspect Hollander had not been human, but Darkyn. An immortal obliged to travel by ship in that era would not have been able to store blood for any length of time, and so would be forced to feed on the crew while at sea. Hollander would also have the Kyn's nocturnal nature, which would compel him to avoid the discomfort of the sun's rays by sailing only at night.

Much of the information on the sites that mentioned Hollander and the *Golden Horde* had been condensed and interpreted; what Jamys needed to see were the actual documents and maps from the seventeenth century. Fortunately for him modern humans who were obsessed with the past preserved such things with great care, and kept them in museums and the libraries of important institutions. When he returned to Charles Gifford's Web site, he discovered the historian had scheduled several lectures at the Miami Maritime Museum, to which he had also donated Father Bartley's journals.

Jamys didn't want to involve Chris in his quest, but his unfamiliarity with Lucan's territory made it almost a necessity. As he made note of the museum's address, he heard a ringing sound coming from his traveling case, and reached in to take out his mobile.

The caller ID displayed the number for his father's private line at the stronghold.

His ruse had been discovered, it seemed. He was tempted to shut off the phone, but if he didn't answer the call, Thierry would order the garrison to begin searching for him.

He pressed the speaker button. "Yes, Father."

"When you bespell a mortal in order to assume his identity, you should remember to adjust his memories as well," Thierry said. "Where in God's name are you?"

He considered how to answer that. "Where I am safe."

"Since you are not here, I disagree," his father snapped. "You are to return to the stronghold by nightfall."

"No."

Thierry growled, "You mistake my meaning, son. I do not make this a request. I am your suzerain as well as your parent, and I say you will come home at once."

It gave Jamys little satisfaction to repeat his father's words back to him. "I am not a warrior."

"You are my son, Jamys." Thierry's tone softened. "There is no need for this estrangement and rebellion. Tell me where you are, and I will come there."

"To bring me back," Jamys amended.

"Yes. No." His father made a frustrated sound. "Permit me to make right this thing between us. You wish to train with the garrison? I will direct my captains to instruct you. I will have my builder construct a villa on the grounds for you so that you may set up your own household. I will give you whatever you wish, boy; you have but to say what you need."

He closed his eyes. "I am not a boy, Father." He felt Chris's hand touch his shoulder and covered it with his own, drawing strength from it. "I am a man."

"Of course you are—"

"Then let me be one." He switched off the phone before Thierry could reply, and set it down beside the laptop, and stared at it. "Forgive me. I did not mean to wake you."

"I was a little cold." Chris picked up the mobile. "I know this is encrypted, but if you keep using it, he'll find a way to track down the signal." She removed the back to extract the battery and the SIM card. "We keep a supply of smart phones downstairs that can't be traced. I'll get one for you to use while you're here."

She said nothing about the conversation she'd obviously overheard. "You are not going to tell Lucan?"

She moved her shoulders. "If he asks me who I've given phones out to lately, I'll have to say you've got one."

"About my father," he persisted.

"I think you should tell Lucan about it." She sat down beside him. "From what I overheard it sounds like you could use some advice. Lucan can seem unfeeling and sarcastic and kind of scary sometimes, but underneath all that sneering superiority and cold-blooded heartless killer thing he does, he's just a guy trying to get by. He'll understand."

Jamys had long suspected the same, and nodded slowly.

"The sun's almost up. You should get some rest." Her eyes strayed to the notes he had been writing. "Are you planning to go down to Miami for something?"

"Yes." He opened Gifford's Web site and tapped the screen where the lecture information was listed. "This."

Chris read it, and then eyed his notes again. "You ran away from home to attend a lecture on piracy? Couldn't you have just taken a class at the local community college?"

He pulled up the account from Father Bartley's journals. "I want to know more about this."

Chris skimmed the page, and then sat back. "Well, no one knows what happened to Hollander and the *Golden Horde*, not even Mel Fisher." Her lips formed an O that she covered with her fingers. "Oh, my God. You're going after the Emeralds of Eternity. No. Really?"

"Yes." He was surprised that she knew about the lost jewels. "You have read the high lord's summons."

"I, ah, heard about it." She jumped as the drapes on the other side of the room began to close. "I thought the curtains closing by themselves would be cool, but they're actually a little creepy." She regarded him. "If you're the one who finds the emeralds, the high lord will give you rule of Ireland, right?" When he nodded, she smiled. "I could help you with that."

Jamys knew how resourceful Chris was, and she knew the region far better than he. Accepting her offer would also allow them to spend more time together, and he wanted that more than the jewels. But while he wanted to have her with him, he had to consider first her position in the household. "I cannot take you from your obligations here."

"You heard Lucan. He said for me to look after you while you're here," she reminded him. "That makes you my number one priority."

Chris spoke as if he were nothing more than a task to be attended to, and yet he detected a subtle alteration of her scent that indicated secrecy. She was not lying, but she was not telling him everything. Jamys couldn't blame her for holding back, not when he was doing the same. He suspected that, like him, she did not trust easily.

It did not matter to him. He would take her however he could have her. "Then we will search for the emeralds together."

Lucan slipped away from his blissfully exhausted Samantha in their bed and left their chamber for his dressing room. Although she thought of herself as his equal, his beloved was still in her infancy as an immortal, and as such spent most of the daylight hours abed. Lucan himself seldom required more than three or four hours of rest, and had discovered he could make do with as little as an hour.

He dressed in silence as he thought on the night's events. While he loved her rather more than anyone or anything in existence, Lucan never took for granted Samantha's own devotion. He could not; she was the only soul in all the world who had ever loved him. He had never expected that, not after walking the night alone for more than seven hundred years. Indeed, she had come to him when eternal life had grown exceedingly tedious, and brought to him the sort of hope and wonder he had never imagined himself feeling.

In the beginning falling in love with her had absolutely appalled him, for he knew very well what he was. He had tried to save Samantha by pushing her away, time and again, only to realize he had not the slightest desire to live without her. Her own love had never wavered, even when Samantha had finally discovered the truth about him, and faced the monster inside the man. She hadn't quailed or run away from learning she loved the most lethal killer among all the Kyn; she had stayed. She had demanded better of him.

For his part, Lucan had learned exactly what he would do to preserve and protect the love that had saved him. When Samantha had been shot and lay dying in his arms, he had ruthlessly dragged her back from the next life by pumping Kyn blood into her veins.

While Samantha rested, Lucan usually went down to his office to work until dawn, but tonight he felt little inclination to attend to business. He'd managed to keep his temper in check when she'd told him about the flowers, but the mysterious gift and her lack of concern over it still aggravated him. No doubt she was right and there was nothing to it, but he wouldn't be able to relax until Garcia made certain of that.

There was one place in the stronghold where he could work off some of his frustrations and assess the new arrivals, and that was where he headed.

At Burke's suggestion Lucan had purchased the five-level parking garage behind the stronghold's main building. After enclosing the open-sided floors with concrete walls, Lucan had been able to do as he liked with the interior. The contractor he'd hired to cover the paved floors with many truckloads of earth had been puzzled, but no more than the lighting designer, the cabinetry installer, or the architect who had designed several auditoriums as venues for professional boxing.

Once the bare bones had been put in place, Lucan summoned his own men, who had oiled and packed down the dirt, adjusted the lighting, stocked the cabinetry, and designated the areas to be used for training and practice bouts. While walking through the completed lists, Lucan doubted any other suzerain or seigneur under Richard Tremayne's rule could boast of having five stories of wide-open fighting spaces for his garrison's use.

Tonight the men who were not on duty or out hunting had gathered on the first level, where training evaluations customarily took place. As Lucan entered through a side door, the guard standing inside straightened and bowed.

"Wait," Lucan said as the guard prepared to announce his presence. He studied the rows of broad backs directly blocking his view of the demonstration area. "Has someone issued a formal challenge?"

"Aye, my lord," the guard said. "'Twas from the visitors' side."

Warriors in strange territory seldom picked fights on their first night among the *jardin*'s garrison. Whoever had started this had plenty of nerve—or was an utter fool. "Which one made the challenge?"

The guard looked uncomfortable. "Their leader, my lord."

Lucan's brows rose. "How interesting. He must have been on his best behavior when I received them." He reached for a hooded cloak hanging beside the door and pulled it on. "Stay here and say nothing of my presence. And for Christ's sake, do not bow when you agree."

The guard's eyes widened before he composed his features and nodded. "As you say, my lord."

With the cloak and the shadows obscuring much of his appearance, Lucan was free to join the crowd of men observing the bout. In the center of a rough, wide circle drawn in the dirt battled two warriors with short copper-clad swords. Both had stripped to the waist, their bodies blooded from glancing wounds that had already closed and vanished. From what Lucan saw, neither had gained an advantage; with their Kyn strength and ability to heal spontaneously they could fight for hours.

His men and the visitors had divided themselves on either side of the circle, and cheered loudly whenever their comrade struck or evaded a blow. Although such bouts were generally fought with some reserve to avoid the infliction of serious injury, the two men hacked at each other with the kind of ferocity seen only on the battlefield.

Sutton, a halberdier who had joined the *jardin* shortly after Michael Cyprien had granted Lucan the territory, displayed his expertise with the short blade by delivering a series of punishing parry and thrust combinations.

The visitors' man, the bullish warrior who had introduced himself to Lucan as Vander, moved with surprising agility for his size. It spared his neck from being skewered by the blade, and lent him the speed and position required to deliver a sideswipe that bit deep into the guard's thigh.

Several of the visitors cried out in one of the old languages for Vander to finish the work, but instead of pressing his advantage, the warrior stepped back and lowered his blade. "Is there no one among this herd of boys to match me?" He scanned the scowling faces of Lucan's garrison. "Or do you all waste your nights swilling wine and swiving wenches while your lord tag tails after that fickle female of his?"

As angry mutters grew loud around him, Lucan turned to Piel, the warrior nearest to him. "Give me your blade."

"Before I have a go at him? Piss off." Piel glanced down at the black velvet glove Lucan extended, and cleared his throat. "Ah, forgive me, Suzerain, I did not see—"

"Blade. Now." While Piel drew his bastard blade from

its simple hip sheath to pass it to him, Lucan stripped off his gloves. The blade had some decent weight to it, and had been maintained with a razor-sharp edge. "Nicely balanced. Turner's work, I presume?"

"Aye, my lord." Piel appeared ready to choke. "Do you mean to kill the braggart yourself?"

"I wouldn't need a sword for that." Lucan pushed his way through his garrison to the front. Before he stepped into the circle, he spoke in a low voice to two of his guards. "Graydon, McNeil, come and take Sutton to the infirmary."

The two men hurried out to lift the wounded Sutton between them and carry him away. The rest of the garrison, now aware of Lucan's presence, fell silent.

"Look at this brave brute here," Vander called to his comrades in the same old language they used. "Twice my size, he is, yet he won't show his face." As the visitors laughed, Vander craned his head, trying to see inside Lucan's hood. In English, he asked, "Come to give me more to carve up?"

Lucan picked up Sutton's sword and tossed it to one of his men before thrusting Piel's sword into the earth at the center of the ring.

Vander looked over at his crew. "Ho. We've a warrior-priest among us, brothers." He sauntered to the center and jabbed his blade into the ground a handspan from Lucan's before glaring over it. "Best you pray for him."

Lucan stepped back to the edge of the circle, and there waited until Vander mirrored his position.

Men on both sides shouted the count in the traditional Latin: *"Tres, duo, unus, ineo."*

Lucan reached his blade in three strides; Vander's shorter legs made it in four, but as soon as he grasped his hilt, he tumbled out of the way of Lucan's attack and came up on his right to deliver a side sweep.

Lucan parried as he pivoted to face the man, who artfully dodged a riposte as well as a boot to his leg.

"The Temple never taught you that," Vander said, grinning as he edged out of striking range. "Can't bow before God on a shattered knee." He feinted to the left before he lunged right.

Lucan, who regularly trained in private with his seneschal, had no difficulty defending himself from Vander's sly attacks. The shorter man displayed some limited skill with the blade, but he had no form to speak of, and depended too heavily on deception and close-quarter strikes as he sought to gain the upper hand.

Amused, Lucan permitted his opponent to come within a breath's width of wounding him before he drove him back again and again. As his frustration mounted, Vander grew more reckless, hacking at Lucan with no regard for his stance or position. At the proper moment, Lucan hooked the man's ankle and sent him sprawling to the ground.

As Vander sputtered and cursed, Lucan stepped over him and kicked his blade out of the circle. He brought the tip of Piel's blade to rest against the back of the man's thick neck, pressing just enough to draw blood.

Both sides of the circle fell silent, and Vander quickly held out his hands in surrender. "You prevail, warrior."

Lucan lifted the blade and nudged the man over onto his back. Only then did he pull back the hood. "As you see, Mr. Vander, I do not spend all of my waking hours swiving *my* wench."

"Forgive me, my lord. Fighting always loosens my tongue." He grimaced. "The match is yours."

"So is this garrison, and they are not accustomed to being challenged by those who enjoy my hospitality." He took in the dismayed faces of the visitors. "While you are welcome to train with my men, you will not pick fights with them."

"Apologies again, my lord," Vander said quickly. "We have been fighting for our lives for so long that we know little else."

Lucan didn't care for mewling sycophants, but he knew too well how it felt to have no place in the world to call home. He held out his bare hand, and after a slight hesitation Vander reached up and grasped it.

"You and your men will report to Captain Aldan for training at tomorrow sunset," Lucan said as he helped him to his feet. "Single-handed combat form to begin. I expect to see some genuine progress within the week."

Vander offered a bow of respect. "As you say, my lord."

"One more thing." Lucan brought the tip of his sword to Vander's throat. "Speak ill of my lady again, and you'll not have a tongue to flap during a fight."

Vander gave a tiny nod of his head.

As Lucan returned the blade to Piel, the men of the garrison parted and formed two-column ranks. Instead of bowing when Lucan walked down the center to leave, they drew their daggers and tapped the hilts against their chest armor, a show of respect usually reserved for a fellow warrior who had distinguished himself in battle.

Ernesto Garcia stood waiting outside the lists. "Good evening, my lord." He bowed and smiled a little. "I take it someone has just greatly impressed the garrison."

"So it would seem." He felt annoyed by how much the impromptu accolade had moved him. "Come, we will talk inside."

Garcia accompanied him to the penthouse, where Lucan directed him to wait in the study. After looking in on Samantha, who had not stirred, he changed into more formal garments and rejoined Garcia, whom he found studying one of his bookshelves.

"You can borrow whatever you like," he told the *tresora*, "but if you crease the spine, I'll rip out yours."

"I appreciate the offer, my lord, but I value my mobility slightly more than a first-edition Oscar Wilde." Garcia handed him a typed report. "The flowers delivered to your *sygkenis* were purchased from a downtown exotic florist. The customer paid for them with cash and signed the receipt with an illegible scribble."

Lucan held up the scanned image of the receipt. "Was he mortal?"

"I cannot say," Garcia admitted. "The proprietor described him as a well-dressed man in his mid-thirties who spoke with a faint European accent. From the florist shop he took a taxi to Port Everglades, and was last seen boarding a private tour boat with black-painted windows."

Lucan kept close monitor on all the major illegal activities conducted in his territory by humans, especially the more inventive operations. To date only a handful had eluded his detection, including one very private casino. "So this secret admirer frequents the Treasure Palace." He walked over to his desk and studied the map of South Florida hanging behind it. "How very interesting."

"Racketeering has never been able to locate the casino or positively identify the operators, as every victim has been found dead within days of filing a police report," Garcia said. "However, in each case the victims who came in contact with the casino's owner gave a description of him that matches that of the man who sent the flowers to your lady. The only name the casino owner used was 'Dutch.'"

"My darling Samantha doesn't gamble," Lucan said as he took his *sygkenis*'s mobile phone out of his pocket, and began scrolling through her call history. "In fact, she refuses to purchase so much as a lottery ticket. Did she investigate the murders of any of the victims?"

"No. In each case, the medical examiner ruled out homicide," Garcia told him, and reluctantly added, "They all committed suicide by hanging."

A crack appeared in one of the windows as Lucan turned on him. "They hung themselves within days of making reports to the police, all of them, and this was not considered murder? Your colleagues are feeble idiots, Captain."

"I am in agreement, my lord." Garcia sounded just as disgusted. "But these cases were never sent over to my department, so I first learned of them only tonight."

In no mood to replace every glass door in his study, Lucan forced back his anger. "So why does he pursue my *sygkenis*? Not to gain access to what the police know about his victims."

"He could learn that by romancing any records clerk," the *tresora* said. "I worry his intentions may be more personal in nature." He nodded toward the mobile. "There is a text that came in for her an hour ago that you should perhaps read."

"Oh, he texts, does he?" Lucan returned to the main menu and pulled up the text messages sent to Samantha's phone. He found one from an unfamiliar number sent just after midnight, and opened it. "He writes, 'The flowers are only the beginning, my lovely. Meet me tonight at the Turtle's Nest, eight p.m.' His lovely, is she? Does he think she's some common tart to be had with a few posies?" He closed his fist, crushing the mobile into a handful of twisted components.

His fury ebbed as unexpectedly as it had come over him, and Lucan regarded the small heap of twisted components that had once been Samantha's mobile. "Garcia?" He looked over the desk at the *tresora*, who had gone to his knees and held his arms over his head.

"My lord." Garcia stood, shedding small showers of shattered glass as he did. He picked one dagger-shaped shard from the back of his hand and calmly wrapped a handkerchief over the wound. "This may have nothing to do with your lady at all. This Dutch could be using her to get to you."

"Then it is working," Lucan said flatly. "What more can you tell me?"

"The Turtle's Nest was the name of a dockside café a mile south of Bahia Mar, but it went out of business some time ago. There are no other businesses operating from that pier." He started to say something else, and then subsided into silence.

"Now is not the time for discretion, Captain."

"Couples have been known to make use of the place," Garcia admitted. "When they cannot afford or acquire a motel room."

"Indeed. How very deliberate a choice." Lucan went to his shelves, reaching through the shattered door to extract a book, which he handed to the *tresora*. "It is yours," he insisted when Garcia hesitated. "You have more than earned it."

"Thank you, my lord." Garcia brushed some glass from the book before tucking it under his arm.

Lucan studied the ruins of his bookcases. "Ernesto, have you ever considered Samantha to be . . . fickle?"

"No, my lord." The *tresora* sounded genuinely surprised. "Even when she was human, my lady was completely dependable. In fact I have never worked with so reliable or dedicated an officer." His expression changed. "She would never trifle with this mortal, my lord, or any other male. You must know that. This Dutch means only to bait you, or do her harm. I can arrange to send a female decoy to meet him tomorrow night, and have men waiting to take him as soon as he shows."

"No, Captain." Lucan smiled. "You will leave this Dutch to me."

Chapter 8

Despite the brightness of the morning sun, Jamys insisted on personally escorting Chris to the private car waiting to take her home for the day.

"For the record, this isn't my idea," she said as her driver, Melloy, came around to open the door for her. "Someone needed my parking spot for his new Ferrari." She rolled her eyes up at the penthouse suite.

"You will return tonight?" The dark shades Jamys wore gave him a teen heartthrob look, but his voice rasped with weariness.

"Sure." She climbed inside, a little startled when his hand supported her elbow. "See you later."

Chris forced herself not to look back through the rear window at him, but as soon as the limo turned the corner, she slid over onto her side and thumped the soft leather seat cushions with her fist.

"You okay back there, Lang?" Melloy asked over the intercom.

"No. Yes. Not really." She sat back up and lowered the partition window so they could talk without using buttons. "Melloy, why do we work for these people again?"

"Well, they pay us a ton of money, and we have all kinds of job security," he suggested. "If you're a night person, the hours are good. If someone wants your parking spot, they lend you me and the limo."

"Anything else?"

He thought for a minute. "They don't sparkle or get you pregnant with a life-sucking fetus."

"Amen, brother." Chris laughed.

Peter Melloy was one of the youngest *tresori* to serve Lucan, and had the unusual advantage of being born and raised in America. While he could behave with the same dreary formality as the European *tresori*, and was as fiercely loyal as any of them, he had a wry sense of humor and a much less slavish attitude toward the Kyn.

"So you and the new guy seem pretty tight." Melloy, whose parents served the Atlanta *jardin*, had not pledged himself to Lucan until a year after Jamys's prior visit. "Got some history going on there?"

"If a couple weeks count, which they don't." Chris rested her arms against the back of the front seat. "Did you hear about the high lord's latest summons?"

"My parents called right after it was delivered to Suzerain Scarlet." He grimaced at the rearview. "Can't talk about it, though. Official *tresori* business."

She waved a hand. "Don't sweat it, Melloy. Padrone Ramas called me about it last night. I know the council doesn't want the high lord to get his paws on the emeralds."

Melloy perked up. "He told you that? Lang, you know what this means?"

I'm totally screwed. "I'm trustworthy?"

"No, you're in. You're going to be one of us." He grinned. "So where are you getting your ink?"

"Haven't decided yet." She couldn't confide in Pete, but she wondered what he would make of her dilemma. He'd tell her to follow the council's orders, naturally; like all *tresori*, he took the secret side of his oath to keep the Darkyn from destroying the mortal world very seriously. "But if the paperwork goes through, I'll probably do the back of my shoulder. *If* I can find an ink shop that offers general anesthesia."

"How can you be afraid of needles?" Melloy sounded perplexed. "You volunteered to serve the Kyn."

"Sam didn't have the fangs when I met her." Chris sat back and closed her eyes. "I was grandfathered in."

As Melloy drove her across town, Chris thought through her impossible situation. She knew enough about Richard Tremayne to suspect the council was right on the money with their orders; once he had the emeralds, the high lord would definitely use them. As cold and ruthless as he was, he might even set up his own private immortal-army-making factory. From there the only thing that kept the Kyn in check—the fact that they couldn't reproduce or otherwise make more Kyn—would be a nonissue. Then the mortal world would be in serious trouble, because Tremayne would be focused on things like wiping out the Brethren, establishing new territories, and taking control of governments. He wouldn't worry about silly little details like who was going to *feed* his armies.

Burke had told her that in order to maintain their strength, heal spontaneously, and use their abilities a healthy Darkyn had to consume a minimum of three pints of human blood per day. Wounded Kyn required much more, often as much as six to eight pints. While the immortals had trained themselves not to kill the humans while feeding, Kyn who had experienced any type of blood loss often became ravenous.

Wounded Kyn could not be trusted to adhere to their practice of not killing humans. If they took too much blood all at once from a donor, a strange psychic reaction, known as thrall and rapture, caused both to lose consciousness. The Kyn fell into thrall, which Burke had described as a sort of state of suspended animation that could last as long as a week. The human donor also slid into an irreversible coma—what the Kyn called rapture—and always died within twenty-four hours.

The average human body held about ten pints of blood, and donors needed six weeks to recover from losing even one pint of that. An army of Kyn wounded in battle could theoretically wipe out an entire village in a single day.

She could explain all that to Jamys, who she was sure would understand. But would it stop him from giving the emeralds to Richard Tremayne? Would he care enough about the safety of the mortal world to sacrifice his chance at becoming a suzerain and having his own country to rule? And what would the council do to her for revealing their intentions to a Kyn?

How do I ask him to choose me over the emeralds? They're his future; I'm not.

Melloy dropped her off in front of her apartment building, and waited there until she waved to him from the third-floor landing. She'd originally sublet the apartment across from Sam's, but once her cop neighbor had turned Kyn, she'd offered the place to Chris.

Sam had insisted she was doing her a favor. "The rent's paid through the end of the year, and by then I might change my mind about living with Lucan."

Chris hadn't been as worried as her friend. While the homicide cop and the immortal assassin's relationship had gotten off to a rocky start, anyone who saw them together felt instant, grinding envy. Chris suspected that alone they'd both been sleepwalking their way through life, definitely too wounded by the past to trust anyone. As a couple they'd woken up and started living again. Before she'd watched Lucan and Sam fall for each other, she'd never thought of love as something that could heal; in her experience it was more like a wrecking ball.

It doesn't have to be that way with me and Jamys. Chris took out her keys. *We could make it work, I know we could. I just have to show him how much he needs me, and what a great* tresora *I'd be. After I ruin his chances of ruling Ireland, or I disobey the council and destroy my future.*

She really needed a third option. And an aspirin.

Once inside her apartment Chris turned to secure the three dead bolts Sam had installed, when she heard a knock, and opened the door to see Jamys standing outside.

It took two tries for her to find her voice. "How did you get here?"

"A cab. I followed your car." He glanced past her. "May I come in?"

"Why? Sorry. Of course." She stepped back, and absently dropped her purse on the fussy little antique cherry table she'd bought with her first *jardin* paycheck. "If you needed me for something, you could have called. I'd have come straight back." He didn't say anything. "Okay, well, ah, come on in."

Chris flipped on a few lights as she led him to the living room. Sam had told her to do whatever she liked with the old furniture, so she'd begun gradually replacing it, donating most of it to Goodwill as soon as she'd bought what she wanted to put in its place. A wonderful old wingback armchair, still clad in faded floral tapestry, took the place of Sam's recliner. The anonymous department store lamps had been sacrificed for four smaller, porcelain versions with glittering bead-fringed shades. She'd sold Sam's still serviceable bedroom set to a new neighbor looking for something cheap for his guest room, and splurged on a gorgeous four-poster in black oak and bedding of white satin.

Sam's battered sleeper sofa had been the last to go, making way for Chris's most expensive buys: an outrageously curvy, completely indulgent long chaise upholstered with soft rose velvet, and a matching settee. Both held an assortment of small pillows and bolsters covered in satin, silk, organza, and velveteen.

Jamys moved around the room, inspecting the old piano shawls Chris had hung as window treatments and the fancy baker's rack that held her television and DVD player. "I do not remember it looking like this."

"Over the years I got rid of Sam's old stuff and bought new old stuff." She watched him reach up to touch a gleaming blue crystal star hanging from the curtain rod. She felt a little embarrassed by her ever-growing collection of shaped, colored lead crystals, which she had suspended by fishing line over every window in the place. "When I open the blinds, the sunlight shines through them and makes little rainbows on the walls." Which made her sound as deep as a six-year-old.

The air seemed a little stuffy, so Chris reached for a pack of matches and lit a gardenia-scented pillar candle by the chaise. She'd been looking forward to snuggling down into the pile of pillows and letting Linkin Park sing her to sleep; now she'd have to drive Jamys back to the stronghold. Unless . . . "Is the cab waiting for you downstairs?"

"No." He released the crystal and looked at her. "What you have done here is very attractive. It is not what I expected."

"I never planned on creating the ultimate chick cave," Chris admitted. "In the beginning I wanted more of a Victorian Goth look. You know, black velvet, scarlet brocade, gilt everything. But for some reason whenever I went shopping and had to choose, I was more drawn to the soft, frilly female stuff."

"There is nothing wrong with it," Jamys said. "I like that you are so . . . female."

"Good, because I like that you're not." A flutter of panic made her grope for an excuse to retreat. "Um, why don't you sit down? I'll be right back."

Chris hurried through her bedroom into her bathroom, where she locked herself inside. *What are you doing, flirting with him? What happens when he finds out you agreed to help him only so you can find the emeralds? Do you think he's going to like you for being such a good liar?*

She hadn't lied to Jamys exactly; she just hadn't explained why she wanted to help him find the gems. Even if she wanted to confess all, Padrone Ramas had slapped a gag order on her; she couldn't tell him anything. Or she could, and say ta-ta to her one shot at being named and recognized with a status among the Kyn.

"Christian?" Jamys called through the door, making her jump a little. "Are you unwell?"

"No, I'm fine. I'll be right out." Chris went over to the

sink, splashed her face with cold water, and straightened her blouse before walking out into the bedroom. Jamys stood beside her dresser and was admiring one of her seashell-covered keepsake boxes. "Jema has a case like this for her photos." He opened the lid to reveal the bundle of papers inside.

"I just keep junk in mine," she said quickly. "Old notes, mostly. Some of them are from you."

He glanced at her. "You save my e-mails?"

Every single one of them, even though she didn't have to because she had read them so often she had them all memorized. "I don't have that many friends who write to me." Disgusted with herself, she went over and closed the lid to the box before she glared up at him. "The truth is, all of the notes are from you. I don't have any other friends who write to me, so I like to save them. It's stupid, I know—"

He pressed a fingertip to her lips, effectively silencing her. "I, too, have saved all of your e-mails."

Chris felt her heartbeat stutter. "Are they in a box on your dresser?"

"I keep them hidden away in my armoire." He traced the top of her cheekbone. "You are exhausted."

"So are you." Which reminded her. "Why did you follow me home?"

"I wanted to know why you have changed so much. And I did not wish to stay in the suite alone. I think I have spent too much time by myself." His voice took on a tired rasp. "May I stay? Only to rest until sunset."

She nodded, and drew him over to the bed. "I'm probably going to pass out the minute my head touches that pillow, so if you need anything, shake me a couple times."

He didn't reply until they were curled up together under her puffy comforter and she had just begun to drift off. "I have everything I need."

Jamys dreamed of blood and pain, and the girl who had saved him from both.

The first time Christian had brought him to her apartment, he had been wounded, bleeding. He had wanted to tell her he could clean up by himself, but after dragging him into the bathroom she had taken out a small first-aid kit to treat his wounds.

"You're a mess," she muttered as she dampened a pad and began cleaning the streaks of dried blood from his face. "You shouldn't have left your blades back at the club. I know you guys are all about the honor and stuff, but that was dumb."

He raised his brows.

"Don't get all Kyn on me," Chris told him. "She could have blinded you." She finished wiping his face and carefully pushed aside what was left of his hair to look at the wound. "It's closed, but it's not healed. You need blood." She began rolling up her sleeve.

Jamys caught her arm. *No, Chris.*

She glared at him. "It's part of my job."

I will not feed on you.

"The honor thing is getting really old and tired now." She yanked down her sleeve. "I keep some bloodwine in the fridge for Sam. I'll get you a glass." She stalked out.

Jamys stood and looked at his face in the mirror. Luce's blade had hacked off most of the hair on the side of his head; he was lucky not to have lost an ear. He searched through the kit until he found a small pair of scissors and went to work on the rest. By the time Chris returned with the bloodwine, he had filled her small trash can with cuttings.

"I liked it better long." She handed him the glass and took the scissors. Shadowed crescents rimmed her eyes, and he could almost feel how exhausted she was. "Sit down and let me do the back."

Jamys sat and sipped from the glass, closing his eyes as the rejuvenating warmth of the bloodwine spread through him. His head felt oddly light without the length of his hair, and the gentle brush of Chris's fingers soothed him.

"It'll probably grow back in a day," she said as she snipped. "I wish mine would. Last year I went blond, huge mistake, and then I tried to dye it over with this gorgeous purple color. It ended up the color of sewer sludge."

He drained the glass and set it aside, but the taste lingered on his lips. He needed to leave and hunt, but Chris's luscious scent filled his head. When she came around to stand in front of him, he latched on to her wrist.

"Ouch." She grimaced. "Little sore there."

He turned her wrist over and saw the stained bandage she'd wrapped around it, and then looked at her pale face. *What have you done?*

"I kinda lied to you. I don't keep any bloodwine in the fridge for Sam." She tried to smile. "It's okay. I've got plenty, and you needed the boost."

She'd bled herself for him. If he could have cursed, he would have. He lifted her into his arms and carried her out, looking this way and that until he found the room where she slept.

"This is nice," Chris murmured as he placed her on

her bed. "Just like in the movies." When he tried to straighten, she tugged on his shirt. "I'm cold."

He wasn't, not with the force of her blood coursing through him. He eased down beside her, gathering her close and pulling the black-and-white geometric bedspread over her shivering body.

"I'd really love to have sex with you," she whispered, "but I think I'm going to be criminally stupid and pass out now." Her eyelids slowly closed, and her body relaxed.

He checked her bandage to make sure she hadn't cut herself too deeply, then rose from the bed to stand at the window. Sunrise was only a few minutes away.

He glanced at the telephone on the bedside table. He needed to warn Lucan about the Kyn who had come here, but even if he could speak, he doubted they would believe what he told them.

Behind him, Chris whimpered, and Jamys went to her. He placed a hand on her forehead. *All will be well, my little friend,* he lied to her. *Forget what has happened tonight and rest now.*

Jamys woke from the dream slowly, roused by the setting of the sun. He could hear the sound of water splashing from Christian's shower, and glanced at the empty space beside him before he rose and left the bedroom. She would want privacy to dress and groom herself, and as much as he would have liked to help her, he doubted her clothes would stay on for very long.

Thanks to her he had rested in a deep state for the entire day; now he felt ready to begin the search for the emeralds in earnest. He would have to speak to Lucan about taking Christian with him, but he expected no difficulty in obtaining the suzerain's permission.

Nothing seemed impossible now.

Chris had called him her friend, but she had saved his e-mails as if they were treasures. She did care for him and, he suspected, not only as a friend. It made him feel hope as he never before had.

He found a bottle of bloodwine in her refrigerator, and drank a glass as he rummaged about in the kitchen. When Chris emerged from the bedroom, he had a pot of tea and a plate of fruit, cheese, and bread waiting for her.

"Hey." She surveyed the table. "You didn't have to make me food."

"You need to eat." She smelled of citrus and flowers, and damp tendrils of her hair curled all around her face. "I would have prepared a hot meal, but I have never cooked."

"I mostly nuke stuff anyway. This is really nice." She nodded toward the bedroom. "Do you want to use the shower before we head out?"

He wanted to sweep her off her feet and carry her back to the bed, this time not to sleep. "Yes, thank you."

Once Jamys had showered and dressed, Lucan's private car had arrived downstairs, and took them back to the stronghold.

"I need to finish up a couple of things," Chris said after they arrived at the club. "Meet you in the suite in thirty minutes?"

Jamys nodded. As soon as she had gone, he went to the suzerain's office, where he found Lucan in conversation with his *tresora*.

"When she asks, my lord—"

"You will lie to her, Herbert. Or, if you find yourself incapable of such a heinous act, you will feign ignorance of my activities." After Lucan inserted a clip into a semiautomatic pistol, he said to Jamys, "My apologies, Durand. I have an urgent appointment to keep."

The scent of night-blooming jasmine hung heavily in the air, but so did another odor. Jamys couldn't identify it as he breathed it in, but he felt it crackling like icy fire in his lungs, and exhaled quickly.

"At least take your guards, my lord," Burke said to Lucan, his tone almost pleading.

The suzerain eyed his *tresora*. "The bitch that whelped me has been dead for well on seven centuries, Herbert. I do not require a new mother."

Jamys offered a polite bow. "May I join you, Suzerain?"

"Nor do I need a boy to trot after me." He tucked the gun inside his jacket. "Burke, look after Jamys until Christian reports for duty, will you?"

Jamys got between Lucan and the door and, when the big man approached him, looked up into his eyes. The ghost gray irises had expanded, reducing his pupils to thin black slivers; a direct indication of the extent of his agitation. Lucan reached to adjust the medallion hanging from the thick gold chain around his neck, running his thumb over the cross in the center of it.

"Excuse me." Lucan strode around him.

The *tresora* almost followed the big man out before he paused at the threshold and stepped back.

"No good will come of this," Burke muttered to himself before he turned to Jamys. "Forgive me, my lord. The suzerain meant no insult; he is . . . in one of his moods. Would you care to take a tour of the underground levels? I don't believe they had been finished during your previous visit."

Jamys nodded at the door. "Where has Lucan gone?"

Burke looked uncomfortable. "The suzerain prefers that I keep his business concerns confidential."

Jamys reached out and removed Burke's spectacles, and showed him the crack bisecting one lens. "Bad business, I think."

"So do I." The *tresora* grimaced as he took the glasses and pocketed them, and then went and closed the door. "My lord, my oath to Lord Alenfar prevents me from voluntarily giving you the information you desire. I am also immune to *l'attrait*." His expression grew hopeful. "However, were you to use your gift to compel me . . ."

Jamys nodded, and rested his hand against Burke's neck. *You wish to tell me where Lucan is going, and why.*

"The master has learned that a casino owner named Dutch sent roses to the lady Samantha's workplace," Burke said, his voice taking on a dreamy quality.

The door behind them opened and closed, and Chris joined them. "What are you doing?"

"Wait." Jamys nodded to Burke.

"My lord then intercepted a texted invitation from this man for Lady Samantha to meet him tonight at an abandoned dockside bar called 'the Turtle's Nest.'" The *tresora* sighed. "He destroyed her mobile and told her nothing. He goes there now to confront Dutch and, I fear, kill him."

"Jesus Christ." Chris went to the desk. "I'll call up to Samantha."

"No." Jamys released Burke to put his hand over Chris's on the receiver. "I will go and stop him."

"Stop him?" Chris chuffed out some air. "I'm sorry, but you can't."

Did she think he was helpless, like his father? "It is what a warrior does."

"It's what a *crazy* person does," Chris corrected. "There are two things on the planet that make Lucan go postal. Brethren, and anyone trying to hurt Samantha. I'm not kidding," she added. "You know the guy who shot her? Lucan touched him with one hand and he exploded. Literally. They had to mop him off the walls."

Jamys put his hands on Chris's shoulders. *There is something wrong about this, Christian. Lucan insisted on going alone. There was a strangeness to his scent.*

Chris bit her bottom lip. "One of the girls up front told me that last night he went to the lists and got into a sword match. Beat the crap out of the guy, too. He never does things like that."

He saw the panic in her eyes. *What are you thinking?*

"Whatever is going on here, it's not about Sam, or he'd be going after her, the way Dwyer did. This guy wants something else." She took in a quick breath. "I think Lucan could be walking into a trap."

Samantha's safety would serve as excellent bait. He removed his hands. "I must go after him."

"I'm driving you." When he started to reply, she glared. "You don't know where the Turtle's Nest is, and you don't know how to drive. I do." She took a set of keys from Burke's pocket. "He's your friend, Jamys, but he's my lord. This is my job; let me do it."

He might have compelled her to think otherwise, but it would take more time they didn't have. "Very well." He reached out to Burke one more time. *You will remember none of what you have told me here.*

Burke's expression blanked and, when Jamys withdrew his hand, grew puzzled. "Lord Durand, Christian, good evening." He glanced around. "Did you, ah, need something?"

"We're good," Chris told him. "I'm going to borrow your car and take Lord Durand for a ride around town, okay?"

"Of course." Burke smiled as he reached into his pocket, and then frowned. "Oh, dear. I seem to have misplaced my keys."

Chapter 9

Chris knew the Turtle's Nest from its brief tenure as a fairly awful bar and its more recent rep as a popular flop spot; when horny tourists weren't getting high or having sex inside the building, runaways and street kids used it for temporary shelter. It stood on the far end of an old pier, and the only way to get to it was by walking the length of the dock.

She parked Burke's Mercedes in a metered curb space directly behind Lucan's red Ferrari. "Well, he didn't stop for coffee." She peered out through the side window, but all the lights of the pier's lampposts appeared to have burned out. Glass never had a chance when Lucan was in a temper; she'd bet her next paycheck that each bulb had shattered the moment he'd passed under it.

"Chris." Jamys pointed to a couple of dark shapes bobbing at the base of one piling. "Boats?"

"Too small." She got out of the car and walked around it. As Jamys joined her, she finally made out the silhouettes of the speedy water vehicles. "Jet Skis. Come on."

He held her back. "You should remain here."

"I should get a day job working for normal people who don't think blood banks are a buffet, but sadly, I haven't." She smiled. "And I don't wait in the car."

The ramp leading up to the pier creaked under their footsteps, but the rush of the waves covered the sound. Chris strained to see any sign of Lucan or a setup, but the dock seemed entirely deserted.

As they approached the old bar, Jamys came to an abrupt halt, holding up his hand to signal her to do the same. When she looked around him, she saw something flash and heard wood crack.

"Gun." Jamys dragged her behind a wall of rusty metal siding.

Chris didn't protest as he covered her body with his. Bullets that would definitely hurt or kill her would only bounce off his Kyn flesh. Unless they were copper, in which case they'd both end up looking like Swiss cheese.

"Come out with your hands up," a man shouted in an ugly tone, "and no one will get hurt."

"There's a guy who loves bad cop shows," Chris muttered in Jamys's chest. "They never say that, you know. Sam always goes with 'Drop the weapon' or 'On the floor, asshole, hands on your head.'"

"There are two of them," he murmured. "Both mortals."

The corrugated metal behind her back suddenly hammered into her as the adjoining wall exploded outward in a burst of splintered studs and chunks of drywall.

"Which one of you is Dutch?" she heard Lucan ask in the pleasant, polite tone he used whenever he was in a full-blown rage.

"Don't move," a man replied. "Dutch sent us to have a little chat with you. I said, don't move."

Jamys went to the edge of the wall to peer around it, and then vanished as a man screamed. Chris followed, only to come up short as she took in the sight of Jamys checking a man on his knees clutching a ruined arm, and Lucan advancing on another who was backing away as he fired directly into the suzerain's chest. The gun emptied quickly, and in true bad cop-show fashion, the thug threw the useless weapon at Lucan.

The suzerain caught it with his bare hand, and crushed it into a mass of twisted metal before dropping it. "Where is Dutch?"

"I don't know." As the man reached the end of the pier, he glanced over his shoulder. "But I got his number, right here. I'll call and find out." He whipped up his hands, but when Lucan kept coming, he cried out, "Don't do it, man. I can't swim."

Lucan seized him by the front of his shirt and lifted him up over his head. "Then you should have no difficulty drowning." He heaved him into the water.

Jamys ran past Lucan, diving off the end of the pier.

Chris looked up from the wounded man as Lucan turned around and walked toward them. She stood. "He's had enough, my lord."

"I think not. He still breathes." When Chris blocked his path, he reached out as if to touch her.

She braced herself. *God, I hope this is worth all the broken bones.*

Something flashed in Lucan's eyes, and then died away, and he lowered his arm and stared at her as if he didn't recognize her. "Christian. What are you doing here?"

He sounded completely bewildered. "I was showing Lord Durand around town and saw your Ferrari parked over there." She glanced over the side of the dock, where Jamys was pulling a limp body out of the surf. "He's busy rescuing that guy you just tried to drown."

"I tried to . . ." He fell silent and still, as if someone had shut off a switch inside him, and then just as quickly came back to life. He seemed to forget she was there as he strode away.

Chris pulled out her mobile and speed-dialed Sam's number as she hurried after the big man.

"Hey, kid," her friend answered, and yawned. "Taking the night off?"

"No, I'm on duty. Hang on." Chris jumped off the steps onto the sand. "Jamys and I are by the old abandoned pier on Loggerhead Beach. So is Lucan, and something's seriously wrong with him."

"How wrong?"

"He just threw a guy who can't swim off the pier." Chris raced through the pilings toward Jamys. "Sam, we need you down here. Now."

"Four minutes." The line clicked.

By the time Chris reached Jamys, he was standing over the coughing, heaving thug and holding a copper dagger.

"Get out of my way, boy," Lucan said as he approached them. He jerked back as Jamys made a quick motion, and looked down at the horizontal slash in his shirt. The edges of the white fabric grew dark as blood soaked through them. "You cut me. You fucking little bastard."

"Stay back," Jamys ordered.

Chris went to the man, and helped him to his feet. "Can you run?" When he nodded, she gave him a push. "Go. That way. Get your friend, and get the hell out of here."

Lucan noticed the thug as he staggered away, and moved to follow. Jamys countered him, still holding his dagger ready.

"I have fought armies, and slit the throats of more men than you could count," Lucan said. "Think you can end me with one tiny blade, boy?"

"We can find out, my lord," Jamys assured him.

"Suzerain, please," Chris begged. "Stop. Just stop."

"And you, you treacherous little slut." Lucan turned his head toward Chris. "I took you into my household, did I not? Gave my protection and my affection, and for what? So you might whore yourself behind my back for this nothing of a boy. Is that how you keep your oath to your master?"

"I haven't taken the oath yet, and I don't whore myself for anyone." It took everything she had to smile instead of bursting into tears. "I think you have me confused with some other treacherous little slut."

"I will deal with you later." Lucan turned on Jamys. "You are no longer welcome in my territory, Durand. You will leave at once, tonight, and you will not return."

"No." Chris felt horrified. "Lucan, please."

Jamys politely inclined his head. "As you say, my lord."

"That's more like it." Lucan bared his fangs. "If I ever find you inside my boundaries again, I will take you apart and send you back to your father in a basket."

"I will go." Jamys lowered his blade. "First you give your word you will not harm Christian."

"My word? I am the master of this territory, and she belongs to me." Lucan grabbed hold of Chris's arm and dragged her to his side. "I will do whatever I damn well please with her."

"If that is how you feel," Jamys said, "I will take her away with me."

"It seems you have a choice, girl." Lucan sneered down at her. "Go with him, or stay with me. Or perhaps you don't care who crawls between your thighs."

Chris blinked. Lucan had a terrible temper, especially where Samantha was concerned, but even in his worst mood he always maintained a frigid politeness, especially toward women. "What is *wrong* with you?"

"Nothing a bit of slap and tickle wouldn't cure." Lucan focused on Jamys. "Shall I have her now, boy? If you watch a real man at it, you might even learn something."

"What about me?" Sam walked up and planted herself in front of Lucan. "You want to teach me something, too?"

Chris didn't know whether to laugh or cry. She settled for cringing. "Sam, he didn't mean it. He lost his temper."

"At last, my lady arrives." Lucan turned Chris loose and pushed her away. "Now we'll each have a whore to plow, boy."

Sam's expression turned to from stone to ice. "Jamys, please take Chris back to the stronghold."

"He can't. I've banished Durand from my territory," Lucan informed her. "He's not taking the little slut any—" His head rocked back as Sam's fist connected with his jaw, and the force of the punch made him stagger.

"Have you lost your fucking mind?" Sam demanded. "Jamys and Chris are our friends. You don't banish him, and you don't touch her. And who the *fuck* do you think you are, calling me a whore?"

Lucan rubbed the fading dark spot on his jaw as he eyed her and sneered. "I am your lord and master, my lady."

"Oh, yeah?" She drew a gun and shot him. "Now you're just beach trash."

Chris couldn't breathe until she watched Lucan pull the tranquilizer dart out of his chest before he toppled over. "Jesus, Sam."

"Lord and master, my ass." Her friend stood over her unconscious lover, aimed, and shot a second dart into his back. "Son of a bitch. If it wasn't impossible for the Kyn to get smashed, I'd swear he was drunk." She turned to Chris. "You feel like sharing?"

"I don't know what's wrong with him. He's been acting so weird, ever since we got here." As her friend's eyes narrowed, Chris felt an irrational surge of guilt. "Listen, Sam, what Lucan said about—you've gotta know he was just talking off his head. He's never even looked at me sideways. Or me at him. Ever."

"Relax, sweetie. This isn't on you." Sam gave her shoulder an absent, awkward touch before she looked at Lucan again. "I don't get it. I've seen him behave like a jackass before, and he never talks trash like that. When he's angry, he's an iceman. Wordy, sarcastic, and vicious, but an iceman." She said to Jamys, "Is this one of the big secrets I don't know about? Some kind of personality change Kyn males go through when there's a full moon, or what?"

"The moon has no effect on us." His dark eyes went to Lucan, too. "I have never seen him like this."

Chris thought fast. "Could he have hit his head on something? Maybe that would have made him forget that he's a decent guy that never acts like this."

"Decency." Lucan pushed himself up from the sand, looking as if he'd never been drugged. "You know nothing of that." He regarded the three of them as he reached back and pulled the second dart out of his shoulder to examine it. "Poison. Pathetic." With a contemptuous flick of his wrist he tossed it to the sand in front of Sam's feet. "At least the whelp there had enough spine to wield a blade."

"Oh, I was only trying to be nice." Sam drew the nine-millimeter from her shoulder holster and pointed it at his face. "This one has copper rounds in the clip, lover. Would you like to find out just how much spine I have now?"

"You'll suffer for this, you farthing bitch." He abruptly turned on his heel and walked off.

The three of them stood in shocked silence, broken only by the sound of Lucan starting the Ferrari's powerful engine before it roared off down the highway.

"Did he just threaten to make me suffer?" Sam's voice sounded hollow.

"Yeah." Chris couldn't believe it, either. "Could he be immune to Alex's tranquilizer, and we just didn't know it?"

"That or maybe the cartridges are defective and he didn't get a full dose." Sam tucked the nine back inside her jacket. "Chris, until I say otherwise, don't talk about what happened tonight to Burke or anyone else in the *jardin*."

"Should I call Rafael and ask him to fly back tonight?" Chris knew that, as Lucan's seneschal, Rafael was the only member of the *jardin* permitted to temporarily take charge if anything happened to the suzerain. Lucan also respected his second more than any other warrior who served him.

"Not yet. First I need to have a serious chat with Alex Keller." Sam turned to Jamys. "Jamie, under the circumstances I think you'd better head back to North Carolina. Chris, will you give him a ride to the airport?"

"Sure, no problem." She shared a troubled look with Jamys. "Is there anything else I can do?"

"Yeah." Sam bent and picked up the dart Lucan had thrown at her and held it up. The streetlights illuminated the glass cartridge, which was cracked and empty. "Pray that Alex has come up with something stronger than this."

The sound of something tapping gently on glass roused Lucan enough to open one eye. He didn't see Burke, Samantha, or any of his *jardin* warriors. He saw a patrolman standing next to his Ferrari. The cop had his nightstick in one hand and a citation book in the other.

With no small amount of relief Lucan pressed the button to retract the window. "How may I be of assistance, Officer?"

"Have you been drinking tonight, sir?" the cop asked.

Lucan checked the roof of his mouth with his tongue, where his fangs did not protrude. "Not yet, I should think."

The patrolman straightened. "Please step out of the vehicle, sir."

Lucan complied, and discovered his Ferrari sat parked on an empty stretch of sand, in which it had also sunk halfway to its wheel wells. He didn't recognize his surroundings but, from the size and architectural style of the mansion sprawled to the left, surmised it was a private beach.

Darkness has no need. Lucan didn't know why that line from Byron's poem echoed in his mind, only that it made him feel a strange, almost unbearable sense of doom.

"Do you know where you are, sir?" the cop asked.

"A beach in South Florida." He hoped. He regarded the shorter man, who shuffled back a step. "Do you know where I am?"

"I'll ask the questions, sir. Would you walk up here, please?" When Lucan had crossed the sand and stepped over the curb, the cop pointed to a faded strip of white painted on the road's edge. "Stand on the white line with your heels together."

Lucan frowned. "Why would I do that?" He breathed in the air. From the temperature and smell of it, he was no longer in Fort Lauderdale. "Where the devil am I?"

"Now, there's no reason to get angry about this, sir." The cop rested his hand on the holster clipped to his belt. "You're going to walk this line for me, and then you're going to blow in a little balloon, and it'll all be over." He inhaled, and his expression became uncertain. "If that's okay with you, sir."

Lucan moved closer, deliberately shedding more scent until the officer's pupils dilated, indicating he was experiencing the full effects of *l'attrait*. "Where am I, and how did you find me?"

"You're in Palm Beach," the cop said, and rattled off an address Lucan didn't recognize. "The owner of the estate called 911 when you drove off the road onto his property. Dispatch sent me to respond. I love that car, man."

"So do I." Lucan reached for the patrolman's arm, and stopped as he saw his hands were bare. "Tell me the time."

The cop glanced at his watch. "Quarter past midnight."

Somehow he'd lost five hours. As he reached inside

his jacket to check his pockets, Lucan discovered the long tear in his shirt and the tenderness of a newly healed wound beneath it. Someone had slashed his chest, and he had no memory of it. "I need a phone."

The cop reached into his pocket and produced one. "Please, use mine."

"Wait here." Lucan dialed the number to Samantha's mobile as he walked down to the Ferrari. When she answered, he said, "Sweetheart—"

"Kiss my ass." She hung up.

"I'd love nothing better." He stared at the phone for a moment, and redialed. The number went straight to her voice mail.

Lucan searched the interior of the Ferrari, finding only a trace of his own blood on the rim of the steering wheel, and some scattered beach sand on the floor mat. Traces of sand also encrusted the seams and soles of his shoes.

He placed one more call, this time to his *tresora*, who thankfully did not hang up on him. "Good evening, Herbert."

"My lord." Burke sounded relieved. "Where are you?"

"Presently, in Palm Beach."

"I see." Burke sounded quite the opposite. "May I ask why?"

"You may not." Until he learned what had happened to him over the course of the last five hours, Lucan could not rely on anyone, even his most trusted human servant. "The Ferrari has had a slight mishap." He gave Burke the address. "Call Triple-A, have it towed back to the stronghold, and summon my mechanic."

"Yes, my lord. Should I send a car for you?"

Lucan glanced at the patrolman still waiting by the curb. "I have already arranged alternate transportation." He hesitated before he asked, "Is Lady Samantha there?"

"No, my lord. My lady departed shortly after eight and has not returned. She did not mention to anyone her destination." Burke waited for his response, and then said, "I could call Captain Garcia—"

"That is not necessary. See to the car, Herbert." Lucan ended the call and walked up to the curb. Along the way he heard again the echo of the poetry fragment inside his head.

Darkness has no need.

What he needed, Lucan decided, was to find Samantha and reassure her, determine what had caused his memory lapse, and then hunt down the bastard responsible and personally thank him.

"Officer," he said to the patrolman. "You will drive me to Fort Lauderdale."

"Of course." The cop opened the passenger door of his squad car for him.

Lucan climbed in on legs that began to shake. "And please, do use your emergency lights."

Chapter 10

Jamys took the keys to the Mercedes from Chris's purse as they walked Samantha to her car and watched her drive off. So absorbed by her thoughts was Chris that she didn't notice he'd put her in the car and was himself driving until he stopped at a red light.

"Hey." She sat up and stared at him. "I thought you didn't know how to operate a motor vehicle."

He shrugged. "When last I came here, I did not."

"You just forgot to mention that since then you learned." She looked out through the windshield. "You're not driving to the airport, either."

"I am not leaving."

"Right." Chris rubbed her eyes. "You did hear my crazy boss when he described the send-you-to-your-Dad-in-a-basket scenario."

"I can stay without trespassing on Lucan's territory." He turned down a side street that led to the Intracoastal, and parked outside one of the many marinas that lined the waterway.

She dropped her hand. "You're going to steal a boat. This is so much better."

"Borrow a boat." He scanned the slips and noted the vessels with lighted cabins before he climbed out of the car.

"I'll assume you know how to sail," she said as she followed him down the ramp to the slip dock. "But where are you going to park?"

"In Miami, near the museum." He stopped by a beautiful wooden-hulled sailboat and nodded at the man sitting in a deck chair and coiling rope. "I will call you soon."

"Take me with you. You need me," she insisted as he looked doubtful. "You'll need a mortal to do stuff during daylight hours, and I promised Lucan I'd look after you. That was before he went psycho, so it still counts."

He wanted to take her with him. What he feared was that if he did, he would not bring her back.

"Christian." He touched her cheek. "You are not my *tresora*."

Her hand covered his. "I could be."

Lucan's sneering threat echoed in his memory: *I will deal with you later.* While Jamys did not doubt that Samantha would do all that she could to protect Chris and the mortals who served the *jardin*—she had appeared fully prepared to shoot Lucan with copper tonight—the suzerain had been a master assassin. He had spent centuries developing his skills and cunning, which were now likely as powerful as his ability to kill with a touch. Jamys also felt sure that Samantha's love for Lucan as well as the bond she shared with him might render her incapable of ending his life. In his current condition, Lucan would not share such compassion.

"I watched my mother go crazy," Christian said, startling him. "Every day for two years." Her hand shook as she pressed it against her shirt, where the cross she wore concealed there hung. "I know Lucan and Sam aren't my parents, and I'm just supposed to be the hired help, but I can't go through that again." Her eyes, now shimmering with tears, lifted to his. "Please don't leave me here."

Jamys pulled her close, and held her until her trembling quieted. Her scent became sharp with fear but not deception; she was genuinely frightened of what was happening to Lucan. As he rested his cheek against the top of her head, he thought of Angelica, and the madness that had twisted and consumed her. Discovering his mother's insanity had made him feel the exact same helpless terror. "We must go now. Do you know how to sail?"

The lightning of her smile flashed, dazzling him. "You forget, I grew up on the beach. Not only can I swim, surf, water-ski and sail—with enough time and materials I could probably build you a boat."

Convincing the sailboat's owner to lend his vessel to them proved no problem; Jamys accomplished it a moment after greeting the man, when he shook his hand. Before he left, the owner showed them the supplies he had stocked for the extended fishing trip he had planned, as well as how to use his new navigational array.

While Chris went below to investigate the cabin, Jamys escorted the boat's owner from the dock to his sports car. "You will return home and enjoy the holidays there."

"Which home?" the man asked.

Jamys's brows rose. "How many do you have?"

"Three. Boston, Atlanta, and Paradise."

"You will go to Boston," Jamys told him, deciding it would be best to keep the man as far away as possible. Out of curiosity, he asked, "Where is this Paradise?"

"It's the name of an island off the Keys," the man told him. "I bought it as a tax shelter. I was going to spend Christmas there. It's a good place to be alone."

"Where is this island?" Jamys asked.

"Ten miles east of Lower Matecumbe. The coordinates are programmed into the navigational computer. Just enter the word 'paradise.'" The man drew out his keys and removed two. "You'll need these to disarm the security system and get into the house."

Jamys pocketed them and, once the man had driven off, returned to the slip, where he found Chris at the helm using the computer to chart a course.

"Commercial boats and barges use the Intracoastal as a shipping lane, plus it's usually clogged with joyriding tourists, so we should probably head out to sea." She pulled up a map and traced an imaginary line from the marina down to Miami. "There's a place we can dock here that's about five miles from the museum. Gifford isn't lecturing there until tomorrow night, so we have plenty of time." She glanced at him. "After we talk to him you should ask him to show the actual journals, too. He donated them to the museum, and he's on the board, so he should have access to them."

He heard the note of anxiety in her voice. "You are worried about Gifford?"

"No, I think you can handle him." She frowned. "I just don't know how much useful information we'll get. I mean, this is the secondhand account of a dying pirate's confession made back in the seventeenth century. Gifford also could have faked the journals. He wouldn't be the first guy to manufacture history in order to boost his professional standing and guarantee a spot on the lecture circuit."

Jamys would have overlooked the change in her scent, but from here they would be entirely dependent on each other. "But that is not what truly concerns you."

She sat down in the captain's chair. "I have to tell you something." When he nodded, she said, "Something that may make you toss me off the boat."

He took hold of her hand. "Nothing you could say would do that, Christian."

"Wait until you hear it," she warned. "The other night I got a call from Italy."

As Jamys listened, Chris told him about her petition to be recognized as a *tresora*, and then related the response from Padrone Ramas. That they would assign such an impossible task to a mortal angered him, but he concealed it from her. It was only when she mentioned the council's determination to prevent Richard Tremayne from acquiring the gems that he understood the source of her anxiety.

"So that's why I originally offered to help you." She sounded ashamed now. "I thought maybe I might be able to find the emeralds before you did, or send you in the wrong direction, or something like that. Then I could give the gems to the council, make them happy, get what I wanted, and save the world in the process."

As clever as Chris was, she likely would have succeeded. "Why are you telling me now?"

"I can't do it." She made a helpless gesture. "Don't get me wrong, I wanted to. I've been working my ass off to train and learn protocol and everything else the council requires. Becoming a *tresora* is all I've thought about for the last three years. I might not have the right bloodlines and pedigrees, but the Kyn are my family. I want them to feel the same about me. But if that means I have to step on your hopes and dreams, I have to give it up. I just can't do that."

She had spoken from the heart, and Jamys felt his own clench in response. The sound of her voice breaking over the last of her words made it impossible for him not to touch her. He tugged her out of the chair and into his arms. He meant only to comfort her, but she lifted her face as he bent to touch his mouth to her brow, and their lips met.

He thought of orange blossoms and honey as he kissed her, reveling in her sweetness. Surely this was why his father could not keep his hands from Jema, knowing that at any moment he could drink from such a delicious fount. The heat of her body poured over him, even as his scent spilled around them, and she sighed his name, the touch and sound of it sending a shudder through him.

Chris was the one to draw back, her face rosy. "So I take it you're not going to throw me off the boat."

"I think not." No, after her admission and that kiss, he had other plans for her. But he should first determine what her desires were. "What will you do if we find the emeralds?"

"I don't know." She gave him an uncertain look. "Type up my résumé. Look into job retraining. Move to Nepal. Why are you looking at me like that?"

"I was imagining you in Paradise," he said honestly.

Sam carried her largest empty suitcase over to the bed, and ignored a knock on the door as she opened it.

"My lady," Burke called. "May I join you for a moment?"

"Not a good time, Herbert." Sam strode into the

closet where she kept her work clothes, jeans, and T-shirts.

Lucan's *tresora* appeared in the doorway. "Forgive me, my lady, but I need some assistance."

"Don't we all?" She grabbed as many hangers off her work clothes rack as she could hold and carried them out to the bed. "If Alex Keller calls, give her the number to my mobile."

Burke came to watch her removing hangers. "I do beg your pardon, my lady, but are you packing to go somewhere?"

"Yes." She stopped what she was doing. "Away from here. Now. You'll just have to deal with this on your own."

Burke began helping her. "You should know that I have sent Triple-A to Palm Beach to tow the master's Ferrari, and he has arranged his own transportation back to the stronghold." When she said nothing, Burke sighed. "My lady, I know at times the master can be difficult, but if you would find it in your heart to forgive whatever he has—"

"He banished Jamys, he manhandled Chris, and he tried to kill not one but two mortals." She eyed him. "Right before he called me a whore. To my face."

Burke paled. "Was Christian hurt?"

"Not physically. She's taking Jamie to the airport, and then I imagine she'll be coming back to pack up *her* things." Sam retrieved some toiletries from the bathroom. "I don't know what brought this on, but it wasn't the usual song and dance. He crossed some serious lines tonight."

The *tresora* grimaced. "Under certain circumstance I know he can be most unkind, but he always regrets it later."

"It wasn't just what he said or did. I shot him with two tranq darts, and they didn't even slow him down." For a moment Sam wondered if she was doing the right thing by walking away, but then remembered how close she'd come to shooting him in the head. "I'm going to talk to Alex, see if she knows what could have caused this. Until we know, you should send the humans home, and tell the men to stay clear of him."

"As you wish, my lady." Burke's locator chimed, and he checked it. "The suzerain has just arrived."

"Elvis has entered the building, has he?" She closed the suitcase. "For now I'll bunk with Chris over at her place." She didn't want to think about long-term arrangements. "Call me if things get ugly, okay?"

Burke nodded, and hurried off to the elevator.

Halfway down to the emergency exit, Sam's mobile rang, and she set down her case to answer it. "Hello."

"Got your message," Alex Keller said over a terrible connection. "We're in Ireland."

"Great." Sam sat down on the steps. "I'd send him to you, but the tranq darts aren't working. Any suggestions?"

"Check your . . . bagged blood," the doctor said. "Someone could . . . tampered with it."

"Tampered how?"

"Added . . . animal blood." Alex launched into an explanation of which Samantha heard only every third or fourth word. Then the connection crackled and her voice came through in a clear burst. ". . . bleed him first, then transfuse him. You'll need six to eight pints, but no more than that or he'll go into thrall."

"I'm sorry, you want me to what? Bleed him?" Sam swore as the line began to break up again. "Alex, can you hear me?"

"There's . . . Kyn . . . mind   control . . . could . . . mess-ing with . . ." The line dissolved into a buzz of static, and then disconnected.

"Shit." Sam tried dialing Alex back, but a polite re-cording informed her that the number she was calling was temporarily out of service.

Although Sam didn't know what Alex had meant by mind control, the possibility that their blood supplies had been tainted made sense. To please her, Lucan usu-ally abstained from feeding on humans and depended mainly on the supply of bagged blood the *jardin* had stockpiled. Because the blood was kept out of sight in a refrigerated room belowground, and was available for any Kyn to use, no one had ever bothered to put a lock on the entry or otherwise secure it.

If someone had spiked their supplies with even a small amount of animal blood, it would definitely affect any Kyn who drank it. At first it would only make them sick, but if they'd continued using the tainted blood, it would gradually begin to change them.

Drinking animal blood for long periods of time caused the Kyn to undergo bizarre physical mutations. After being forced for decades to live exclusively on cat blood, the high lord had become a part-human, part-feline hybrid known as a changeling. Sam and Lucan had also battled a snakelike Kyn who had lost most of his humanity by living on the blood of reptiles.

Remembering Faryl Paviere and his grotesque ap-pearance didn't bother her as much as recalling the fero-cious and violent behavior he'd displayed. Sam had personally witnessed him using his jaws to rip the head off the body of a Kyn warrior as easily as a human might pop a grape from a stem.

"No, it can't be the blood." She and many of the men among the garrison also made use of it, and none of them had fallen ill or shown any drastic changes in behavior. *Unless someone tainted B positive blood,* she thought. Ever the connoisseur, Lucan preferred the taste of that particular type over all the others. She and the rest of the Kyn were aware of this, which was why they usually set it aside for his use. . . .

Sam left her suitcase on the stair and trotted down to the first-floor landing, where she inputted the code to access the secondary stairwell leading down to the tunnels.

At the blood-stocks room she found the captain of the guard supervising a group of *tresori* wearing protective shrouds and working in bucket-brigade fashion as they removed bloodstained white bags.

"What the hell happened here?" Sam asked Aldan.

"Nothing good, Lady Samantha." He sketched a quick bow. "Someone deliberately destroyed our stocks. They used a blade to pierce the bags, let them empty out, and strewed coin on the shelves and flooring."

Samantha peered inside the room again and saw the hundreds of pennies that had been scattered everywhere. "Why throw coins in the blood?"

Aldan looked uncomfortable. "'Tis like a thing that was done in the old days, during the *jardin* wars. A traitor would come into a stronghold and poison the blood stocks by dropping coppers into the kegs."

"You kept *kegs* of blood?"

"During the winter season, when humans remained indoors and were harder to hunt, the cold kept it sound." He saw her expression and quickly added, "'Twas not taken by force, my lady. We collected the blood bled from the sick by leeches hoping to heal them. Our *tresori* would also give what they could to help sustain us."

"The only thing we have in kegs now is beer, right?" When the captain nodded, she looked back in at the mess. "I don't get it. This isn't the Dark Ages. We can buy all the blood we want and have it here in a few hours. So destroying it was a waste of time and perfectly good pennies."

"Often such a thing is done to provoke, my lady." Aldan gestured for her to follow him, and led her out of earshot of the mortals. "It is not the act but the doing of it that harms. Lord Alenfar is as feared as he is respected. For an enemy to successfully elude detection and the guards to infiltrate his household and make worthless that which sustains it . . ."

She stared at him. "You're saying they did this to make Lucan look bad?"

"Not bad. Weak," Aldan said. "Or perhaps unworthy of rule."

This on the same night Lucan had driven off the only son of another, highly dangerous Kyn lord, leered over a girl he'd always treated with affection, and nearly pushed Sam, his life companion, into shooting him. "You may be right, Captain. What is the general procedure when something like this happens?"

"We must make it known to the garrison," he said. "They are the first line of defense. Our mortal allies should also be advised. For that, I would call on Mr. Burke."

"All right. I'll head upstairs and talk to him. If you would, call Lady Jayr and ask if she can spare some of her blood stores. Send one of the men to Orlando to pick it up."

He bowed. "As you say, my lady." When he straightened, he drew the short sheath containing his *sgian dubh* from his boot. "I would ask you to ease my mind and carry this." He offered it to her. "Pistols require bullets," he explained. "A blade does not."

Sam curled her fingers around the Celtic knots carved into the stag-horn handle, and drew out the blade. It had been honed to razor sharpness, and forged from folded bands of copper and steel, which would make it effective against mortal or Kyn. "Thank you, Aldan."

"My lady." He nodded and went back to the cleanup.

Sam resheathed the small dagger and tucked it into her own boot before she headed for the lift, which she took to the first floor. As soon as the doors opened, music blasted in her face and red lights danced before her eyes. She wove through the milling patrons, wishing as she did that she could pull a giant plug and shut the whole place down.

Burke's office adjoined Lucan's, but she found it empty. Then she heard a low moaning sound on the other side of the door between the two, and kicked it open.

The love of her immortal life sat in his custom-made executive chair. On his lap sat a pretty twentysomething with a killer tan, a tiny black dress, a white silk bandeau around a messy beehive of raven hair.

Lucan lifted his face and had the incredible balls to look relieved. "Samantha." The girl slid to the floor with another low moan as he stood. "You are—"

"Pissed off." She went to the girl and helped her up. "Look at me." After she checked her pupils, Sam removed the bandeau, folded it over, and pressed it against her throat. "Did you have sex with her?"

"No. I had no desire to—"

"You can shut up now." Sam shed enough scent to blot out Lucan's, and told the girl, "Ask the doorman to get you a taxi, and take it home. Forget everything that happened here."

"Doorman. Home. Forget." Like a sleepwalker, the girl drifted out of the office.

Sam looked down to see she stood in the exact spot where Lucan had kissed her for the first time. Or at least she assumed she did; after he'd felt her up, he'd wiped the memory of it from her then-mortal mind.

"Our blood stores have been destroyed," Lucan said. "I haven't fed in three nights."

She stared at the little bulge Aldan's blade made in the side of her trouser leg. "I know."

"Samantha." He came up behind her. "Why won't you look at me?"

He had such a beautiful, seductive voice. Even before she'd fallen in love with him, Sam had been entranced by it. He had a huge vocabulary, which he loved to use, and could converse better than anyone she'd ever known, including Herbert Burke and Ernesto Garcia, two of the most educated men she knew.

Sometimes, after they made love, Lucan would tell her stories about some of the places he'd seen during his travels, and she enjoyed that almost as much as the sex.

Burke came through from his office. "My lady." His voice chilled a few degrees when he added, "My lord."

Sam made herself look at the lying bastard she loved. "All right, start talking."

"Herbert." Lucan watched Samantha's face. "Tell my *sygkenis* what I intended to do when I left the stronghold tonight, and what time I departed."

My lady.

"You left at seven so you might intercept the man who sent flowers to her office," Burke said stiffly. "I believe you also intended to kill him."

"That is the last thing I remember," Lucan said. "When I came back to consciousness, it was midnight and I was in Palm Beach. My Ferrari had been driven into the sand and left to sink in it, hardly something I would do to my favorite vehicle. But I could not remember driving there or anything that may have occurred after I left the stronghold."

"That's convenient." She should have been angry with his bullshit excuse, but it added another piece to the puzzle. "So you're suffering from amnesia."

"I haven't forgotten a thing. What I lost was time." He stretched out the fingers of one hand. "Five hours, gone." He snapped his fingers. "Like that."

Something about his voice. It had started to chew on her nerves, this feeling. *About his words. About what he called me.*

"My lord," Burke said tentatively, "when you awoke in the Ferrari, were you injured?"

Lucan opened his jacket. "It appears someone slashed my chest."

"Jamys did that," Sam murmured, distracted by the two words that were bouncing back and forth in her head. *My lady.* Why were they so important?

"Samantha?"

"Quiet. Let me think." Lucan wasn't the sort of guy who used a lot of pet names, but when they were alone he'd call her 'love.' And when he was angry, he always addressed her as 'madam' but occasionally he'd use—

Burke cleared his throat. "My lady, perhaps I should—"

"That's it." She felt a fierce satisfaction as she glared at Lucan. "You called me 'my lady.'"

"Did I?" He didn't seem impressed. "How mysterious. I imagine that would be because you *are* my lady."

"You didn't say 'my lady.' You said it all slurred together. You made it into one word. Say it now." When he didn't, she stepped forward and slapped him.

"Lady Samantha." Burke tried to get between them.

"Stay out of this, Burke." She saw Lucan's eyes turn to chrome. "Say the goddamn word."

Her lover folded his arms. "Milady," he drawled with insulting slowness. "Does that satisfy you, madam? Or would you care to hear me recite more niceties?"

"You say it with a short *i*. 'Mih-lady.'" A strange sensation churned in her stomach, and for a moment she thought she might be sick. "Son of a bitch."

His jaw tightened. "Oh, that I am, but what does it matter how I say anything?"

Of course, he didn't get it. He had no memory of saying it. "That's not how you said it on the beach. You said mee-lady. You used a long *e*." She turned to the *tresora*. "Burke, in all the years you've served Lucan, have you ever heard him say 'my lady' like that, with a long *e*?"

"I cannot say that I have," Burke admitted. "Perhaps if he were to imitate someone else, a peasant or a commoner, he could manage it."

"When did I call you that, Samantha? In Palm Beach?" Lucan demanded. "Were you there when I wrecked the Ferrari?"

"Burke, whoever did this didn't think about pronunciation. It came out of his mouth, but Lucan wasn't the one speaking." A laugh escaped her as her knees turned to jelly and she had to catch the edge of his desk to brace herself.

Lucan began to reach out to her and then seemed to think better of it. "Burke, clear out the club and tell the men to secure the stronghold."

"We have visitors, my lord," the *tresora* reminded him.

"Send them to one of my hotels," Lucan said. "Under guard."

When Burke left, Lucan came to stand beside her. "Samantha, obviously we have much to discuss, but I want you to know that I only made use of that girl to feed. When I returned tonight, I was so weak I could hardly walk."

"That's because tonight at the beach I shot you with the tranq gun. Twice." She leaned against him. "It wasn't you. You didn't lose five hours, Lucan. They were stolen from you."

His arm came up around her. "By whom?"

"The same bastard who I think took control of your mind and body." Her mobile rang, and as she flipped it open, she looked up at him. "Someone who says mee-lady." Into the phone she said, "Brown."

"Sam, I need you to come in," Captain Garcia said. "We've got the guy who murdered Coburn in custody."

"What?" She straightened. "Who collared him?"

"No one. He turned himself in."

Chapter 11

Once they were under way, Jamys insisted Chris go below to eat and rest while he manned the helm.

"I will wake you at dawn," he promised.

She'd watched him handle the boat long enough to gauge his experience, which exceeded her own. He'd even done something to the rigging to make the sails more effective, which worked so well he cut off the engines as soon as they were out on the open sea.

Chris scanned the horizon for storm clouds, wide breakers, or anything that might spell trouble. "All right, but yell down if you need me. I'm a light sleeper."

"Are you?" He seemed amused by that.

In the cabin belowdecks Chris found some clean clothes and took them into the head. The boat offered a surprisingly large shower and heated water, which she quickly put to use. The clothes proved to be several sizes too large for her petite frame, but she made do by belting and cuffing the jeans and knotting the hem of the T-shirt.

The owner liked his comfort foods, she decided when she opened the small fridge and examined the contents.

Two bottles of excellent wine stood next to a whole herb-roasted chicken, bags of fresh fruit, and a container of salad greens. More meat and frozen veggies packed the little freezer section, and in the cabinet next to it she found enough canned and dry goods to keep them fed for weeks.

Not us, me, she corrected herself, and felt a little depressed. Jamys might manage to drink a small glass of wine, but nothing else. Now that they had left the stronghold behind, there would be no more convenient supplies of blood. As a *tresora* it was her responsibility to keep her Kyn lord strong, so she'd have to feed him herself until she could buy some units. Or he could go out each night and hunt. . . .

The thought of Jamys holding another woman while he fed on her made Chris's stomach turn. *No, I'll steal the blood if I have to.*

Although she had no appetite now, Chris forced herself to eat a few slices of chicken and some fruit and drink two full glasses of water. Fluid replenishment was one of the *tresoran* secrets to countering blood loss; Burke had taught her to drink as much water and juice as she could every day in order to keep hydrated.

Burke, who by now was probably frantic.

Chris took out her mobile and dialed the *tresora*, gnawing at the inside of her lip as she did. She couldn't tell him much, but she could let him know she was all right.

"Christian." Burke answered before the first ring had finished. "Thank God. Where are you?"

"I'm fine and so is Jamys." She could lie to him and say she was at the airport or her apartment, but her heart wasn't in it. "Have you seen Sam? Is she okay?"

"Our lady is well. Christian, the master has been attacked, and we have secured the stronghold. You must return at once."

There would never be a good time to tell him, so it might as well be now. "I'm not coming back, Mr. Burke. I don't serve Sam or Lucan anymore."

"I cannot justify his actions," Burke said slowly, "nor even explain them. But whatever the master said or did to you, he was not himself. I think it safe to say that he deeply regrets his behavior, and any harm it may have caused you."

"It's not because he was acting like such a jerk," she assured him, and glanced at the upper deck. "I have other priorities now that are more important to me. I'm sorry."

"Are you quite certain about this?" he asked gently. "I believe in a few days this ungodly situation will have sorted itself out, and all will return to normal. I would not trouble you about it, but you have worked so tirelessly for your position. It seems a pity that all that effort should go to waste."

"I know what I'm doing, I promise." She took in a deep, steadying breath. "I am grateful for everything you've taught me. I'll always owe you."

"Nonsense, my dear." He sniffed. "Wherever you go, perhaps you would take a moment now and then to drop a note to an old man, and let him know you're well?"

"Absolutely." She was never going to get a good-bye past the lump in her throat. "Take care, Mr. Burke."

"Godspeed, Miss Christian."

She kept the tears away by tidying up the dishes and putting away the food. The subtle shift of the hull as it cruised through the calm water soothed her frazzled nerves. She'd just walked away from the only real friends and family she had, which might turn out to be the biggest mistake of her life. By revealing her orders to find the emeralds and keep them from Tremayne, she'd betrayed the council. As soon as they found out—and they always found out things like that—they'd erase her name from their list of potentials and forget she'd ever existed. With as much as she knew about the Kyn, they might even try to have her mind-wiped or killed.

Chris wandered over to the bunk in the back corner of the cabin, and lay down on the plaid coverlet. Although it was comfortable and roomy for a single, obviously the owner slept alone on the boat. She saw a row of buttons in the wall panel over her head and touched one.

From two small speakers on either side of the cabin the distinct sound of a cello colored the silence. Yo-Yo Ma, she recognized, performing Bach's prelude from Cello Suite No. 1. It was one of her favorite classical pieces, and when she closed her eyes, she thought of the acclaimed musician in an overcoat and scarf, his talented hands clad in fingerless gloves as he played his beautiful instrument in the snow.

Whatever happened after she and Jamys found the emeralds, she would call Burke, Chris decided. She'd write to him, too, every month. It didn't have to be a big thing, just a card or an e-mail to let him know she was okay and happy. She was going to be okay, and very happy.

She had every reason to be. Jamys cared about her, and trusted her. She'd make a new life for herself being his *tresora*. She didn't need the council's permission or a title or anything. Jamys was still Kyn, and if he wanted her, he'd have her. From the way he'd kissed her tonight, he definitely liked her.

Chris stared up at the ghostly reflection of her face in the mirror-polished wood ceiling. *So why do I feel so miserable?*

Like father, like daughter.

What her conscience suggested made her roll over and bury her face in the pillow. She was not like Frankie Lang; she wasn't running away from a marriage or a kid. Sam and Lucan and Burke would be fine without her. They had a stronghold filled with devoted humans and immortal warriors, allies in Orlando and Atlanta, and more money than God. Once they got over the name-calling thing, they'd have each other.

No, she wasn't like Frankie at all.

Chris had just turned thirteen a few days before her constantly battling parents had had a huge fight over money. The next morning Adele left to go shopping, and Frankie had picked up his board, kissed Chris on the top of her head, and took off.

"See you later, baby," he called as he walked out to his Jeep.

Chris never saw him again.

Once Frankie had abandoned them, he'd stopped long enough to clean out what was left in the bank account, leaving Adele with nothing. Despite this, Adele refused to get a job, a divorce, or otherwise deal with reality. She repeatedly told her daughter that they would simply wait until Frankie came to his senses and returned home to take care of her and their daughter.

When her checks had begun bouncing and the credit cards stopped working, Adele had been furious. She had spent weeks on the phone demanding more time, more credit, and getting neither. Adele's Chrysler disappeared in the middle of the night; in the process of filing a police report she learned it had been repossessed. As their food dwindled and the collection notices mounted, she remained in denial, sending Chris off to school each day with the promise that everything would be fine.

The bank began calling about the imminent foreclosure proceedings; Adele refused to speak to the loan officer up until the morning two sheriff's deputies arrived to evict them from the property.

Some neighbors had first stared through their windows at them, and then closed their blinds so they wouldn't have to watch.

One of the deputies had been kind enough to offer them a ride to a local shelter for homeless families, where Adele sat in a dead silence as Chris filled out the intake forms. The shelter manager told them they could stay for a week to give Adele time to find a job or someone who could take them in. Adele had said nothing, and moved like a sleepwalker until the manager took them to the dining room to have a meal.

The sight of the tray Chris had fixed for her seemed to rouse Adele from her stupor. "What is this?"

"I don't know." Chris, who'd been living on canned food for weeks, sat down beside her and started eating. "It's not bad. Some kind of stew, I think."

"This is garbage." Adele had slapped the fork out of her hand. "We don't eat garbage." When the shelter manager came over to speak to her, Adele threw the tray of food at her before dragging Chris up by her arm. "We are going home, Christi. Right now."

Her arm throbbed as her mother's thin fingers dug into her skin.

"Mom, please, calm down." Chris saw flashing red and blue lights coming down the road, knew instinctively the police were coming for them, and tried to dig in her heels. "Let's go back inside. You don't have to eat anything. We could just rest for a while."

"We don't belong here," Adele said, her voice as hard as her grip. "We're going home."

The cops reached the end of the driveway before they did, and blocked it with their squad car.

"Ma'am?" One of the cops got out and directed his flashlight at Adele's face. "We got a call from the shelter that there was some trouble inside. You and your girl okay?"

Adele looked down her nose at him. "Those people tried to feed my daughter garbage. You should go and arrest them at once."

"Calm down, ma'am." The cop gave Chris an assessing look. "Everything's going to be fine now, honey. Don't be scared."

Her mother yanked on Chris's arm and hauled her around the cop car. When the officer followed and called for her to stop, Adele broke into a run, dragging Chris alongside her. She tried to keep up, but something caught her foot and sent her sprawling.

"Easy, sweetheart." One of the cops helped her up.

"Please don't hurt my mom," she begged him as Adele began screaming and pummeling the other officer. "She's just really upset."

"It's okay," the cop told Chris as his partner handcuffed her mother and hustled her into the back of the squad car. "Your mom needs some help, so we're going to take her to a hospital."

She saw the shelter manager hovering a few feet away

with a plump, white-haired lady in a blue wool coat. "Can I go, too?"

"No, but there's a safe place downtown where you can stay until she's better," he assured her. He beckoned to the woman in the wool coat. "This is a friend of mine named Miss Audrey. She's going to give you a ride there."

Miss Audrey came over and bent down, putting her face too close. "What's your name, young lady?" When she didn't reply, her smile became a tight line. "Answer me."

"Christi."

Miss Audrey straightened. "Very good." She marched Chris over to another police car, but when she shoved her into the back of it, the seat vanished and four marble walls shot up around her, closing her into an airless tomb.

Chris scrambled to her feet and beat her fists against the cold stone. "This isn't real. This didn't happen to me. Let me out of here."

Her shadow doubled, and Chris spun around to see the towering figure of a man in a monk's robe. For a moment she thought it was Lucan, until he extended the torch he held, and she saw the network of scars covering his fingers and hand.

"Who are you?"

I was the maker of the scroll, and the keeper of the cross. It was I who washed it in my blood. You and your mortal family were my army, my guardians, each sworn to protect the secrets of eternity. Now you number but two. You will not fail me as your sister did.

The smell of burning metal was making her stomach clench. "This is just a dream, and I don't have any sisters, you asshole."

You have the loyalty to protect the mortal world from

eternal damnation. But do you have the conviction to do what needs be done?

He talked like one of the Kyn, Chris thought, but he was dressed like a Brethren. "Are you Hollander? The guy who stole the emeralds?"

The monk began to laugh, a deep and frightening sound that bounced around the inside of the tomb, each echo growing louder until Chris pressed her hands over her ears and called out for the only hope she had left.

"*Jamys.*"

The sky had softened from black to deepest blue by the time Jamys guided the sailboat into Biscayne Bay. Other vessels of various sizes sat anchored in a vast web of light and shadow cast by the brightly lit condominiums and hotels crowding the shoreline. One mortal who had risen early glanced up from the bobber on his fishing line and raised a hand in silent greeting as Jamys passed.

He returned the wave and then studied the assortment of piers, boathouses, and landings jutting out from the bay's edge. Chris had said they might make use of one of the public docks, but he would need to consult a more detailed map to locate them. He turned the boat back into the wind, dropped the headsail, and back-winded the mainsail. As the boat slowed to a near stop, he secured the rigging and dropped anchor.

Chris still slept below, and it took all his resolve not to go down to join her. After sharing a kiss with her, however, all he could think about was stealing another, and another. He suspected he could kiss her for days and never grow weary of it.

His present dilemma was that he wanted more than kisses from her. Much more.

Jamys checked the horizon again, where the coming dawn had pinked the edges of the clouds. They would have to secure a vehicle to use whenever they were on land, he decided, or perhaps hire—

Jamys.

Chris's voice called to him with such power and terror that for an instant he stood frozen. Only when he had pulled the door belowdecks from its hinges and jumped down into the cabin did he feel the echo of it through his thoughts. She had not called to him, as he could plainly see her in the cabin's only bunk, her body still. The only sound he heard came from the soft rhythm of her breathing.

Why had he imagined her shouting his name when she was sleeping so peacefully? It had not been a memory or some fancy of his imagination; he'd heard her as clearly as if she had screamed his name in his ear.

Jamys went to the bunk, where her scent bathed the air and told him that she had been asleep for hours. He saw that she had been so tired, in fact, she had simply dropped on top of the covers. He reached for a blanket that had been left folded atop a chest, shaking it out before bending down to drape it over her. He hated the thought of waking her, and decided against it as he reached to brush a lock of hair from her cheek. He could give her—

Jamys please Jamys help me Jamys find me—

Jamys fell to his knees, blinded and deaf to everything but the bellowing storm that came roaring into his mind. It was as if he had been swept into the heart of a tornado, and as he fought to hold on to consciousness, he heard inside the terrible winds her voice and his name, distant and ragged, as if Christian were calling to him as she fought for her life.

Christian.

I'm here. Jamys, hurry.

Now Jamys felt the psychic barrier between them, as tall and wide as the wall of a fortress. Another Kyn had entered their dream and was using ability to prevent Jamys from reaching Chris's mind. Without hesitation he threw himself at the other immortal's barrier, battering it with his thoughts. At first it held fast against him, but as he continued to pour his power against it, he felt it flex and then grow thin. Just as he gathered himself for one last barrage, in his mind appeared a panel of smooth stone that changed from solid white to an opaque gray, and showed on its other side Christian, who stood beating her fists against it.

Such determination for such an untried warrior, another voice said, and the strangeness of it crawled through Jamys's mind like a swarm of hungry, burrowing insects. *In the face of eternity, will you be as steadfast and valiant? Would you kill her to save a hundred, a thousand, a million?*

No, Jamys thought, lashing out in pain and rage at the other alien mind. *I would die so that she might live.*

Save her, and you are lost. Kill her, and then perhaps you both shall live. The other immortal's power abruptly vanished.

Jamys!

He caught her in his arms, and they fell together through the voice and the wind and the darkness. Jamys landed on his back with Christian thrashing blindly on top of him.

"I have you." He closed his arms around her, holding her still until she opened her eyes and stared down at his face. "I have you."

She looked up and all around at the boat's cabin before she collapsed against him. "Oh, God."

Jamys cradled her as he sat up, turning her so that he could hold her as he braced his back against the frame of the bunk. He felt as weak as if he had not fed for a month, and it took all his self-discipline to stifle the tremors vibrating from his very bones.

"I thought I was having a nightmare." Chris shifted, tucking herself into the curve of his arm. "What was that?"

"Not a dream." The rapid beat of her heart distracted him; he could hear it humming through her limbs. Wherever they touched, it pulsed beneath the thin silk of her skin. "It felt like the nightlands."

"That's where you go when you sleep?" She shuddered. "I'd rather stay awake for eternity."

Exhaustion and hunger made his fangs emerge into his mouth. "Sometimes it can be frightening." He needed to put her aside, moor the boat, and leave her to hunt. And as soon as his head cleared, he would.

She lifted her face from his shoulder. "But I thought the Kyn were the only ones who could cross over into the nightlands. Why was I there? Jamys, your eyes."

"Forgive me." He eased her off his lap and tried to stand, and was vaguely alarmed to discover he could not. "Go to the helm, Christian, and take care of the boat. I will rest now."

She ignored him and pressed her fingers to his neck. "Damn it, you barely have a pulse."

Jamys felt her move away, and his body responded with a sluggish flow of need. That he couldn't act on it was his only relief. He would rest through the daylight hours, and when he woke, he would hunt.

The unyielding wood made a poor pillow, he decided, until he felt warm hands lifting his head onto something much softer.

"You're a lot heavier than you look." Cloth slid from beneath his cheek. "Well, Burke said not to let it show."

Her words made no sense to him, but he smelled her blood spill into the air a moment before a drop of it touched the corner of his mouth. Jamys tried to turn his head away, but her hand prevented it.

"Right now you need it more than I do," she chided softly. "Go on. Drink."

Her command was his wish, and the undoing of all his resolve; his lips sought the source of the blood and covered it. The taste of her made his fangs stretch out, eager to penetrate and take more, but to spare her more pain he used the last dregs of his strength to only suckle at the small wound.

Even that thin flow poured life and strength into him with astounding speed. Soon he brought up his hands, expecting to feel her forearm beneath his lips and instead grasping the tight muscles of her thigh. He raised his head to look at what she had done to herself, and saw a small wound marring her flesh, high up on the inside of her thigh. She had cut herself for him.

Her hand stroked over the back of his head, gently pressing as if to urge him back to the source of his delight. He ran the flat of his tongue over the wound, gathering the bright red beads that had welled there, and heard the soft sound she made. He could smell the arousal darkening her body's scent, and followed it until his mouth found the edge of her panties. The sharp points of his fangs easily sliced through the flimsy fabric, and he peeled it back from the pretty flower of her sex.

"Oh. Boy." Her fingers curled into his hair. "Burke didn't mention this."

He looked up at her flushed, startled face before he deliberately pressed his mouth to the center of her dark curls. "And this?"

"Not a word." She watched him through drowsy eyes, and when he used his tongue to part her, she shivered. "Jamys."

He drew back a little to take in the fragrance of her desire, and look upon her hidden beauties. If she were his, he would take her away to some sultry deserted island where they would never have to wear clothing, and he could look upon her and touch her and take her whenever he wished.

Jamys put his hand over her to feel her heat against his palm, and her hips moved so that her damp mons rubbed against his skin. He eased two fingertips between her folds and found the slick entrance to her body, which instantly clenched around him in reaction. He could feel her tension in her thighs and the tightening of her belly, but when he glanced at her face, he saw only longing and excitement.

"Do you like that?" he murmured.

"No." A dimple appeared in her cheek. "I love that."

Slowly he pushed his fingers deeper, penetrating her sheath and filling her soft, wet channel. When she tightened again, he put his mouth against her, stroking her open with his tongue and rubbing the small, hooded nub of her clit. Like a pearl it swelled and emerged, satiny-soft, pulsing along with her heart.

As he lavished long, slow strokes of his tongue on her, he used his fingers to play within her, turning them in a rhythmic glide against the fluttering, grasping grip of her body.

This was how she would feel on his cock: hot and wet, tight and trembling.

The thought of fucking her that way made his muscles knot and his hips jerk as his fangs shot out into his mouth, and then she convulsed, scoring herself on the sharp tips as her body spasmed.

The taste of her sex and her blood released all the dark wanting inside him, and Jamys thrust his fingers in and out of her, harder and deeper with each roll of his wrist, driving her from one peak to another as he rode her with his mouth and tongue.

Her hands fisted in his hair, and she curled over, bringing his mouth to her lips. The carnal explosion of that kiss brought him to the edge, but it was the feel of her hand reaching into his trousers that sent him over. The moment she touched him he groaned and shoved the head of his straining penis against her palm, and released the first aching stream of his seed.

"I have you," he heard her sigh.

Chapter 12

Sam looked through the two-way mirror at the suspect sitting in the interrogation room. A tanned, somewhat overweight man in his early forties, he wore an off-the-rack business suit, a wide and rather ugly yellow tie, and a fake Rolex. "*That's* our killer."

"Alleged killer." Garcia glanced down at the clipboard in his hands. "He's Eugene Gates, forty-three, divorced, no children. A pharmaceutical rep. Couple of speeding tickets." He handed her the arrest report. "He gave the desk sergeant a bloodstained diamond necklace, but hasn't offered a motive."

Sam looked past him at Jonah Massey, who stood just outside talking with one of the janitors. "What's he doing here?"

"I want Massey in there with you." Before she could reply, Garcia shook his head. "The DA wants a full confession on videotape. That means two officers present, my lady."

It also meant she couldn't use *l'attrait* to compel the suspect to tell her the truth. "Massey," she called, and was momentarily distracted by the hamster-wheel squeak of the janitor's wheeled bucket as he pushed it out of sight down the hall. "Can you run a video camera?"

Massey ducked inside. "In my sleep."

"Then you're in charge of taping and typing." She handed the clipboard off to him.

Inside the interrogation room Sam pulled out the chair on the opposite side of the table, noting the complete lack of reaction from Gates. The suspect, who seemed content to continue staring at a long scratch in the table's Formica top, didn't even twitch when she went through the introductions.

"Mr. Gates, I'm Detective Samantha Brown." Sam turned the chair around, straddled it, and nodded at Jonah. "This is Detective Jonah Massey. Have you been informed of your rights?"

Gates nodded slowly.

Sam breathed in but didn't smell any taint in the air that might indicate the man was stoned or drunk. "Sir, I'll need you to answer me with verbal replies."

"Yes, I've been informed of my rights," he told the scratch. "I murdered Noel Coburn."

Gates spoke in a monotone. That, combined with his vacant expression and lack of body language, suggested he was mentally handicapped, was in a state of shock, or had been sampling his wares a little too liberally.

"We're going to videotape this interview, Mr. Gates. What you say in this room will definitely be used against you in court. Do you understand, and consent to that?"

"Yes."

Sam nodded to Massey, who switched on the camera and recited the time, the date, and their names for the record. What she needed to do first was see if she could shake Gates out of his parrot act. "What's your middle name, Eugene?"

He looked up at her as if expecting her to provide a hint. When she didn't, he frowned and thought about it. After thirty seconds, he said, "Victor."

"Do you know what day it is?" After he answered that just as slowly, she sat back and studied his face. He had the remains of a summer tan, but it had taken on a yellow cast, and the skin around his mouth and under his chin looked loose. He smelled of soap, and his clothes were clean, but his fingernails looked as if he'd been digging in the dirt for days. "What did you have for breakfast this morning?"

He licked his lips with a dry tongue. "Nothing."

"How about dinner last night? Lunch yesterday?" Before he could answer, she asked, "When was the last time you ate anything, Eugene?"

It took him a full minute before he replied, "Three days ago."

Massey whistled. "That long, huh?" A candy bar landed on the table in front of Gates, and when Sam glared at Massey, he shrugged. "The guy's probably hungry, right?"

"Hungry." Eugene reached out with his cuffed hands to pick up the candy bar. "Right." He tore off the wrapper and crammed the entire bar into his mouth, closing his eyes as his cheeks bulged and he chewed.

"If he chokes on that, you're writing up the reports," Sam told Massey. She waited for the suspect to swallow before she said, "Mr. Gates, I can get you some real food, if you want."

"Real food." He nodded, and seemed unaware that tears were rolling down his face.

He's been starved. Sam felt an unwilling sympathy for the man. "Before I order a meal for you, I'd like you to tell me about the last time you saw Noel Coburn."

"The last time . . . was in the garden."

"Was this your garden?"

He shook his head. "She made it for us. She was nice. She kept us in the garden as long as she could."

Sam frowned. Murder suspects could invent all kinds of imaginary reasons to be found temporarily insane at trial, but Gates didn't seem to be phonying it up. "Eugene, have you been using some of the stuff in your sample case?"

"No." He turned his right wrist back and forth, jangling the cuffs and a bracelet around his wrist.

Sam leaned over and tugged back the end of his jacket sleeve. Gates wore a MedicAlert bracelet, and when she turned over the oval tag, she saw a list of serious allergies to substances that included opiates. "Did anyone else give you drugs?"

"No." He stared down at his bracelet. "Gold."

The bracelet was the classic MedicAlert red and silver on a silver chain, so he wasn't talking about that. "What's gold, Eugene?"

His eyes met hers. "Hell."

Massey uttered a soft, urgent sound, and when Sam looked at him, he made a swirling motion with his finger beside his temple.

Sam felt inclined to agree with him, but she had to press for details before they could write him off as a potential nutcase. "Eugene, what was the name of the woman who kept you in the garden?"

"Whore." He lunged across the table at her, trying desperately to claw at her with his hands.

Sam stood and moved out of reach, and just as quickly as he had attacked, Gates subsided back in his chair. "Why did you kill Noel Coburn, Eugene?"

His face reddened as his voice returned to the flat monotone. "He owed me money and he wouldn't pay. So I killed him." He looked up at her, his eyes hard and ugly. "You whore."

"Hey," Massey said. "Watch your mouth."

Sam watched his face. "How did you kill Coburn, Eugene?"

He stared at her, his expression confused. "I tied the rope around his wrists, and held it when . . . when . . ."

"When what?"

Gates bent over, his face darkening to purple as he tried to open his jacket.

Sam hurried around the table. "Massey, call for a rig." She loosened the knot in his tie and popped his collar. "Now. He's having a heart attack."

Massey ran to the wall phone as Sam released Gates from his cuffs and lowered him to the floor. He looked up at her, his eyes wide as he tried to speak, but nothing came out of his mouth.

"Starting CPR." Even as she began compressions, Sam knew it was hopeless; she could smell the rot that had already begun to seep into his scent.

Fifteen minutes later Sam stood and watched as the responding paramedics lifted the gurney holding Gate's draped corpse and wheeled him out of the room. She followed them to the hall, where cops from other departments had come to stand in clusters of twos and threes to watch the body being removed.

As Sam walked past them, she heard one of Dwyer's old buddies mutter, "Another notch for her nightstick."

"What did you say?" Suddenly Massey was there, in the jackass's face, and he looked ready to shove the old-timer through the wall.

Sam stopped and tugged at Massey's arm. "Forget it." She glanced at the blustering cop. "No marks on your nightstick, huh, Dave? Keeping it stuck up your ass is working."

As the other cops snickered, Massey backed away with insulting slowness, and then walked with Sam to see the paramedics to the elevator.

"I didn't know how much shit you put up with. You've got to dodge it all the time," he said as soon as the doors closed. "But you never report it. Why?"

"Dave Kernan has already racked up two internal suspensions since January," she told him, "and since he's managed to alienate or lose all the friends he had in the department, he can't afford a third. He's only about eighteen months away from retirement."

"Fuck his retirement," Massey said promptly. "He's an asshole."

"True. He's also got two mortgages, an old crap Caddy that really needs a transmission job, and a wife on an insulin pump." She regarded him. "As for his nightstick, he's shoved it so far up his ass you can see the top of it when he yawns."

Massey grinned. "Now I get you."

As they walked back to the squad room, Sam noticed a bucket and mop sitting by the stairwell exit, and stopped. "Your pal the janitor needs to learn how to clean up after himself."

"Sorry, what janitor?"

She eyed him. "The one you were talking to right before we questioned Gates."

"I wasn't talking to anyone. I don't even know any of the janitors." His scent radiated truth. "You sure you saw me?"

"You were standing out in the hallway, talking to the guy, right over there." She strode to the spot where the janitor had been standing, and breathed in deeply. She could smell hot metal, and beneath that a trace of something cold and green. Just as she had another time before, but where?

The hallway dimmed as a voice came into her mind. *This is nothing to concern you. You will forget it.*

Sam couldn't move. The thing in her head held her somehow, and she could feel it sifting through her memories even as it erased them. She couldn't stop it—and in a minute, she suspected, she wouldn't want to—so she focused on what it was. *Are you Kyn?*

I am like you. A guardian.

No, you're not. I don't freeze people's bodies or rummage through their brains.

Yet you jail and question your suspects. The voice sounded amused. *You know Death so well, Samantha. You have devoted your life to the study of it. Yet you remain blind to the gifts it has given you.*

I can see fine, pal.

Then look upon what you never saw.

The hallway outside Homicide shifted into the penthouse suite at the stronghold, where she could see Lucan sitting outside on the balcony. A blanket fell from either side of the oversize rocking chair he occupied, and as she walked to him, she saw the limp bundle he was holding in his arms, and her own white, still face pressed against his chest.

He looked exhausted, his handsome face almost as

pale as hers, but he sat and rocked her like a baby as he watched the sun rise.

Burke walked past her, a silver tray with a glass of bloodwine in his hands. "My lord," he said softly. "Has there been any change?"

"None." Lucan didn't even glance at the tray. "I want nothing. You may go."

Burke bowed and turned to leave.

"Herbert." When the *tresora* returned, Lucan looked up at him. "If she dies, I fear my sanity will not survive it. Under such circumstances I expect I will lay waste to anything that steps in my path. Rafael mentioned to me that you are a marksman."

Burke's throat moved as he swallowed and nodded.

Lucan handed him a pistol. "I've loaded it with copper rounds. One to the head to slow me, and the second to the heart to finish it." He bent to press his mouth to Sam's brow and tuck her in closer to him. "If you would, carry the weapon at all times."

Something glistened in Burke's eyes. "I will, my lord."

Samantha tried to reach out to her lover, but the balcony vanished, and she stood again in the hallway, still frozen in place. *Why did you show me that?*

When he tells you that you are his life, daughter, you should know the true meaning. The voice grew more insistent. *What the mortal said during your questioning is not important. You will dismiss it.*

She smiled. "I can do that, sure."

Return to the stronghold now. He's waiting for you, my lady.

"My lady?"

Sam shook off what felt like a vague daydream about Lucan as she turned to Garcia. "Sorry, what did you say?"

The captain frowned. "Were you able to get anything out of Gates before he died?"

"Nothing important." She rubbed the back of her neck. "I'm going to head back to the stronghold. He's waiting for me."

Chris had never used her no-limit *jardin* credit card to buy much more than office supplies, and briefly worried that Lucan had canceled it, but the agent had no problem putting through the charges for the rental car.

"You're all set," the agent said as he handed her the keys to the black Lexus. "May I ask why you chose Enterprise for your rental needs?"

"You picked me up at a dock. The only other people who do that are sailors." She winked at him. "I've already got a guy and a boat."

She drove from the rental agency to the nearest cluster of shops, where she bought a warm jacket and comfortable shoes, along with two weeks' worth of casual wear and lingerie for herself, and some trousers and dress shirts for Jamys. After brooding over a pair of ripped jeans that she loved but wasn't sure he'd even wear, she added them to the pile.

One of the salesgirls intercepted her on the way to the cash wrap. "Excuse me, but I would love to show you something special."

Chris glanced at her overflowing pushcart. "I haven't bought enough stuff already?"

"Oh, no, it's just, well, you're perfect for this unbelievable dress we have in Petites." She glanced at a thick-bodied overdressed woman rummaging through a nearby rack. "We don't get many petites in here."

Chris glanced at her watch. She had left Jamys sleeping in the cabin, and the sun wouldn't set for another three hours. "So show me this dress."

In the Petites section the salesgirl went to a rack of holiday dresses and removed a sleek, shimmering black sheath that looked as if someone had slashed it with scissors.

"I know it looks like crap on the hanger," the salesgirl said quickly, "but it's totally different on. It was made for someone with your figure."

Chris looked down at herself. "I have no figure."

"Yeah, which is why I'm kind of hating your guts right now," the girl admitted.

Chris chuckled as she took the dress and headed into the dressing room. A few minutes later she came out and went to the nearest full-length mirror, where she saw a gorgeous stranger wrapped in long, slinky ribbons of black.

"Holy cow." She had no reason to buy something this beautiful and useless, but she wasn't sure she could make herself take it off again.

The salesgirl appeared behind her holding a pair of matching black platform heels, a tiny beaded black bag, and a headband of black crystals. "Could you? Just so my hatred is *completely* justified?"

Chris added on the accessories and then gazed along with the salesgirl at the results. "Damn. You have a business card, right?"

"Yeah." The girl absently dug one out of her pocket and passed it to her as she kept staring. "Damn."

Chris paid for her purchases and packed the bags into the trunk of the rental before she walked over to a sandwich shop to grab something to eat. She discovered she didn't have much appetite, but forced down a salad and a tall glass of orange juice anyway.

Her next stop was a drugstore, where she bought a selection of first-aid supplies and took them into the customer restroom. The cut on her thigh had already started scabbing over, and thanks to Jamys probably wouldn't become infected, but as per her training she cleaned it and applied a new adhesive bandage.

Chris had always imagined taking on the responsibility of providing blood for a Kyn lord would be a little revolting. It wasn't that she was squeamish; she didn't mind the sight or smell of blood or the pain of the small wounds required to start the flow.

The thought of being used as someone's food was what had troubled her; she was a person, not a Happy Meal.

Helping Jamys this morning had dispelled all her worries. When she'd realized how weak he'd been, she hadn't even hesitated. Watching him drink from the cut she'd made on her thigh had made her feel strangely protective, almost possessive. That had quickly turned into very divergent feelings as soon as his hands grasped her leg.

She should have known. Burke had warned her that sometimes blood wasn't the only thing Kyn wanted while feeding on a mortal, especially if there was any kind of physical contact. He hadn't mentioned how badly the *tresora* would want it, though, and maybe that had been on purpose, to keep her from finding out.

She didn't regret being intimate with Jamys. How could she? He'd made her light up like Las Vegas, and after that horrible nightmare of being trapped in that tomb, she'd needed it. Her only real regret was that she hadn't done much for him in return—but secretly she'd loved that, too. How many women could honestly say that they got their guy off with a single touch?

Chris parked outside her final stop, a community blood bank that was one of many owned by the *tresoran* council. All she had to do was show her *jardin* identification at the desk and they'd bring her a large cooler stocked with fresh units. Two coolers, if she wanted that much. She had no reason to feel guilty about getting it.

I can't go on feeding him myself every day, and it's too dangerous for him to hunt. This is the only alternative.

At the desk inside a smiling young woman greeted her, and then inclined her head in the public shorthand for a bow as soon as Chris placed her ID on the counter. "Will your lord be coming to Miami tonight, Miss Lang?"

"No, this is for a visitor." She had decided against mentioning Jamys's name; she had no idea if it might get back to Lucan. "I'll need a two-week supply of stores. Also, if you have one, a nine and a couple of clips."

The girl nodded. "Right away."

As she waited by the counter, she looked over at the people waiting in the lobby. All of them were mortal, and she was pretty sure two of the men in suits were *tresori*. With their backs to the walls, the pricey but discreet style of their clothes, and the clean-cut hair, they gave off that sort of official vibe. Both seemed to be ignoring her in favor of the magazines they were reading, which seemed a little odd. *Tresori* always checked out everything around them; their training instilled a kind of professional paranoia that became almost second nature. That was exactly why she'd taken a hard look at the people in the lobby.

One of the men seemed engrossed in the latest issue of *People*, while the other was thumbing through a copy of *Time*. The only problem with the second guy was that the mag in his hands was upside-down.

Maybe he's dyslexic, Chris thought as she wandered down the counter, pretending to check out the literature while getting in better position for a closer look. Out of the corner of her eye she saw both men shift subtly in response. *Nope, they are watching me.*

One of the men rechecked her position by bending down to untie and retie his shoe. As he did, his jacket sleeve slid back to reveal part of his forearm and half of a black cameo tattoo, the center of which should have contained the profile of the man's Kyn lord, but was instead covered in scar tissue.

Chris, who had never seen a *tresora* with partially mutilated ink, had to force herself to read the front of the pamphlet she wasn't reading.

Tresori assigned to guard the blood bank would have been stationed at the entry points to the building; watchers wouldn't have allowed themselves to be seen at all. Chris wandered back to check the number of names that hadn't been crossed off the sign-in sheet, which was seven; she'd counted nine people waiting in the lobby.

More than anything, the man's scarred tattoo frightened her. She'd never seen anything like it. And why would a *tresora* hack out of his own flesh the face of his Kyn lord?

Chris waited until she saw the receptionist emerge with the cooler from a back room. Chris vaulted over the counter and ran to the girl, whose eyes went wide.

"Side door?" When the girl gestured, Chris took the cooler and smiled. "Thanks. And the nine?"

"In the cooler."

She ran for the exit, bolting through it and sprinting for the rental car. She had enough time to get in and

drop the cooler on the seat before she saw the two *tresori*
run around from the front of the building. She ducked
down and slipped the keys in the ignition as they trotted
past her, both looking in every direction before they hurried to a big black cargo van.

As soon as they'd climbed inside the van, Chris
started the Lexus, reversed out of her space, and sped
out of the lot. They were good, she thought when she saw
the van appear in her rearview. She floored the accelerator as she scanned the road ahead for an intersection
with some cover, and once she reached one with a green
light, she coasted to a stop and turned on her emergency
flashers before she reached into the cooler.

Chris left the engine running as she got out of the car,
raised the hood, and waited in front of it, watching for
the van. It slowed as it approached, and then as she'd
hoped, it stopped behind her rental.

She stepped out from behind the hood and threw a
unit of blood at the van's windshield; it burst and covered the glass and part of the hood with blood. With the
nine-millimeter she'd taken out of the cooler, she shot
out both front tires, and put another three rounds into
the van's engine before she dropped the hood on the
rental, climbed in behind the wheel, and sped off.

Where there were *tresori*, there were bound to be
backup *tresori*, so Chris drove around Miami until she
was certain she wasn't being tailed. Dumb and Dumber
didn't belong to Alenfar or she would have recognized
their faces, which meant they'd been brought in from another territory. She could describe them to Jamys and
see if they matched anyone who served his father, but
most American *tresori* wouldn't have fallen for her
stalled-car routine. She'd bet money they were Euro-

pean—maybe a couple of trackers working for the council or even Tremayne.

But why follow me? In the grand scheme of things, Chris knew she was less than nobody.

The sun was setting by the time she returned to Biscayne Bay, and once she parked the rental, she walked down the dock to the boat. None of the fisherman she passed seemed out of place, and none of her internal alarms were going off, but once she and Jamys saw Gifford tonight, it would probably be safer to move the boat to a different spot.

She could hear the shower running belowdecks as soon as she climbed on board, and smiled a little as she brought the cooler down and left it on the table. She had to make another trip to the car to get the rest of her shopping bags, but by the time she returned, Jamys was waiting on deck for her.

"Christian." He took her bags and set them aside before he lifted her from the dock to the boat. "What is all this?"

"Clothes, shoes, girl stuff, that kind of thing." She hugged him, drawing back only when he didn't return the embrace. "You found my note, right?"

"Yes." He took her right hand and brought it up to his face, but he didn't kiss it. "You smell of blood and gunpowder."

"I had to shoot a van. I picked up some stores for you, did you see the cooler?" She carried the bags below, where she began to put everything away. "I bought the most amazing dress. You have to take me somewhere nice someday so I can wear it and make all the other women hate me."

He was staring at her. "You shot a van?"

"Yeah, after I threw blood at it." She checked her

watch. "We should leave soon; Gifford's lecture starts in an hour." She held up a jumper to her front. "Does this make me look scholarly, geeky, or just sad?"

He took the jumper from her and tossed it onto the bunk. "Tell me about this van."

Chris dropped the perky-teen act. "Two guys followed me into the blood bank. Clean-cut, dark suits, not too bright. I tried to outrun them, and when I couldn't, I took out their ride, which was the van."

His expression darkened. "Were they mortals or Kyn warriors?"

"I think they were *tresori*." She went and sat down on the edge of the bunk, and rested her elbows on her knees. "But one of them had a really creepy tat." After she described the mutilated black cameo, she glanced up at him. "The scarring was too perfect for it to be accidental. Would the Brethren have done that to him? Wait, never mind." She mentally kicked herself for reminding him of his own ordeal.

"They have been known to cut off tattoos from captured *tresori*," he said slowly, "but it would be in their interests to preserve the likeness of any Kyn lord." He sat down beside her. "Do not be afraid to speak of anything to me, Christian. I am your friend."

"I know, I just hate reminding you of the bad old days." She used her shoulder to give his a gentle bump. "We should get going."

Jamys pulled her onto his lap and kissed her until she forgot to breathe. When he lifted his mouth from hers, he said, "Wear the dress."

"It's a lecture in a museum, not a night at the Mynt Lounge," she reminded him. "But I could model it for you later."

Chapter 13

Lectures at the Miami Maritime Museum were well attended, and Jamys and Christian arrived shortly before all the folding chairs provided for the audience filled up. Others stood as the museum's director introduced Professor Charles Gifford, a short, thick-bodied man who looked distinctly ill at ease in his tweed suit.

"He looks like a repo guy," Christian murmured.

Jamys spotted the scars on his hands and forearms. "He was a fisherman."

"Good evening," the professor said, and launched immediately into a talk about piracy and its evolution through the ages.

Jamys paid close attention to the details Gifford offered about specific ships and captains, but at no time during the next hour did he mention Hollander or the *Golden Horde*.

"Today we apply the label of piracy to any number of crimes: copyright infringement, illegal audio and video transmission, even unsavory corporate acquisitions," the professor said in his summation. "We hear news stories about drug runners who hijack and kill fishermen for their powerful boats, or lawless Somalians who attack cargo ships and ransom their captains."

"Or have our Facebook pages hacked," someone among the audience muttered, causing a ripple of laughter.

Gifford nodded. "While the savage nature of any sort of piracy appalls us, it is in reality a seafaring tradition that has existed for thousands of years." He curled his big hands around the edges of the podium. "Pirates are alive and well, ladies and gentlemen, and they aren't going anywhere. Not as long as there are ships in the sea, treasures to be coveted, and men willing to kill for them. Thank you."

As the audience applauded, Jamys noted the bashful reddening of Gifford's blunt features, and the speed with which he left the podium. While the museum's director took his place to invite the audience to help themselves to refreshments, the professor shook a few hands and then disappeared into an adjoining exhibit room.

"Seems like he's better with history than people," Christian said as she rose from the folding chair next to his. "Time to put my sad little jumper in action."

"It is not sad." He guided her around the exodus of people heading for the buffet tables. "It is modest."

"So is a chastity belt." She sighed. "But I think I look geeky enough to pass, while you"—her eyes shifted to the tattered blue jeans she'd asked him to wear—"are making me and every other female under this roof very hot and bothered."

Jamys bent his head. "I should like to bother you again," he whispered against her ear, and enjoyed the shiver he felt hum down her back. "Until you drench me."

"Journal first." She tightened her fingers. "Wet and wild later."

They made their way into the exhibit room where Gifford had gone, and found the professor standing in the middle of a treasure display and adjusting some lighting.

"Barry," he said as they approached. "These bulbs are too bright. Have we got any forty-watt back in the maintenance closet?"

"I can go check for you, Professor," Christian said, "but my name's not Barry."

"Huh?" The historian glanced over his shoulder before climbing out of the display case. "Sorry, kids. This exhibit won't be opening until the weekend." He gestured at the door. "There's punch and cookies out there."

Christian gave Jamys a wry look. "We've already had our cookies, Professor. We were wondering if we could ask you a couple of questions about Father Bartley's journals."

A shuttered look came over the historian's face. "I'm afraid I don't have time for that. I wrote some articles about the journals. You can read them on my Web site."

"We will, thank you." Jamys reached out, and as soon as Gifford began to shake his hand, he nodded to Christian and sent his thoughts into the other man's mind. *You want to answer our questions completely and honestly.*

Gifford's tight expression smoothed out. "What would you like to know about the journals?"

Christian quietly closed and locked the door before rejoining them. "Professor, are the journals authentic?"

"Yes, they are. I bought them from a private collector who let them go for a song." He grinned like a boy. "Would you like to see them? They're right over here."

"We would," Jamys said.

Gifford led them over to another display where a small collection of leather-bound books had been arranged inside a glass case. "The priest wrote everything in Latin, so it's difficult to read, but I can translate it. I went to Catholic school and I almost became a priest."

Christian made a face. "What changed your mind?"

"Sex. I discovered I liked it too much to spend my life as a celibate." Gifford unlocked the case. "Father Bartley was much more devoted to the church. He came to Port Royal in the late sixteen hundreds, but on the day he arrived, he decided to move his mission to the north side of the island."

"Why?" Jamys asked.

"The governor of Jamaica at the time was Sir Thomas Modyford," Gifford said. "Sir Thomas didn't care that England was no longer at war with Spain; he hated the Spaniards, and by extension loved the pirates who attacked their ships. He protected them from prosecution, allowed them to use the port as safe haven, and was rumored to have personally funded a few raids."

"Like a private army of cutthroats," Christian said.

The professor nodded. "Sir Thomas had a strategic advantage as well. Jamaica lay smack in the center of the major shipping lanes in what at the time was considered the Spanish Caribbean, so for the hundreds of pirate ships that were based out of Port Royal, it was like fishing in a barrel. Their raids made Port Royal one of the wealthiest—and most decadent—cities in the world." Gifford stopped at one page. "Ah, here it is. Father Bartley wrote this the day his ship came into port: 'Never in my most despairing moment could I have envisioned such a garden of demons. Everywhere I turn there are pirates, assassins, and prostitutes, all engaged in the most brutal of behaviors, and the vilest of carnal acts. The port is riddled with gaming houses and grog shops, each packed to the very walls with villains. From the windows of the brothels, which occupy every fifth building, women lean out with bared bosoms to proposition those passing on the street below. I fear if I were to remain in this New World's Sodom, I will be torn apart by the very beasts that inhabit it.'"

"Sounds a little like spring break," Christian murmured.

"Leaving was a wise decision, because Port Royal was already doomed," the professor told her. "A few weeks after Father Bartley went to the north side of the island to set up his mission, a major earthquake and tidal wave leveled half the city. Two thousand people were killed instantly, and another thousand died from injuries, starvation, and cholera in the aftermath. The survivors attributed the disaster to God's wrath, visited upon the wicked as judgment for their countless sins. A few claimed to have seen a blood-drinking angel of death stalking pirates at the docks just before the tremor started. Whatever the cause, the city never recovered."

Jamys exchanged a look with Christian. "Did the priest write anything about this 'angel of death'?"

"Not a word," Gifford said. "He never returned to Port Royal. Would you care to hear a passage about an interesting conversion of the native heathens, or how to conduct mass in a grass hut?"

"We are interested in the confession the priest took from the dying pirate," Jamys said.

Gifford sighed and shook his head sadly. "I promised

I wouldn't talk about that, but okay." He reached for one of the journals.

"Who made you promise?" Christian asked.

"A man who gave me a lot of money I didn't report to the IRS," he admitted. "I buried it in some airtight cases in the backyard but the dog kept digging them up. So I donated most of it to the museum. Anonymously, of course."

"He seems to be volunteering a lot of information," Christian murmured to Jamys. "Does that usually happen?"

"No." Although his ability was powerful, humans under its compulsion always responded directly to the suggestions he made. "Professor, why do you tell us of these private matters?"

"The man who gave me the money said that if anyone made me break my promise, I should tell him all the terrible things I've done. Like the time I dressed up in my seminary clothes and pretended to be a priest having sex with my girlfriend." Gifford thumbed through the journal. "Here's the passage. It begins with the priest offering absolution."

Jamys frowned as Gifford launched into his reading. "I am not the first Kyn to compel this mortal. I can feel a trace of another lingering in the patterns of his thoughts. The Kyn who questioned him may have left a command in Gifford's mind to expose his most guarded secrets."

"Do you know any Kyn who can do that?" When he shook his head, Christian studied the historian. "If the Kyn who got here before us meant it to be a self-destruct button, it wasn't a very good one. I mean, cheating on taxes and playing X-rated Confessional won't get the

guy arrested. At best there'd be a month of scandal mon-
gering by the local papers and TV stations. He'd probably get kicked off the museum board."

"Which would destroy his reputation." Jamys reached
out to Gifford and touched his shoulder. He intended to
command the mortal to stop reading and tell him everything he knew about the man who had paid him for his
silence, but as soon as he connected with the professor's
mind, he felt a now-familiar barrier.

Instead of hurling his ability at the wall as he'd done
with Chris, Jamys held back, sending tendrils of his mind
in all directions. In a distant corner of the human's
thoughts he found a gap in the barrier, and slipped into it.

You will show me who you are, Jamys thought, easing
into the powerful presence and permeating it from
within with his own ability.

A parade of mortals and immortals began flashing
through Jamys's thoughts: a slave-collared thrall, the
leader of a slave rebellion, a haughty courtier, a devout
Templar, a brooding monk, a defiant sailor. Each of the
males had the same brutally handsome and eerily familiar face, one that grew gaunt or sleek by turns but never
aged. Each carried the hammer of a smith, and in their
cold gray eyes an eternal fire burned.

Jamys saw the sailor become an avenging angel, and
the angel a secretive explorer, and the explorer a reclu-
sive farmer. As the man changed, so did his garments,
becoming more fitted and modern as he changed lives
again to work as a train conductor, a wealthy business-
man, a laughing showman, a dreadlocked common la-
borer, a bald-headed janitor.

Jamys finally recognized the man as he shifted into

the casual garb of the sailboat owner, and reached deeper.

The immortal had lived hundreds of different lives, changing himself to suit the demands of each new era, but he had never been happy. He carried a terrible burden, one he shared with his human kin, who had slowly dwindled away over the centuries. Something else had happened to the immortal, was yet happening, something wondrous and terrible that had sent him back out into the world. He had to bring together the last of his mortal bloodline with the sons he had sired so long ago, the three medieval knights made immortal like him—

Jamys staggered as he was forced out of the professor's mind by a surge of power unlike any Kyn ability he had ever encountered.

Gifford's eyes grew unfocused. "You are clever, boy," he said, his voice dropping to a resonant baritone. "But I have wiped clean from the mortal's mind everything he knew of Hollander and the *Horde.* You will learn nothing from him."

Christian stepped back. "I know you." Her voice shook as she added, "You were in the tomb with me."

Gifford's eyes glowed as he turned his head toward her, but the voice Jamys heard speak next came from inside his own mind. "Live, and you kill a hundred, a thousand, a million." He looked at Jamys, and the voice inside his head grew icy. "Kill her, and you shall save them."

Jamys stepped closer, and gazed into the historian's eyes. "Touch her," he said clearly, "and you will never again live another life on this earth."

Gifford began to laugh and shake as his eyes rolled back into his head. A moment later he sank to the floor.

Christian grabbed him in time to keep him from hitting his head. "Okay, I think the professor's had enough."

Jamys crouched down beside her and checked the mortal. Gifford appeared unconscious, but his breathing was regular and his heart beat steadily. "He is asleep."

Christian picked up the journal Gifford had dropped along with a page that had fallen out of it, handing the journal to Jamys before she unfolded the page. "This is a map. Looks pretty old, too. No *X* marking the spot, but there's a ship's course marked on it from what looks like Jamaica to Florida." She showed it to him.

He eyed the date and some words scribbled at the bottom of the map. "This had to be the final course of the *Golden Horde*. The pirate must have drawn it for the priest before he died."

"If we follow the ship's course, maybe we won't need an *X*. Let me see that journal again." When Jamys handed it to her, she turned to the front leaf before she went still.

Jamys inspected the rectangle of red-bordered black paper in the front of the journal. In the center were two inverted, overlapping scarlet triangles with the letters *LHS* stamped in gold across them. "What is that?"

"It's a bookplate. Collectors use them to tag their personal libraries." She closed the journal and stood, her shoulders rigid. "I know the guy who sold this to Gifford."

"How could you know this man?"

"Easy." She gave him a bleak look. "I used to work for him."

Once the nightclub had been cleared and closed, armed guards emerged from the tunnels to take their assigned positions throughout the stronghold. In the largest of the conference rooms Burke met with the mortal household staff to brief them, while Aldan assembled the garrison in the lists to do the same.

Lucan remained in his office to review the last week of video recordings from the security cameras, in hopes of finding some clue as to the identity of the Kyn who had tampered with his mind and taken control of his body. He saw no one and nothing unusual, save for the most recently arrived group of refugees, who were now being kept under guard at a nearby resort hotel.

He looked up as his captain and his *tresora* entered. "What have you learned from your people?"

Aldan nodded to Burke, who said, "The household staff have not noted anything out of the ordinary, my lord. The visitors have kept to their rooms for the most part, and what minor disruptions they have caused have not been intentional. No one has been observed on the penthouse level, near the stores, or anywhere inappropriate. Earlier I sent a sample of the stock that was poisoned over to the blood bank to be tested, but that will take some time."

"Copper-tainted blood could not do this to me," Lucan said. "Captain, what of the men?"

"They've no love for the visitors, Master, but they've seen naught to alarm them. The strangers have shown no untoward behavior." He hesitated before he added, "Vander, the one you fought the other night, has remained behind under guard. As appointed leader, he requests a moment to speak with you about his men."

Lucan had no interest in listening to any complaints about ill-treatment, but Vander had served with the other men in his group, and had likely witnessed some or all of them using their talents. "Bring him to me."

Glenveagh and Sutton flanked the visitors' leader as he strode into the office. "Suzerain." Vander performed a shallow bow. "My brothers have asked me to speak on their behalf and ask as to why we have been removed from the household."

"Some cowardly bastard has used his ability in an attempt to challenge my rule," Lucan told him. "My first thought was to kill all of you; that would instantly eliminate the threat and give me an enormous amount of personal pleasure."

Vander looked confused. "My lord, my men and I would never use ability against you. You have provided us with—"

"Shut up," Lucan said as he rose from his desk. "One of you is going to die tonight; answer my questions truthfully and it may not be you. Now, what ability have you, Mr. Vander?"

"I am a treasure finder," he muttered. "Nothing of great value can be hidden from me."

"How exceedingly profitable." Lucan came around the desk. "Demonstrate it for us. Now."

Vander jabbed a thumb at Glenveagh. "This one carries in his left pocket a watch and chain."

"Which I consult often enough for it to be noticed by anyone," Glenveagh said. "Hardly hidden treasure."

Vander gave him an unpleasant look. "What of the woman's locket in the pouch on your belt? Is it meant as a love token for your Scot?"

Before the guard could lunge, Aldan clapped a hand on his shoulder. "I'm not so easily won, little man. You must romance me first."

Lucan resisted the impulse to smash their skulls together. "Glenveagh, open the pouch."

The guard unsnapped the flap and took out a delicate chain. "I purchased it as a gift for Christian," he said as he held it up to show Lucan the heart-shaped pendant. "Next month is her birthday."

"The Pearl Girl." Vander smiled. "I fancy a piece of that myself. Think earbobs would persuade her to spread her—"

Aldan plowed his massive fist into Vander's face, and watched him sag. "Forgive me, Master. I fear my knuckles are overly fond of Miss Christian."

"Aye, and my sword," Glenveagh muttered.

"Enough." Lucan picked up the glass of bloodwine Burke had brought him earlier and dashed it in Vander's face, rousing him. "You will keep a civil tongue in your head, or my men will cut it out."

"As you command, Suzerain." Vander spit out a shard of tooth. "You have seen my talent. What more do you want?"

"Who among your men can control the mind and body of another?" Lucan demanded.

"None." Vander looked bewildered. "I have never seen such a . . ." He stopped and licked his lips. "No man I serve with has that ability."

Lucan leaned in. "Do you think me a fool? You have seen this done. Who was it?"

"It was when I sought out the girl, Christian," Vander muttered. "He used it to compel her to deny me. Your particular friend, the one who looks like a lad."

"Jamys." Lucan straightened. "His ability only affects mortals. Try again."

"But I heard him say . . ." Vander averted his gaze. "It must be another unknown to me, my lord."

Every lightbulb in the office exploded as Lucan

grabbed him by the throat and rammed him into a wall. "Tell me, or die."

"I heard him talking to the girl," Vander wheezed out. "He wishes territory of his own. And when I tried to take her to my rooms, something happened."

Lucan released him. "What?"

"I cannot say. One moment I was with the girl, the next I was in my rooms." Vander rubbed his throat. "I could not say how I got there. I had no memory of it."

"Captain, take the guards and search the stronghold for Jamys Durand." He helped Vander to his feet. "Burke, find Christian and bring her to me."

"A moment, Captain," the *tresora* said, and then informed Lucan of the phone call he had received from the girl. "I know from the manner in which she spoke that she was not under Lord Durand's or any Kyn's sway," he added, giving Vander a disgusted look. "Nor would he have left with her if he meant to challenge your rule."

"Perhaps he feared being found out," Vander suggested. "Your lady saw him with you at the pier, did she not? And no other Kyn there but him."

"My knuckles begin to itch, Master," Aldan said. "Might I scratch them another time?"

"Leave him with me," Lucan said. "All of you. Get out."

The men left with reluctance, and as soon as Lucan closed the door, Vander shuffled to his feet. "I regret exposing your friend's betrayal, my lord, but 'tis better to know there is a knife at your back before it is used."

"I have known Jamys Durand his entire life." Weary now, Lucan returned to his desk and dropped in the chair. "And his father, all of his kin. They are obsessed with honor." He shook his head. "He could not have done this."

"That may be. I have heard talk of the boy's mother," Vander said carefully. "Is it true that she handed her family over to the Brethren?"

Lucan thought of how he had found the Durands in Ireland. "Yes, and the evil bitch died for it."

"My own mother was a common street whore." Vander came to the desk and began idly straightening the objects nearest the edge. "She led my father on a merry chase, right to the gallows. She held me in her arms so that I might watch his neck being stretched." He picked up a framed photo of Samantha standing on the beach and looking out at the sea. "Your lady is as clever as she is lovely. She understands this time, and the strangeness of the world. Any man would count himself fortunate to own her."

"I don't own Samantha." Lucan took the photo from him, and then went still as he saw the web of cracks in the glass covering Samantha's image. "I love her."

"Doubtless she knows it," Vander assured him. "What I most admire is your patience with her, and her determination to live a separate life from yours."

Lucan turned the frame facedown on the desk. "We share the same life."

"Yet she is gone from here at the worst possible time, to do this . . . police work, is it?" Vander shook his head. "Were she mine, I would never let her wander from my sight. Not when an enemy is poised to attack. But perhaps there is another reason for her absence now."

Lucan looked up. "Samantha would never betray me."

"Of her own accord, no, perhaps she would not. But this boy, Jamys, can seize minds, and control bodies, you said." Vander looked sympathetic. "I pray she has not fallen under his influence. Given your feelings for her, he would be a fool not to use her against you."

Lucan picked up the phone and dialed Samantha's mobile, but the line went immediately to her voice mail. Panic welled up inside him, but when he tried to rise, his legs refused to obey him. "Help me to my feet. I have to find her. I have to get her away from him. If he has used her—if he has so much as touched her—"

"That is not all you must do, my lord," Vander said, and smiled as he reached out to touch his shoulder. "But please, do let me help you."

Jamys didn't ask any questions as they left the museum and drove back to the boat, which gave Chris time to consider how much to tell him. She tuned the car radio to a Cuban-American station she liked and let the lively beat of salsa fill the silence.

If she had believed in God, by now she'd be convinced he was punishing her. After all she'd done to forget the past and make herself a better person, he probably wouldn't be able to resist dragging all that old shit back into her life, or dropping it right in front of Jamys. Maybe this proved there was a God, because nothing else could have hurt her more than this. It was the perfect celestial fuck-you.

She parked the car and stared at the boat for a while.

"Come and rest with me," Jamys said. "We need not begin following the map tonight. You are tired."

That she was. "I don't think we should wait. I can't come with you on the boat, either." She ran her hand over the top curve of the steering wheel. "I'm going to see the guy who sold the journal to Gifford, and find out where he got it."

"I will go with you," Jamys said.

She shook her head. "We can cover more bases if you follow the map and I check out the journal."

"Is that the only reason?" he asked gently.

"No." She unfastened her seat belt and faced him. "There's a lot you don't know about me. I was a really messed-up kid, and after my mom died, I didn't really care what happened to me. I just . . . shut down, you know?"

"I did the same when I learned how my mother had betrayed us to the Brethren." He took her hand in his and stared out at the bay. "Alexandra Keller said I was catatonic, but she was wrong. I was aware of everything. My shame kept me locked inside myself."

Chris had known street kids who had done that, withdrawing into themselves so far they became like ghosts. "When I was in school, I used to wish I could take an eraser to myself, rub out all the mistakes, and do things over the right way. Life would be so much easier if you could do that."

"Only if you live in the past."

"Which we don't." She forced a smile. "Come on, I'll program the navigational computer with the map's course."

"Christian." He waited until she looked at him before he said, "There is nothing you could do that would make me think less of you."

Jamys said such beautiful things, as if he knew exactly at the right moment what she needed to hear. He probably even believed some of them. "Thanks." She leaned over to kiss his cheek before she climbed out.

It appeared as if all the dockside fisherman had called it a night, and most of the boats moored near theirs looked likewise unoccupied. Chris almost started to relax when she spotted a figure sitting in the shadows at the edge of the dock. He had a line in the water, but no tackle box or bait bucket, and had pulled the hood of his jacket up over his head. As they drew closer, she spotted the black gloves on his hands and stumbled.

Jamys caught her arm, his gaze also on the hooded man. *I see him. Get on the boat and go below.*

Chris took out the gun in her purse and concealed it and her hand in the side pocket of her jumper. *No, I'm not going to do that.*

The man's back straightened, and he reeled in his line before standing and turning toward them. "Evening."

The voice wasn't Lucan's, but Chris didn't relax. "Howdy."

The fisherman walked toward them, still holding his pole, and then stopped beside the sailboat. He inspected them and the boat with casual interest. "This yours?"

Jamys shifted in front of Chris. "Yes."

"Beautiful craft." He pulled back his hood to scratch at his close-trimmed beard, which looked like snow against his dark complexion. "You run charters?"

What Chris assumed was a glove was just the natural color of the islander's dark skin. "No, sorry."

"Truly a shame. I imagine she flies over the waves." He nodded to Jamys and walked on.

Chris thumbed on the safety before returning her gun to her purse. "I don't know about you, but I feel like an ass." She glanced at Jamys, who was still watching the fisherman depart. "It's all right. He's not a threat to anything but the fish around here."

"As you say." He still waited until the man disappeared from sight before he followed her onto the boat.

Chris charted a course on the nav system and chose a small marina where they could meet when Jamys reached the Keys. "I'll probably get there first, so I'll take care of renting a slip for the day." She saved the data and checked the maritime weather forecast feed. "You've got clear skies and calm seas, but if you run into any problems, just give me a call on the mobile."

He switched off the equipment. "You have not told me about the man you are going to meet."

Chris didn't like to think about Stryker, much less talk about him, but she could give him the edited version. "His name is Leonin something long and Russian, but he goes by Stryker. He operated some specialty nightclubs and private party houses in Fort Lauderdale, until the city got tired of his activities and invited him to relocate anywhere else. He moved his entire operation down to Key West, where the locals aren't nearly as judgmental."

"Why would they judge him?"

"Stryker collects old books only as a hobby. His real business is the personal fantasy trade. He dabbles in fetish and same-sex clubs, but the big money comes from his private parties. He rents houses and sets them up as theme scenes for swingers."

Jamys looked perplexed. "Swingers?"

"They're people who like to have sex with multiple partners," she explained. "He throws orgies for the ones who like to dress up in costumes and role-play."

"What do they pretend to be?"

"Ancient Romans. Movie stars. Anime characters." She sighed. "And vampires."

Chapter 14

Chris made sure she would reach Key West before Jamys did by driving there as fast as she could without stopping or getting caught in any of the tourist speed traps. Crossing the Seven Mile Bridge that connected Marathon with the Lower Keys was considered passing the halfway mark, but she wouldn't relax until she hit mile-marker zero.

She hadn't lied to Jamys about Stryker; she simply hadn't volunteered certain details. While she didn't know exactly where Stryker himself was, she knew precisely how to find out.

Once Chris drove into the downtown area of Key West, she parked the Lexus in a metered lot and from there walked three blocks past the open bars and the closed gift shops to Free Wheeling. Although the front windows of the garage were dark, and the doors locked, she knew the owner kept the place open twenty-four hours a day.

Chris made her way around to the back lot, where rows of cars and bikes in various stages of repair sat parked behind a razor-wire-topped chain-link fence. The warped sheet of plywood that currently served as the garage's back door hung slightly askew on its hinges, but it opened shortly after she rapped out an SOS on it.

The grizzly bear of a man who peered out at her didn't offer a welcome. He did take a pull from his beer bottle before he demanded, "What the fuck you want?"

"It's me, Bug." When he didn't react, she added, "Chris Lang."

"Well, well. Little Christi Lang, all growed up." He drained the bottle in his hand and tossed it in the garbage barrel to her left. "Your old man owes me two hundred bucks."

Good luck collecting, she thought. "I need to find someone, and I'll pay you four hundred to help me."

"Cash?" When she nodded, Bug shoved the plywood out another foot. "Come on in."

Chris followed him through a dirt-and-grease-encrusted labyrinth of car parts, toolboxes, and motors to a card table with four folding chairs, two men inspecting the cards in their hands, and several mounds of poker chips.

"You remember Cody," Bug said, nodding to the rail-thin mechanic in filthy coveralls on one side of the table. "Loot you don't."

Chris eyed the man in the polo shirt, whose appearance was so clean and neat that next to Bug, Cody, and the garage around him he resembled an alien life-form. "Hello."

"I'll see the cash first," Bug said.

As a gesture of good faith, Chris took out her wallet and counted out eight fifties onto the table. That left her with a couple of twenties and change, but if she needed more money, Jamys could convince a mortal to donate to their cause.

Bug picked up the bills and held each one up to the light to see the embedded security strip before he shoved the money into the front pocket of his bib overalls. "Who's worth this much to you, little girl? Not your daddy."

Chris tucked her arms around her waist. "I need to find Stryker."

"Shit, no, you don't." Bug went over to an ancient cooler and rummaged around in the floating ice until he pulled a fresh beer bottle from it. "Here." He held it out to her, but when she tried to take it, he pulled it back. "You old enough to drink this, now, right?"

"You got wasted with my dad at every one of my birthdays," Chris reminded him. "So, what, you can't count now?"

Bug chuckled and gave her the bottle. "Still a mouthy little twerp. I always liked that about you, Christi. Forget about that ass-peddler and play some cards with us." He sat down and picked up his hand. "Go on. Deal her in, Cody."

"Bug." Chris sat down in the chair beside him. "I'm not a little girl anymore. A lot is riding on this. Tell me where he is."

Bug regarded her over the fan of his cards. "I'll tell you after you play a hand. Bitch, and you're outta here."

Chris took a swig of the icy beer and sighed. "Deal me in, Cody."

She hadn't played poker since Frankie had taught her how during one of the summers they'd spent in the Keys. Still, it was like riding a bike, and in no time she had assembled a full house.

"I'm done." Loot tossed his cards down. "You've known Bug for a while, Christi?"

"It's Chris." She parked the rest of the chips they'd fronted her in the pot. "And yeah, I've known him since I was in diapers."

Loot leaned forward. "Do you know how he got his name?"

"No one does," Cody put in. "But they think it's because he won't wear a face shield when he rides."

"That's not it." Chris glanced at Bug, who threw his hand down in disgust. "You never told your friends?"

"No one's fucking business." He grinned as he looked over her head. "Your old man owes me two hundred bucks, though, Christi."

"I heard you the first time." Chris turned to Loot. "It's not because of the bugs he eats on the bike. He's named after the letters B-U-G, for—"

"Christi?"

The sound of the voice behind her made the cards fall out of Chris's hand. She gazed over her hand-winning full house at Bug. "You knew he was coming here?"

"Whose chair do you think you're sitting in, sweet cheeks?" Bug jerked his head as he stood up, and Cody and Loot followed him outside, leaving her alone with the man behind her.

"Christi. Jesus. What are you doing here, honey?"

"Buying information." Chris waited as he moved around to face her. "Hi, Daddy."

He stared at her before he headed for Bug's cooler. "I need a drink."

Chris watched him. Over the eight years since the last time she'd seen him, Frankie Lang had put on fifty pounds, tanned himself to a muddy bronze, and lost most of the hair atop his head. He wasn't fat, exactly; she could still make out some of the muscles in his arms and chest, and his surf-god face hadn't bloated too much. Older chicks in dimly lit bars were probably still receptive to his bullshit.

But here under the naked bulb hanging over Bug's card table, Chris could see that the booze had busted a hand's width of capillaries on and around his nose. He'd always loved Southern Comfort, and from the faint yellowing of the whites of his eyes SoCo had returned the favor by fucking with his liver. She saw a scar on his chin she couldn't remember, and the sulking droop of his mouth that she'd never forgotten. Unlike her, Frankie Lang had never growed up.

"Bug tell you to come down here?" her father asked as he sat down across from her. "I'm fine, you know. I laid off the hard stuff last summer." He lifted his bottle and drained a third of the contents before taking a breath. He seemed to realize then that she hadn't said anything, and tried again, this time with a wavering grin. "So, how have you been, kid?"

"How have I been?" She pretended to think. "When you didn't come home that night, I was confused. When Mom started to fall apart, I was scared. Hungry, too—the food started to run out right after you and the money did. When the bank foreclosed on the house and kicked us out on the street, I was terrified. When they put Mom in the nuthouse and me in foster care, I was a basket case. But then, so was Mom."

"That's too bad." He reached across the table and tried to take her hand. "Your mom's doing okay now, though, right?"

Chris couldn't believe it. Could not. "Mom killed herself two years after you bailed. Exactly two years to the day."

He drew his hand back. "Sorry to hear that. Adele never was right in the head. Hey." Frankie jolted back as Chris shoved the table into his chest. "It's the truth, Christi. And it wasn't because of me, either. She'd been seeing shrinks all her life, long before me."

"So, what, you think she was better off slitting her wrists and bleeding out in the bathtub?" Chris demanded.

Frankie swallowed. "They told you how she offed herself?"

"I know how she did it because I'm the one who found her." She wanted to describe every horrific detail so he could enjoy a few nightmares, but if she did, she'd puke up the beer. "After the funeral my grandmother blamed me for Mom's suicide and turned me over to the state. I went back into foster care. Don't you look at me like that. Like you're sorry for me."

"Can't help it," he muttered. "I am. No kid should have to deal with what you been through. If I could go back and change things, Christi, I would."

"The hell." The laugh that tore out of her hurt her throat. "I can't believe you've been here in the Keys, all this time. I should have guessed. Drinking and screwing around were the only two things you were ever good at. Well, at least now I know." She gestured at the door. "You can run away again now."

He started to get up, and then dropped down. "I got one thing I gotta say."

Her eyes narrowed. "Oh, I've heard all I ever need to, Daddy."

"It's why I took off," he snapped, and then looked immediately ashamed. "The night before, Adele got drunk and we had a fight about you. She said you weren't my kid. That some other guy got her pregnant."

"Mom told you that you're not my father?" Chris asked, to be sure she hadn't heard it wrong.

"Yeah." He moved his shoulders. "I always suspected anyway. You don't look nothing like me. When you were born, she swore you were two months early, but the doctors didn't put you in that baby microwave thing after you came out. You were just little."

For Chris it was a toss-up between weeping with relief and shooting him in the head. "Did Mom happen to mention who *is* my biological father?"

"It was some French guy she met a couple months before me, when she went to the Riviera with her folks. By the time we met, she was already a month gone with you." He got to his feet. "So, okay, you need anything? Money? A place to stay?"

"I need you to get away from me, Frankie," she said honestly. "Right this minute."

"Yeah, sure." He gave her one last guilty look. "I'm sorry, kid. I just can't . . . sorry." He edged around the table and hurried through the back door.

Chris sat there and stared at nothing in particular until she smelled the sour citrus blend of hand cleaner and Budweiser. "You know about this, Bug?"

"He stayed with me right after he left Addie." He parked a fresh beer in front of her before he sat down. "He's not a bad guy, you know. Only reason he stayed with your mother long as he did was 'cause of you."

"Until he found out I wasn't his kid," she tacked on. "Then he couldn't get out fast enough."

"Yeah, well, that was a real kick to the dick. If it helps, he stayed plastered for close to a year after." He beckoned to Cody and Loot, who came in and took their seats. "You deal, Christi." He shoved a new deck to her.

"Another time." She pushed it back. "Where is Stryker?"

Cody made a ticking sound with his tongue. "That pussy has shark teeth, little girl."

"Do you need the cop to leave the room before you tell me, is that it?" As Bug choked on his beer, Cody's bottle slid out of his hand, and Chris looked at Loot. "Would you mind giving us a minute?"

"How do you know I'm a cop?" he countered.

"There's an unmarked unit parked at the curb. You've got a standard-issue thirty-two in that ankle holster you think I haven't noticed. Your haircut is regulation. There's no money on the table because outside the rezes gambling is illegal in Florida, and occasionally you have to take a random department polygraph." Chris offered him a polite smile. "And, of course, Loot isn't your name because you're loaded. It's biker shorthand for Lieutenant."

He smiled slowly. "You do know cops."

"My best friend works homicide in Fort Lauderdale." She eyed Bug. "Stryker."

"He bounces around Sundown Estates on the east side of the island," Bug said. "Worked out the deal with a Realtor who's into whips and chains." He removed a slip of paper from his bib, wrote on it, and handed it to her. "Entry code for the gate."

She slipped the note in her purse as she watched Loot's face. "You're not interested in pursuing justice here, Officer?"

"I'm not KWPD." His smile was serene. "I fly copters for the Monroe County Sheriff's Department. Aviation Division, Undercover Operations."

"A black-ops chopper copper." She whistled a single descending note. "Glad I'm not smuggling anything past our borders." Something occurred to her, and she turned her gaze on Bug. "No wonder you're so damn antsy. You're helping him, you narc."

"Confidential informant," Bug corrected, and gave her a wary look. "I don't need that advertised, either."

"My lips are Superglued." She handed him the beer and got to her feet. "Nice seeing you again, Bug. Gentlemen, have a lovely evening."

"Hey," Loot called after her. "You never told us what the B-U-G means."

She glanced back at Bug, who squirmed a little. "Only exactly what he is. Big ugly guy."

Jamys diverted from the course Chris had set long enough to sail by Paradise, the boat owner's private island. Photosensor lights illuminated one small pier that led from a cover into a dense thatch of palm and pine trees. Nestled in the center he spotted the tin roof of a large structure; that was likely the house. No vessels were moored to the pier, and the island appeared deserted. If Christian had been with him, he would have persuaded her to spend the coming day there with him, but she was waiting in Key West.

Would she be there waiting, or was it all a ruse?

Jamys had known something had changed the moment Chris had found the strange symbols on the journal's bookplate. He thought at first she had been frightened, but then he detected the complexity of the dark change in her scent. She felt fear, yes, but there was more to it than that. He knew only too well how mortals smelled when they felt despair, and rage, and disgust. She had felt all those things, and winding through them an abysmal amount of regret.

Whoever this Stryker was, Christian despised him. He

could hear it in her voice each and every time she uttered his name.

Jamys returned to the *Golden Horde*'s mapped course and reached the marina rendezvous point at Key West some two hours later, and saw Christian waving to him. He guided the boat to the empty slip she indicated, securing the sails and mooring lines before he climbed out onto the pier.

"You made it." She hurled herself at him. "I was beginning to worry."

"I took a slight detour." When she began to pull away, he wrapped his arms around her and kept her close. "I think we should stop our search for the night. There is a place I want to take you. Come on board, and we can go there now."

She looked up at him. "Someone else might find the jewels, and you'd miss the chance to rule Ireland. Isn't that everything you want?"

"I know what I want tonight." He caressed her cheek. "It is not Ireland."

Her smile slipped. "I get it. You figured out that I didn't tell you everything about Stryker." She bumped her forehead into his shoulder three times. "Okay. He hired me to work at some of his parties. I didn't have sex with anyone, at least, not . . ." She made a frustrated sound. "Look, everything I did, I did by myself, with people watching me. I'm not proud of it, but I was fifteen and alone and no one else would give me a job."

"Was there no one to help you?" he asked. "Your family?"

"My family." She made a bitter sound. "My father— the man I thought was my father—was a drunk and a beach bum. He didn't like finding out I wasn't his kid, so he left me and my mom. That drove my mother crazy, and she killed herself two years later. My grandparents blamed me for all of it and turned me over to the state. I don't know who my biological father is, and everyone who knew his name is dead or won't speak to me, so he's out of the picture." She made a dismissive gesture. "That pretty much covers my family."

Now he understood so many things about her. "You cannot blame yourself for their actions."

"Jamys, I'm the only reason my parents got married, my father left, my mother committed suicide, and my grandparents disowned me." She blinked a few times. "I didn't do it on purpose, but yeah, I destroyed my entire family."

"Christian."

"I've learned to live with it," she assured him. "I didn't ask to be born. I loved my dad and my mom. I tried to love my grandparents. I was a good kid—at least, I think I was—until I met Stryker."

This was her secret shame? "Christian, you were a desperate child, alone in the world. You did what you had to in order to survive."

She shook her head. "I was old enough to know better. I could have stayed in foster care after my mom died." Her hand went to the cross hidden under her shirt.

"The cross you wear," he said, startling her, "it belonged to your mother?"

She nodded. "She gave it to me the night before she killed herself. Took it off her neck and put it around mine, and said I'd have to carry it now. I thought she was just being crazy again." She pulled the cross out from her shirt to look at it. "She never took it off, not even when she went swimming or showered. I don't know why; she wasn't religious."

"Do you wear it to remember her?"

She shrugged. "I kept it to spite my grandmother; she wouldn't let me take anything with me when she dumped me in foster care." Her eyes met his. "I hate what my mom did, but I loved her, too. It's all I have left of her. And it's all I have to remind me not to be her." She sighed. "You wouldn't understand."

"I know what it is to love someone you hate." He thought of all the nights he had spent alone in his tower chambers and, before that, locked inside his silence. "I knew what my mother had done, and I didn't tell my father. I let him think she had been tortured to death in Dublin." He met her gaze. "It drove him mad, Christian. I let my father become an animal because I could not face what my mother had done to us. Because for all the horror she had brought upon us, I loved her still. So yes, I do understand."

"I hope you still feel that way after we do this." She climbed onto the deck and went below.

Jamys followed. "You know where Stryker is."

"His operation is about a mile from here." She wouldn't look at him. "I need to shower and change, and then we'll have to put together an outfit for you."

Sensing she needed some time alone, Jamys went up on deck, and waited until she called his name.

As soon as Jamys entered the cabin, he saw a glittering dark column. It was Christian, standing with her back to him, her slender body wrapped in shimmering black ribbons. She had woven her hair into an intricate braid, and a spray of long, gold-tipped scarlet feathers hugged the right side of her head.

She turned, an altar goddess carved from jet and

ivory, and the dusky allure of her darkened eyes dueled with the luscious red pout of her lips. Both won his soul.

"Say *something*."

Speak? Jamys could barely think. He lifted his hand to touch an inch of silken skin bared by the bewitching material. Naked, in his bed, covered by nothing but moonlight and shadows, she would look like this. "Magic."

"It's the dress and the makeup." Pleasure glowed briefly in her eyes before she turned away. "It should get us into the party." She offered him a jacket made of gleaming black leather and too many zippers. "I found this in his trunk. It should fit."

He didn't want any other eyes on her but his. "Forget this Stryker. We can be in Paradise in an hour. Let me take you there."

"I want to." And she did, he could hear it in her voice. "I think if it was just you and me, I would. But we have to find these emeralds. Not for Tremayne, and not for the council. We've got to do it for the right reasons. To keep everyone safe."

"Very well. We will talk to Stryker together. If what he knows leads us to the gems, we will decide then what to do with them." He stepped closer. "But when this quest is finished, Christian, I am taking you away with me."

"You don't take a *tresora* away with you," Chris said slowly. "I know, because I've memorized all the rules. You do something like that with a girlfriend, or a lover, or a *sygkenis*."

"I am not your master, and you are not my servant," Jamys said quietly. "We were friends, and we always will be, but now I want more. I want you as my woman, and my lover. I want to give you my heart, Christian. I want yours to be mine."

"You don't know what you're asking." Her mouth tightened. "It'll change everything between us."

"Will it?" He touched her cheek. "We have slept in the same bed. We have kissed, and touched, and given pleasure to each other. Are we not lovers now?"

"Don't play with me, Jamys," she whispered. "This isn't my job we're talking about. I've only got one heart, and it's already been broken a bunch of times."

"I will never hurt you." He folded her into his arms. "You can trust me."

She trembled, her face hot against his neck, and then she nodded. "All right."

Tall, wide gates protected the entrance to Sundown Estates, but as Jamys reached for the door handle to get out and open them, Christian retracted the window and pressed some numbers on a small keypad.

"I got the code from an old friend," she said as the gate swung inward and she drove through to a small shack. "I might need your help with this guy."

The uniformed guard had a gun on his belt and a clipboard in his hand, and bent over to give them an unfriendly look. "Help you, ma'am?"

"We're here to have anonymous sex with a lot of people," Christian told him. "Can you point us in the direction to the latest orgy?"

"I'm sorry, ma'am, but you have the wrong place." The guard straightened as Jamys got out of the car, and looked over the roof at him. "Sir, I have to ask you to get back in the vehicle."

"Yes, of course." He walked around the car. "I merely

wish to change places with my lady friend. She is a terrible driver." He held out his hand. "Enjoy the remainder of your evening."

The guard hesitated before taking his hand. The moment he did he went still.

"You wish to tell me where Stryker is," Jamys said.

"Seven-five-one Albatross Avenue." The guard smiled at Christian. "Your lady sure is pretty."

"She is beautiful," Jamys corrected. "You want to return to your station and forget about this conversation." So that Christian couldn't hear, he added one last mental command. *When you see our car drive out of the complex, you will telephone the police and report to them Stryker and his activities here.*

"Sure." The guard wandered back into his shack.

Expensive cars had been packed into a vacant lot beside the mock-plantation home at the end of Albatross Avenue. A bored-looking man dressed in formal wear didn't remove the white buds blocking his ear canals as he gestured at a spot by the curb.

Christian turned off the motor and looked at the draped windows of the house. "Did they have orgies back in the Dark Ages?"

"They have them in every age," he assured her. "I have seen mortals engage in such acts, but I have never taken part myself. The Kyn prefer privacy."

"One more reason to love you guys." She got out of the car.

The man who answered the doorbell wore a black spandex bodysuit and a red-lined black cape, and flashed pointed canine veneers at Chris. "Welcome to the Dark Side. May I see your invitations?"

"We're just here for the cookies." Chris pushed past him.

When the doorman started after her, Jamys clapped a hand on his shoulder. "You wish to be silent, go home, and never again dress like this or work for Stryker."

The man's mouth clamped shut as he nodded and walked out.

Jamys joined Chris, who was looking around the room. The home's furnishings were being used by several dozen mortals in various stages of dress and gathered in loose groups. A third were engaged in physical inter-course; the remainder were watching the couplings, drink-ing, talking, and laughing. Waiters, nude but for small black aprons tied around their waists, circulated with trays of champagne, liquor, appetizers, and baskets filled with small shiny packets. Nude females and males in the center of each group were in the process of climbing down from black-painted platforms.

"He's over there." Chris nodded to a well-dressed, indolent-looking male being attended to by a group of adoring young women.

He caught her arm. "I will speak to him."

"I need to do this, for me. Please?" When he nodded, she squared her shoulders, gripped his hand, and started toward Stryker.

The man seemed wholly preoccupied with the girls competing to use their mouths on his genitals, but as soon as he glanced up at Chris, he smiled and began pushing their heads away.

"Patience, my darlings," he chided when they began to plead with him. "It seems for me Christmas has come early this year. You are looking exquisite, Tian."

Christian inspected the pouting faces around him. "You're looking at about twenty years for statutory rape."

"I'll have to advise the district attorney. Perhaps I'll wait until he's finished sodomizing the circuit court judge over there." Stryker's eyes shifted, and he fastened the front of his trousers. "Who is your delicious-looking friend, and does he have an open mind?"

"Don't even go there." Christian eyed the girl closest to her. "Where did you get this bunch? The beaches, or the bus station?"

"These are courtesy of a local church." He picked up a martini glass from a side table and sipped from it.

Jamys frowned. "You take these children from a place of worship?"

"No, dear boy. Every Saturday the church feeds the homeless in a park not far from here." Stryker plucked the olive from his glass and fed it to one of the girls. "I find the selection often overwhelming."

"Stryker likes to hire runaways," Chris said, her voice flat. "He knows how desperate they are. The younger the better."

The mortal raised his martini glass. "You told me you were twenty-one, my darling. How was I to know you were such an accomplished underage liar?"

Chris faced Jamys. "I was wrong. We need to get out of here before I jump across that table and yank his tonsils out through his nostrils."

Jamys glanced back at the smirking mortal before he drew her out of Stryker's hearing range. "I will not permit him to speak to you like this and live. But if I kill him, the information he has dies with him. I will have to get closer to him and use *l'attrait* to compel him to talk."

"Then I'd have to spend the rest of the night spraying you down with Lysol." She took a deep breath. "Look, I know the jerk, and I can handle him. Trust me." She turned around and went back to the table. "Stryker, we're here about the old journals you sold to Professor Charles Gifford."

"Did I? Let me recall." Stryker sat back and slowly fondled the girl beside him as he pretended to think. "You mean Father Bartley's earnest but largely boring chronicles of life among the wild native islanders?"

"Yes. We want to know who sold them to you," Chris said.

"A lovely, rather dangerous man who collects precious things," Stryker said. "He had the oddest obsession with emeralds, and had amassed a collection of them that was simply breathtaking. I recall three in particular that he had in his safe. He claimed they were cursed and had to keep them locked up."

Jamys exchanged a look with Chris. "When did you see this?"

"I can't remember the exact date. Some years ago." Stryker eyed Christian. "You know, I think it was just after you left me, my darling."

"Give us his name and we will leave."

"But you've only just arrived." Stryker rose, displacing his adoring acolytes as he approached Chris. When Jamys stepped in front of her, he halted. "Your boy plays bodyguard. How charming." He inspected Jamys from head to toe and back again. "How does he look without the clothes?"

"Sorry," Chris told him. "You'll just have to dream."

Jamys's attention strayed to two men in dark suits who had entered the house and were moving quickly in their direction. Both fit the description of the men who had pursued Christian from the blood bank in Miami. "*Tresori.* We should go."

She followed the direction of his gaze. "Damn it."

"Not to worry, my darlings." Stryker made a deceptively lazy gesture, and four men converged on the pair, discreetly disarming them before escorting them over to Stryker.

"We are Interpol agents," one of the *tresori* said with convincing authority. "This man and woman are wanted for murder. You will put them in our custody."

Stryker smiled. "Dear man, Interpol agents do not personally arrest suspects. They investigate, they coordinate, and then they issue warrants and arrange for local authorities to do the dirty work for them. I suggest the next time you decide to impersonate a law enforcement agent that you first read up on their procedural methods."

The other *tresora* scowled. "We will pay you ten thousand American dollars to give them to us." When Stryker merely lifted his brows, he added, "Twenty thousand."

"Do you have the money on you? No? What a shame. I don't accept checks or credit cards." Stryker tapped his chin with one long black-polished nail. "I can give you the name of the seller, Tian, as well as his current location. He's quite obsessed with collecting emeralds. I will even go as far as to detain these two impostors long enough to give you and your friend a reasonable head start when you leave. But as you well know, nothing in life is free. If you want my information and my services, you'll have to offer me something in trade."

"No." Jamys took Chris's hand. "Let them go. We will take our chances."

"Wait." Chris squeezed his hand. To Stryker, she said, "What do you want in return?"

Stryker's eyes drifted to the couple gyrating atop the center table. "Entertainment. All my regular performers are on break now, so you and Tian give my clients a little show." He glanced at Chris. "It's not as if it's her first time." He beckoned to his entourage, who followed him over to the center table.

Chris's scent darkened and heated as she stood and stared after the buffoon. "How badly do we need this?"

"The three gems he saw have to be the emeralds," he admitted. He wanted to ask her what Stryker had meant by his last remark, but she was too angry. "We will leave. He wishes only to hurt you."

"No, that's not what he wants." She gave him an odd look. "Do you trust me?" When he nodded, she said, "We have to perform together for him. It'll be like a dance."

He frowned. "I do not dance well."

"You won't be the one dancing." She led him toward the platform Stryker had indicated, and once there used a chair to climb atop it.

Jamys ignored the catcalls and hooting of the spectators as he looked up at the hand she held out to him. "You are sure you wish to do this?"

"No." Her hand remained out.

Jamys took it and climbed up beside her. All around them the lights dimmed while spotlights lit the platform.

"Quiet," Stryker called out. When every voice stilled, he grinned up at them. "What should the DJ spin for you, Tian? You used to be fond of the Backstreet Boys, as I recall."

"Evanescence," she said, moving behind Jamys. " 'My Immortal.' "

"Ah, classic Goth. How painfully predictable." Stryker made a gesture, and a few moments later the first gentle piano notes spilled out from the wall speakers.

Jamys felt Chris's hands at his waist, and heard her voice beneath the sad music. "I'll dance. All you have to do is stand still."

She rubbed up against his back like a cat, turning to press her shoulders to his. He could feel her arms moving, and heard the slither of a zipper being released. She slid down him, her buttocks caressing the backs of his legs, and then curled a leg around his calves.

Her body arched with serpentine ease as she took hold of his belt and used it as a handhold to swing herself around to face him, and then pull herself up. He felt the buttons of his shirt being popped one by one out of their holes as her fingers inched over them. When he looked down, he saw she'd hiked up the skirt of her dress, exposing a long swath of thigh.

This is what he made you do? he couldn't help thinking to her.

She stood on tiptoe, pressing her cheek to his. "No. He paid me to perform alone."

His jaw tightened as he felt her lips against his throat, and his temper thinned as he heard the suggestions being called out by those watching them:

"Give it to her, boy."

"Get on your knees and suck his dick."

"Fuck that tight little ass."

"Jerk him off."

"No, jerk her off."

At last he understood what Stryker had demanded of her. *You need not do this.*

"Forget about them." She cradled his face with her hands, and looked into his eyes as her smile flashed, all bright and brilliant delight. "It's just you and me. We're not in hell. We're in paradise, and this is for us."

What followed tested Jamys's self-control to the brink, as Chris used her mouth and hands and body in a slow, deliberate seduction. As she worked herself against him and around him, she managed to peel down her bodice and slip her arms free of her dress, baring herself to the hips. She brought his hands up to cover her breasts, rubbing her peaks in circles over his palms before she lowered herself again, this time nuzzling her way from his chest to his groin.

The torment continued ceaselessly, endlessly. With her mouth she toyed with him, with her fingers she stroked him, and just as he thought he could not bear another moment, she would move to his back. His shirt slid from his shoulders to the table, and he felt the blunt scrape of her teeth against his shoulder even as her fingernails lightly scored his chest.

Jamys reached down to tuck his arm under her bottom, and lifted her up until her thighs spread and she wound her legs around him. The small soft curves between her legs nestled over his erection, and he flexed his arm to work her subtly against him.

As she tried to speak, he covered her parted lips with his mouth and poured his hunger into her mind. *Like this, I want you like this.*

Chris latched on to his shoulders, her hips rolling as she used her body to stroke him. The fabrics separating their sexes added more friction as their movements came in sync.

He wanted to be inside her so much he curled his fist into a handful of her hair, and pressed her face against his neck, praying he would not rip the dress from her and sate his most desperate need. He heard his name rushing out with her short, rapid breaths, and then her body began to tremble violently. He splayed his hand across her buttocks, pressing her to him as she shook, and then jerked in response as the semen came jetting from his cock.

"Wow." Her arm curled around his neck, and her damp, hot cheek rested against his heart. "That makes up for a lot of bad memories."

He kissed her brow and the tip of her nose and bow of her upper lip before he looked into her dazed eyes. *You are my every pleasure, Christian. All the wants and dreams and longings of my soul. I am yours, my lady.*

The music swelled and ebbed, and finally drifted to its sorrowful end. Chris unwound herself from him, going to her knees before him, lifting her arms to press her hands to his thighs as she bowed her head.

Stryker stood up and clapped his hands together slowly several times. "How quaint and conventional." He eyed the soaked material at the front of Jamys's trousers. "At least someone enjoyed it. Now, Tian, perhaps after one final solo performance, for old times' sake, we may—"

"Oh, so you think you're going to welsh on us now?" Chris accepted Jamys's hand as he helped her down, and gave him a small nod before she offered Stryker a cool smile. "Not this time."

Sound and colors blurred around Jamys as he moved to Stryker and grabbed him by the throat. When his men moved in, Jamys snarled at them, and they slowly backed away. He then applied just enough pressure to see Stryker's bloodshot eyes bulge before he eased his grip. "You wish to tell me the name and location of the man with the emeralds."

"His name is Noel Coburn. He uses a jewelry store as a front for selling weapons." After an extended coughing fit, Stryker wheezed out, "He had them in the safe at the shop."

"That's the guy Sam found murdered downtown. She said his safe and shop had been cleaned out." Chris stepped closer. "Did you have him killed? Do you have the emeralds?"

"No. The office safe was purely for show." Stryker gasped as Jamys tightened his fingers. "Second safe. Hidden under the rug in the front of the store. I swear."

As Jamys released him, Stryker fell back into the arms of two shrieking girls, and took them down to the floor with him. He stepped over the writhing bodies to grab the two *tresori*, slamming their heads together hard enough to knock them unconscious before dropping them.

Chris pulled her dress back in place and zipped up the side. "Come on," she said to Jamys, "before I let you kill him."

Chapter 15

Halfway between the station and the stronghold traffic suddenly came to a standstill, and when Sam leaned her head out to look ahead, she smelled smoke and blood, and heard shouts from a block away. Using her emergency flashers, she eased out of her lane and drove on the shoulder until she reached the accident at the intersection.

Crumpled front ends conjoined an SUV and a small pickup, which both had air bags deployed. One man with a nose streaming blood was shouting and pounding on the roof of the truck.

Sam parked to one side and ran out in time to keep the angry motorist from trying to drive his fist through the window. "Sir, you need to come away from here."

"Sonofabitch ran the red. Come outta there, goddamnit." He tried to jerk his arm from her grip, and then stared at her. "He *ran* the *red*."

"I can see that. Let me get him out." Sam shed more scent as she pointed to a nearby bus stop bench. "You go sit over there and be quiet."

The dazed motorist lurched off, and Sam called it in

on her mobile as she pried open the truck's door. The boy inside lay unmoving against the deflating air bag, half a joint still tucked in the corner of his mouth.

"What happened to 'just say no'?" Sam muttered as she carefully lifted him out of the seat. She carried him across the glass-strewn road to the opposite curb, where she lowered him onto the grass. The air bag had done a number on his chin and the front of his neck, and blood oozing from the friction wounds wet her scarred palm as she felt for the pulse she didn't find.

"Shit." She tipped his head back and cleared his airway, trying at the same time to hold back the images pouring into her mind.

"May I be of assistance?" a low voice asked.

Sam looked up blindly at the blond woman. "You know CPR?" When she nodded, she said, "Take over compressions for me."

As soon as the woman did, Sam stopped fighting the death vision, which dragged time in reverse, hauling her across the intersection and down the road two miles, dropping her behind the steering wheel of the truck.

Sam saw a rawboned hand thumb a lighter and touch the flame to the end of a freshly rolled joint. She smelled the harsh, sweet scent of the marijuana as puffs of smoke billowed up in front of her eyes. The tip of the joint flared as she inhaled, and a seed inside it popped, blowing off the glowing end. She heard a young voice swearing as a hand swatted the burning sensation on the top of her right thigh.

She couldn't stop the boy from looking down to search for the burning ember, or warn him that the green light he'd just seen had turned yellow. She could only brace herself as the yellow switched to red and he roared into the intersection and collided with the SUV. The impact threw her forward into an explosion of sound and whiteness.

The sound of coughing brought her back to reality, where the boy lay struggling for breath on his side.

The blond woman kneeling behind him made soothing noises as she held his shoulders and smiled at Sam. "He's breathing again on his own."

"Thank you." Sam staggered to her feet, scrubbing her palm against the side of her trousers. "You saved his life."

"So did you," the woman said simply.

It took another a minute before the downtown patrols and paramedics arrived at the scene. Sam used the time to check on the other victim, who was still sitting quietly on the bench. "How are you feeling, sir?"

"That kid almost died, didn't he?" He gave her a dazed look. "I got a fifteen-year-old, just got his restricted permit." His eyes shifted to the scene across the street. "That could be him."

She nodded. "Talk to your boy about this. Let him know how it feels." She touched his shoulder. "And check his pockets occasionally."

After she gave the details to the patrolmen, Sam walked back to her car. The smell of the blood made her throat dry and her fangs ache, but the last thing she wanted to do was hunt.

The urge to hurry back to the stronghold had disappeared as well. Although Lucan hadn't been responsible for what he'd done or said, she still felt bruised inside. She'd never taken his love for granted, but the bond they shared was supposed to guarantee it would last forever. Discovering that someone else could make it and Lucan go away had left her feeling brittle, as if one more knock might smash her to pieces.

"Excuse me." The blond woman walked up to her, and held out her mobile. "You dropped this on the grass."

"Thanks." Sam took it and pocketed it. "You should go and talk to the officer over there; he's going to need a statement from you."

"I've already done that." She glanced around. "I was wondering, Detective, if you knew where I might get a glass of wine at this hour. I'm still feeling a bit shaken."

"You certainly don't show it, and my name is Samantha." Sam noted the soft English accent and the pale skin; the woman must have just arrived on vacation. "There's a decent pub just around the corner, and I'm off duty now, so how about I buy you the drink?"

"That's very kind of you. I'm Werren." A smile briefly warmed her cool features. "I don't want to keep you from going home."

Home was Lucan, but she didn't want to go there. Not until she was ready to be his *sygkenis* instead of a screaming bitch. "It's okay. Come on."

Neptune's Bar and Grill had lost the grill to a kitchen fire some years back, and cut its losses by sticking to the better-selling liquid comforts: beer, wine, and liquor. Sam scanned the faces of the patrons, mostly men, nursing their bottles and glasses as they watched a sportscaster on the big plasma TV in one corner. A few glanced at them as they sat at the end of the bar, and Sam made a mental note to accompany her Good Samaritan every step of the way back to her car or hotel.

A baby-faced bartender came over and greeted them as if they were swans in a desert. "Ladies, what can I do you for?"

"Red wine okay?" Sam asked the other woman, who nodded. "Got something that won't burn off our tonsils with the first sip?"

"Cases of the stuff," he said, and rolled his eyes. "Boss's wife comes here with her girlfriends. They're all like French or something."

"Then please do bring us something that you can't pronounce," Werren said politely.

Sam held on to her chuckle until the bartender reached the cooler at the other end of the bar. "I love how you Brits make a snappy comeback sound like Shakespeare."

"While I am ever astounded by the generous nature you Americans possess." As the bartender delivered two glasses of dark red wine, she returned his silly grin with a regal nod. "You're always willing to jump in and save someone, whether it be car-crash victims"—she lifted her wineglass—"or a stranger whose insides resemble the Gordian knot."

"Well, then." Sam held out her glass. "God save the Queen."

"And Mr. Obama."

The wine tasted surprisingly good, and Sam thought she might be able to drink most of hers if she took it slow. Fortunately her companion seemed in no hurry to knock back her glass.

"So what brings you to South Florida?" Sam asked. "Vacation, business, family?"

"Business. My employer sent me to acquire some property, but I have a little time for myself." Werren lifted a hand to the high collar of her blouse before she took another sip from her glass. "What is it like to live here, in this beautiful place?"

"As places go it's usually hot, crowded, and busy, and

that's just in the off-season." She ran her thumb along the thin stem of her glass. "But there are some wonderful places to explore. The Riverwalk, ballet at the performing arts center, and all the neat shops at Las Olas. There's a wildlife preserve a little south of here that has nature trails and a walk-through butterfly garden. It's beautiful *and* peaceful."

"Sounds lovely, but I'm more of a night person." She flinched as two of the men hooted loudly over a touchdown on the television.

Sam glanced sideways and what she saw nearly made her fall on the floor.

"Not terribly fond of loud noises, either." The other woman frowned at her. "Is something wrong?"

"Tired eyes." Sam rubbed them before she studied Werren again. Her blond hair gleamed, every strand brushed neatly in place, and her ladylike outfit looked equally immaculate. *So why for an instant did I think she was wearing an old potato sack only slightly filthier than the rat's nest on her head?* It couldn't have been a vision; the woman wasn't bleeding or dead.

Werren picked up her glass, and then wrinkled her nose and set it down again. "I think this lovely wine is actually giving me a headache. Would you mind terribly if I cut this short?"

"No problem." Sam dug some bills out of her wallet and tucked them under her half-empty glass for the bartender. "I'll walk with you. Car or hotel?"

"I've a lovely little cottage by the water, about a mile down the road," Werren said as they left the bar. "But you needn't walk me there. I won't get lost."

"This time of night? You'll get mugged," Sam advised her. "Come on, I'll give you a ride."

Traffic was again flowing through the intersection where the collision had occurred, and as Sam reached her car, she looked for the wrecked vehicles, which were gone. The city's accident-response department must have already towed them away. Even as she thought that, something else about the scene seemed wrong.

"It's strange," she said to Werren as she merged into the southbound lane. "That accident caused such a mess, but now it looks like it never even happened."

"I wish it hadn't." Werren sounded distant, as if her thoughts were elsewhere.

Sam saw the way she was rubbing her fingers against her right temple. "Headache getting worse?"

"It's only just beginning, I'm afraid." She nodded at the street corner they were approaching. "It's right there, at the end of that walkway."

Sam found an empty space at the curb, and looked up at the dark windows of an exceptionally pretty little beach house. "Now this is *really* strange. I've driven past this corner a couple thousand times and I've never once noticed this property." She saw the way the other woman was frowning. "This is the place, right?"

"It is, but I always leave the light on in the front room and now it's off." She turned to Sam. "Would it be completely wretched of me to ask you to walk up and have a look?"

"Wretched, no. Smart, yes."

Sam got out and scanned the surrounding area as she approached the front wraparound porch. The wind played with hanging chimes of pipes, shells, and sea glass, and the sound of the tide retreating added a soft background rush. The front door and windows bore no marks of being forced open, and when Sam climbed up the steps, she couldn't smell or feel any sign of a mortal who might have done the same.

"I think you're okay," Sam said as Werren joined her. "Just keep your doors and windows locked, and if you want to go somewhere at night, you should . . . call . . . a cab." There had been no glass on the road at the accident scene, Sam suddenly recalled. Not a single shard. While county usually did a decent job cleaning up after a collision, they weren't that meticulous.

"I had no choice, my lady," the other woman murmured.

She stared at Werren, whose face had lost all expression. "What did you call me?"

"If you fight them, you will be made to suffer." The cool eyes closed.

The beach house melted into dark water, and the porch began rocking under Sam's feet. On either side of her the bright lights from the hotels and clubs on the beach receded to the east, while the wooden deck built atop itself an empty cabin with blacked-out windows.

Sam didn't bother to watch the changes around her anymore; she lunged at Werren. A thin cable wrapped around her neck and burned into her flesh with the hot-acid bite of copper. It shocked her so much she froze.

"Take her weapon," a rough voice ordered beside her ear.

Werren approached, darting back as Sam lashed out with a vicious kick. "Please. They will hurt you if you resist."

Sam brought her boot down as hard as she could on the man's instep, making him howl and shove her away. She dragged the copper garrote from around her neck as she reached for her pistol with her other hand, only to find herself shoved back into the confines of a body-size cage, the door to which was slammed in her face.

"Another illusion? This time I know it's not real." She tried to wrench the bars apart. "Goddamn it, let me out of here."

Werren walked up to the cage, and reached in to take her weapon. When Sam tried to stop her, she found herself manacled by huge metal cuffs attached to the bars of the cage.

"Everything is real, my lady." She sounded sad as her hair snarled into wads of dirty knots and her pretty outfit sagged into a rotting potato sack. "I am the only illusion."

So now he knows.

Chris wouldn't let herself look at anything but the scenery as Jamys drove them back to the marina. Since they'd left Stryker's orgy, he'd been very quiet, and all she could think of to say were a bunch of pathetic excuses and inadequate apologies. She'd just shown him what Stryker had made of her, and forced him to have sex in front of a houseful of perverts; even the most sincere "I'm sorry" wouldn't redeem her behavior.

It's better that he knows. At least she wouldn't have to pretend anymore that the years between her mother's suicide and the day she met Sam didn't exist. She had to put this behind her and go on as if nothing had happened, something she was becoming an expert at doing.

To give her hands something to do besides twist her fingers into knots, Chris took out her mobile. "I'm going to try to call Sam. If she can meet us somewhere, away from the stronghold, then we can keep Lucan from finding out that you didn't go home."

"I have no home," Jamys said. "I cannot return to my father's stronghold, and even if he would permit it, I have no desire to serve another Kyn lord." He gave her a sideways glance. "Once the high lord learns of my situation, he will have me declared a rogue."

Chris knew a little about rogues, the loner immortals who were considered outcasts among the Kyn. If they did anything to hurt humans or piss off Tremayne, he had them killed. Sometimes he had them killed simply for turning rogue. Sam had told her how often Lucan had been sent to execute them before Cyprien had made him a suzerain.

"Then you go back to North Carolina," she told him. "You make up with your dad and take an oath to him or whatever you have to do, but you don't go rogue. You don't ever go rogue."

"By leaving my father's stronghold without permission, and disobeying Lucan's orders by remaining in his territory, I have already." He parked the car in the marina's lot and shut off the engine. "Finding the emeralds is my only hope of redemption now."

"Oh. So you've decided to give them to the high lord." Although she understood his motives, her heart sank a little. "Okay. Maybe he won't use them to decimate the mortal world."

"He would not use them for that specific purpose." He got out of the car and came around to open her door. "But I believe he cannot be trusted with them, so no, I would not give them to Richard."

"Immortality might tempt someone on the council to act like an idiot, too." She climbed out and walked with him toward the slip. "If we can't give them to either side, then why are we still looking for these rocks?"

"In the summons, Richard said that the guardian of the emeralds is dead." He stopped and looked down at her. "I think you and I were fated to become the new guardians."

"Us?" She frowned. "I could see you doing that, but I'm human. I'm only going to be around for maybe another fifty, sixty years, and that's not . . ." She realized what he meant. "No, Jamys."

"Think about it." He cradled her face between his hands. "If you were made immortal, Christian, we could be together forever. I could take you as my *sygkenis*, and neither of us would ever have to be alone again."

"You'd make *me* your life companion." She tried to wrap her head around that. "What are you talking about?"

"I am in love with you." He drew his knuckles down along the side of her cheek. "I have been these three years."

She walked away from him and went to the boat, where she turned on the navcom and pulled up the course that would take them back to Fort Lauderdale. She felt him the moment he stepped onto the boat, but kept her back to him.

"Why are you so angry with me?"

"Three years." She hammered the coordinates into the keypad. "The last three years, do you know how I spent them? Training."

"I know—"

"You're Kyn. You don't know." She saw the faint reflection of her face on the navcom's small monitor, and her features were so drawn they resembled a too-tight mask. "Every single day for the last three years, I've been training. I learned how to fight with my fists, my feet, my elbows and knees. I practiced how to use knives, clubs, swords, Tasers, and anything else Burke handed me. I spent fourteen months going to the firing range every day to master every pistol, every rifle, every assault weapon in the stronghold armory, until Turner qualified me as expert on all of them. I can outshoot a SWAT team, Jamys, and I don't even *like* guns."

She switched the computer screen to the maritime report, but she couldn't focus on the readout.

"What has this to do with us?" he asked at last.

"It has nothing to do with us. See, there *was* no us. There was just me, and what I had to do. I've never been book smart, so the French lessons almost made me quit." She sounded bitter, and realized she didn't care. "Your language has too many damn irregular verbs in it, and why can't you pronounce the ends of words? What's wrong with the ends of words? We say them in English."

"I know," he admitted. "It took me a long time to remember to say them."

"Well, you're immortal; you have the time to spare," she reasoned. "Oh, and then there was tolerance training. For that, I got tapped for blood every hour until I passed out cold. Then Burke would wake me up, make me drink a barrel of juice, and then give me work to do and evaluate my performance on the job. I'm actually pretty good at that; it only took me eight months to work up to losing three pints without compromising my ability to think straight and observe proper protocol."

He turned her around to face him. "Christian, why are you telling me this?"

"I'm telling you I did all of that," she assured him,

"and a lot more, because that's what *tresori* do for the Kyn. We serve every need you have, and I thought if I could do that for you ... if I could be the perfect *tresora* that you'd ... and you're telling me that all this time, you've been in love with me? With that girl I used to be, the homeless loser with the funny hair, the pierced eyebrow, the checkered sex-trade past?"

"It matters not how you appear, or what you have done," he said, running a hand over her hair. "That is not who you were to me."

She went to the starboard side of the boat and sat down on the edge of the hull to stare down at the murky water in the slip. "I can't believe this."

Chris tried to hold it in, but her shoulders began to shake, and then the rest of her body joined in.

Jamys came to sit beside her, putting his arm around her shoulders. "Please, Christian, don't cry."

That did it. The first laugh rolled out of her, followed by another, and then she really let go.

Jamys frowned. "You are not crying."

"I know. I should be," she gasped between eruptions of giggles. "But it's just so funny. I was so sure it was the only way we could be together. Three years, trying to be so perfect, so ladylike, so boring ..." Overwhelmed again, she shook her head and just let it out.

"I should probably tell you," Jamys said, "what I have been doing all this time."

"Sure." Chris heaved in a breath and wiped the tears from her cheeks. "You had to listen to my stuff."

"I have been training as well. I have been learning how to fight. First with my father, and then by myself." His mouth hitched. "I was never a Templar, you see, so I had never taken up the sword. One cannot rule warriors unless one can prevail over them, but I had a more personal motive. Thus I set myself to study and learn the techniques of Kyn warriors, and practice until I was ready to challenge the warriors of my father's garrison."

Chris sobered. "How long did you have to train?"

"Every night, from dusk until near dawn, for three years." He smiled. "I did it for you, Christian."

"Why on earth would you want to turn yourself into a warrior for me?" As he gave her an ironic look, she understood. "Oh, my God. So you'd have the right to take a *tresora*."

He nodded. "I convinced myself that it was the only way you and I could be together."

It was a good thing she'd exhausted her supply of laughter for the time being, because what they'd done for each other was almost hilarious. Sad, too, because they could have avoided all of it.

"You are not laughing," he murmured, drawing her closer.

"How can I? You sold your watch to buy combs for my hair, and I cut off my hair and sold it to buy a chain for your watch." She sighed. "Don't take that literally, it's an analogy. Something two other misguided lovers did in an O. Henry story."

"'Gift of the Magi.'" He nodded. "I know it well."

"So do I, and yet we both made the same mistake anyway." She looked up at him. "I know we have a couple million things to talk about, and then there's the emeralds and Lucan and Sam and saving the world, but I need a break. You wanted me to spend the night with you in Paradise. Is that offer still good?"

"Oh, yes." He drew her to her feet, and led her back

to the navcom, where he put in a new set of coordinates. "If you'll cast off, I'll see to the sails."

"We're actually *sailing* to Paradise?" She'd thought he'd used the word as a euphemism for making love.

Jamys caught her around the waist, lifting her up for his kiss. "Wait and see."

Chapter 16

Werren watched the cage containing Samantha Brown being lowered by the crane. "Has the master returned?"

"Not yet." Clemens, the first mate, made a pushing gesture above his head for the crane operator to stop the winch. Beneath their feet the shouting continued, joined now by a furious rattling sound. "She stays in the cage until he does."

His scent had gone sour with the stink of fear, something Werren found fascinating. "She cannot go anywhere, and if she tries to hurt someone, the men will kill her." *Unless she kills them first.*

"You'd better go talk to her," Clemens said. "Explain how we do things, and what Dutch expects from her."

"I have no authority to speak for the master in his absence." Werren regarded him. "I believe that is your place, Mr. Clemens."

"Don't play your mind-fucking games with me, whore." He gave her a push toward the stairs. "Tell her how it's going to be. Otherwise she'll be hanging from the mast in shreds at dawn."

As Werren descended the narrow staircase, she considered using her gift once more to disguise herself. Altering physical appearance was the most difficult illusion to maintain, however, as movements and speech constantly demanded thousands of tiny adjustments of the facade. Places and things required much less of her gift, usually no more than a single flick of thought. In this instance, however, her actual appearance might be more effective in convincing the lady to listen.

Werren found Samantha kicking at the base of the cage with her boots, alternating left and right as she worked at creating a gap between the bars. The scent of blood and copper made Werren's stomach clench, and she saw the raw wounds the detective had inflicted on her wrists while trying unsuccessfully to free them from the manacles.

"If you will stand still," she said, causing Samantha to do precisely that, "I will remove the shackles."

"Go to hell, you fucking bitch." She resumed kicking the bars.

"I regret deceiving you as I did," Werren said, raising her voice to be heard over the racket. "I had no other choice but to carry out my master's commands."

"You can drop the pathetic human act now," Samantha said, wedging her boot against one bar and trying to push it out with no success. "I know you're Kyn."

"Like you," Werren said. "But you are of this time. How did your master change you without killing you?"

Narrow hazel eyes glittered. "Let me out of here and I'll tell you all about me, my master, and our secrets."

She sounded pleasant, even sincere, but Werren knew better. "Dutch will have all of his secrets once he brings him under his control. You cannot escape. The men will not permit it, and when you try, they will hurt us both."

Samantha stopped kicking. "Do you really believe I give a rat's ass what happens to you?"

"No. Not now, not when you're this angry. But I can explain myself, my lady. Once you hear what has been done to me and the others, you will understand how desperate our situation is." Despair made her go to the cage and grip the bars. "Please, allow me to—"

A bloody hand shot out and gripped her by the throat, cutting off her voice. "Open the fucking cage. *Now.*"

"I cannot." Werren felt the other woman's nails stabbing into her flesh, drawing blood, and her gift exploded out of her, transforming her into a snarling beast.

Samantha held on. "Sorry, no sale this time, sister." She tightened her grip. "Drop the illusion, or I'll rip your throat out."

Werren forced back the roiling power pouring out of her and resumed her honest appearance. "What do you want, my lady? You hurt me, but I am like you. A prisoner."

"Funny, but I don't see your cage anywhere." She dug her strong fingers in deeper. "Who are you? The truth this time."

"No one of importance." Werren tasted her own blood on her tongue, and with it the temptation to goad Samantha into killing her. She was so weary of the nightmare of her existence, and death would be her only release. The women she left behind, however, would suffer—including this one, who had yet to understand the horror that awaited her. "My name is Werren Reed, and I have been a prisoner here for a very long time."

"Why? What did you do?"

The same two questions she had been asking ever since Dutch had taken her. "My master purchased me from my mother's employer. I have been his slave ever since."

The hand tightened. "Slavery isn't legal."

"It was when he took me," Werren said simply. "He kept me in his bed for weeks, using me for sex and slowly draining me of my blood. I prayed for death, my lady."

Something flickered in Samantha's angry eyes. "You're still breathing."

"Not by any choice of my own. When I died from the blood loss, I thought, 'At last, it is finished. I am free of him.'" She curled her fingers around one bar. "I woke up in a cage much like this one, naked, helpless, hopeless, and there I stayed."

"You're breaking my heart." Despite the harsh tone she used, some of the pressure of her hold eased. "You said there were others. Did he buy them, or did he let you out the cage to grab them for him?"

"In the beginning he did not know how I had been changed. He dragged me out of the cage to service him and the crew." She didn't care to think on those wretched years of her existence. "When I fought them—and I did fight, lady, every time—he would punish me until I blacked out. The master's punishments were terrible, but no matter what he did, I never died again."

Samantha shook her head. "He had to know you were Kyn."

"He did not know what he was," Werren pointed out. "None of us did. And so I would wake up tied to a cot with some grunting, sweating sailor atop me, my wounds healed. When the men were satisfied, the master put me back in the cage. I was left there to starve for weeks, sometimes months."

"So you saved your own ass by becoming his partner

and getting other women for him?" Samantha shook her. "You think that makes it okay?"

"I am not his partner. I am his possession." Werren touched her snarled hair. "This is my latest punishment for speaking out of turn. I'm not permitted to wash myself or comb my hair until the master says I may again. If he is pleased when he returns, he may allow me a bucket of water and a sliver of soap. That will be my reward for capturing you, my lady: permission to bathe."

A powerful stream of seawater blasted down into the cage, knocking Samantha off her feet and freeing Werren from her hold. She staggered back to see the fire hose Clemens was using on the detective.

She wanted to shout at him to stop, but that would only make him angrier, so she went to the cage and released the shackles around the detective's wrists.

"Let me out of here," Samantha shouted, only to be knocked to the floor of the cage.

"Keep your head down, and your mouth shut," Werren called above the sound of the water.

The first mate hosed the detective for another minute before he shut off the spray. "Take her to the others and have them school her," he shouted down in a tight, ugly voice. "We leave in ten minutes."

She nodded, and waited until he disappeared from sight before she went to the cage and crouched down. Reaching in, she helped Samantha into a sitting position.

Seawater dripped from the hair hanging in the detective's furious eyes. "Is that how you take a bath?"

"Only when they are angry." She propped her shoulder against the bars and studied her hands, which looked cleaner than they had for days. "I'd rather have the bucket. The salt makes me itch."

"Stop talking to me like we're friends." The other woman checked the raw, torn wounds circling her wrists, watching the edges shrinking before she eyed Werren. "He said you're leaving. He meant you with him."

"Yes." Only one more trip, and it would be finished. "It will not take long."

"I don't care," Samantha said. "How many humans will he leave behind to guard me?"

"Twenty. Each of them knows what you are, and how to hurt you," she warned. "If you approach any of them, they will kill you."

She wiped the water from her eyes. "Then why bother to kidnap me?" Before Werren could answer, she sat up with a jerk. "Lucan. He did this to get to him. Does he have any idea what Lucan will do to him when he finds out?"

"Of course he does." Werren stood up. "But he will not allow it. Nothing and no one can harm Dutch. He can make anyone do as he pleases. When he finds the treasure that was stolen from him, he says he will become the most powerful man in the world."

"That's what every sick, twisted jackass thinks." The detective got to her feet and scanned their surroundings. "Where are these other women?"

"I'm taking you to them now. They will try to help you understand." She took the key from the peg on the wall. As she unlocked the cage, she added, "I was not jesting about the men. They are armed and they will shoot you. They use only copper bullets."

Once Werren opened the door, Sam shoved her aside and ran for the stairs. It would be simpler, and more merciful, to let the detective get herself killed. Yet Werren followed, climbing up on deck to see Samantha standing by the mainmast and staring at the sea that surrounded them.

"Where am I?"

"The ship is called the *Golden Horde*." Werren joined her and pushed back the tangled hair the wind blew into her eyes. "Welcome to hell, my lady."

"I know you're probably tired of hearing me," Chris said into the mobile, "but I've left three voice mails, Sam, and now I'm getting worried. Call me, say you're okay, and I'll quit bugging you."

Chris left the phone on the bunk as she went to the closet and took out a T-shirt and jeans. Stripping out of the dress was a relief; as beautiful as it was, she didn't think she could ever wear it again, at least, not in front of anyone except Jamys.

He loves me. She couldn't stop that thought, or the idiotic smile it summoned from her lips. *He's loved me ever since we met.* A fairy godmother couldn't have done better by her with a thousand waves of a magic wand.

The rabid little organizer that inhabited her soul wanted to make plans, but Chris felt curiously detached about the future. If she and Jamys were able to make it work, they'd definitely have problems—some rather large, especially when she began aging and everyone who saw them together assumed she was his mother, or his grandmother—but there were plenty of ways to turn back time. Alex Keller had been a plastic surgeon before she'd been changed to Kyn; when the wrinkles came, Chris could probably talk her into doing some strategic nips and tucks.

The Darkyn were incapable of reproducing, so they'd never have kids. Chris thought babies were cute, but she'd never once felt the urge to start popping them out. Adele and Frankie had done too good a job as nightmare parents while destroying her childhood; her biological clock had been smashed along with it.

As for plans, Chris suspected she'd be better off living in the moment, and making the most of every night she spent with Jamys. She couldn't do anything about death, so she'd devote herself to making their life together amazing.

The motion of the boat under her feet changed, first slowing and then shifting to a subtle bob. Above her head, Jamys's footsteps moved from the helm to the port side, and she heard the drag of rope across the deck.

Chris climbed up to see the silhouette of palm and mangrove trees against the moon, and the silvery path of the narrow pier leading from the boat across a small cove to an island.

"This is Paradise?" she asked Jamys as she went to help him with the last of the mooring lines.

"Paradise Island," he corrected, and without warning scooped her up into his arms. "The owner of the boat suggested we might enjoy visiting his house here."

"I bet he did." She wriggled a little as he stepped from the deck to the pier. "You don't have to do the bride-over-the-threshold thing. We're not married, and I can walk."

"You agreed to become my *kyara*, my human wife." He brushed his lips over hers. "So, yes, in the eyes of heaven, you are my bride, and we are newly wed."

Jamys carried her the entire length of the pier, across a curving walkway of cut bleached coral studded with mollusk shells, and up to the front door of a very modern-looking beach house. Slightly overgrown bushes with dark green leaves flanked the entry, the frame of which had been inlaid with different types of antique brass compasses. The door opened easily and he stepped inside with her.

"I guess on an island you don't have to lock up when you leave," she said as he set her back on her feet, then lifted her face as rosy light illuminated them. The source, flame-shaped bulbs enclosed in seven garnet-colored glass floats hanging from an artfully draped old fishing net, brightened the hall enough to show a keypad next to a large framed mirror.

"I have the disarm key." Jamys went to put it in.

Chris walked up to the mirror, which had been framed with weathered, carved deck planks. Primitive gold-painted cutouts of the sun, moon, and stars adorned the frame's top and sides, but someone had carved words into the bottom plank: *Do You See What I See?*

The automatic lights and the mirror's question made her feel slightly uneasy, but as she moved into the next room, she spotted a tiny light near the baseboard that flickered from red to green, and bent down to examine a small metal box similar to those she'd had installed in the Winterheart Suite. "I think he has the lights controlled by motion sensors."

Hurricane lamps and hanging lanterns provided illumination for the front room, which had been furnished with a sturdy bamboo living room set upholstered in palm-frond green. Bookcases built into the walls held a bewildering assortment of new and old paperback books. Chris went over to read some spines, and saw they were arranged in a specific order.

Jamys moved around the room. "What does he read?"

"Dark fantasy novels." She glanced back at him. "He's

got them arranged by subject matter." And something was wrong with that, but she couldn't put her finger on exactly what. "He's got novels about angels, demons, ghosts, psychics, warlocks, werewolves, witches. . . . Hey." She plucked a new novel from the shelf. "This one doesn't come out until March. How did he get it before the rest of us?"

Jamys inspected the shelves. "There is one subject missing."

"I read a lot of dark fantasy." She looked for her favorite authors, and saw several who were not represented at all. A shiver ran through her as she realized why. "I don't see any vampire books."

"Nor do I." He replaced the novel on the shelf. "Perhaps we should check the remainder of the premises."

"Maybe he doesn't like vampire fiction," she reasoned as they walked through the rest of the rooms on the first floor. "Not everyone does. Sam can't stand it."

The open layout of the house flowed with soft tropical colors, airy spaces, and translucent fixtures fashioned from ordinary glass objects. As Chris admired the dining room table, made from a sheet of frosted, bubbled glass over a layer of vertically standing driftwood boughs fitted together like puzzle pieces, Jamys investigated the adjoining rooms. She looked over at the massive tapestry of intricately woven cloth hanging across from the table, which at first glance looked no more interesting than a bedsheet in need of ironing. When she moved closer, she discovered that what she had assumed was painted linen was actually made of metal.

Not metal. She trailed her fingers over the tiny strands of the weave. *Gold.* She tried to lift the edge to see the back of it, but it weighed so much she could barely shift it. If it had been made from real gold, and she'd bet her next twelve paychecks that it had, the tapestry could be worth millions.

Jamys reappeared. "Are you hungry?"

"I'm not crazy about coconuts," she admitted, "but I can get something from the boat later."

He held out his hand. "Come and see the kitchen first."

The brand-new kitchen, as it turned out, had been outfitted with every appliance and convenience Chris could want. The fridge had been stuffed with fresh vegetables, fruits, and meat, and more nonperishables crowded every shelf of the peroba cabinets.

There was enough food, Chris thought, to feed a houseful of guests until New Year's. "Maybe this guy invited some people to stop by or something."

Jamys shook his head. "He told me that he always came here alone."

"Then how did this stuff get here? Why so much for just one man?" She hugged her waist as she looked around. "No one could have set this up as a trap. No one knew we were coming here but us."

"There are no other humans on the island, and before we docked, I sailed around it to assure there were no other vessels." He came up behind her and encircled her with his arms. "I should feel threatened, but I do not. I feel safe here. I believe someone is helping us, Christian. Someone who wants us to find the emeralds."

"Well, they're going to have to wait one more day." She dropped her arms as she turned around to face him. "If I'm going to be your wife, then I want my wedding night. And it starts right here, right now." She stood on her toes to press her mouth to his.

Kissing Jamys was like being drugged and electrified in his hands. He lifted her up in his strong arms, and carried her through the house, the lights dimming around them as he slipped into one of the back rooms.

A single bedside lamp came on, illuminating a white master suite. A massive oversize king dominated the room, and offered a simple retreat of sand-colored linens heaped with large pillows shaped like shells. When Jamys lowered her to the mattress, she looked up at a ceiling that shimmered and moved as brightly colored koi swam lazily across it.

"There are fish on the ceiling," she murmured as Jamys stretched out beside her. "No, there's an aquarium on the ceiling. Or the ceiling is an aquarium. How do you feed the fish if they're all the way up there?"

His hands cupped her shoulders as he moved over her. "I imagine with great care." He brushed her hair away from her throat. "And a ladder. Christian."

"Jamys." She lost interest in the fish, and shifted under him as a deep, pervasive throb spread through her pelvis and up into her breasts. "I have been thinking about this for so long ... and now it's happening, and I still don't believe it."

His voice went low and soft as he stretched her arms up and over her head, pinning them to the mattress. "You cannot have wanted this as much as I have."

He brought her palm to his lips, using his tongue to trace the mound at the base of her thumb. It brought back the memory of him doing the same, and much more, between her thighs, and she lifted her hips, rubbing herself against him with the same sensual languor. "Keep doing that and you'll never get rid of me," she teased.

His long fingers found and traced the outline of her

mother's cross under her shirt. "I will never leave you, Christian. From now until the end, whatever may come, we will face it together."

She put her hand over his. "And when it's my time to die?"

"There is nothing in this world for me if you are gone from it." He touched his brow to hers. "You will have to take me with you."

"No argument here." She curled her arms around his neck. "We'll never have to be alone again, here or in the next place."

They slowly unwrapped each other from their clothes, giving gifts of kisses to the skin they exposed. She could touch him anywhere she wanted, with her lips and hands and tongue, and there was so much of him she wanted to learn and know and pleasure: the elegant stretch of his back, the long muscles of his thighs, the sexy dent of his navel.

Everything about her seemed to fascinate him, too. He kissed every inch of her breasts, tracing their contours with his tongue and lavishing suckling tugs of his mouth on the peaks. He rolled onto his back so he could stroke her from shoulders to bottom with his palms; she spread her thighs to do the same with her slick folds against his shaft.

She couldn't keep her hands away from his penis; the velvety texture of his foreskin excited her as much as the length and hardness of his erection. Playing with him as he touched her made her feel powerful and dizzy; she could taste her racing heartbeat when she put her mouth to his.

They came together on their sides, face-to-face as he draped her thigh over his hip and she guided him to her

She wanted to feel every inch of him coming into her, and kept her fingers curled around him as he pressed deep. The sensation made her eyelids droop and her lips part; she'd never felt more a part of anything than this, than with him. It shook her, it completed her.

He looked at her with the same astonished relief. *Now I know why it was you, why it was always you. This is where we belong.*

Jamys moved, flexing and rubbing himself inside her as he tested this new symmetry they had discovered. The slick tightness of her body gloved every inch of him.

She could feel the nudge of his cockhead as he forged deeper, and the tiny, thrilling burst of sensation when he touched the mouth of her womb. Her clit pulsed as he drew out and the bulge of his shaft glanced it; his eyes burned into hers as he pulled her closer to work against it.

Chris felt her whole body tighten, and she clutched at him, rolling her hips as she tried to get more of him. "Jamys, please, please, I need . . ."

"What do you need?" he murmured as he splayed his hands over her bottom, and worked his cock in and out of her folds. "Tell me, my lovely one."

Chris rolled over, dragging him with her, groaning as he held back. "I need you. Please. Give me more. Give me all of it."

He pushed inside her in one long, slick motion, his hands easing her thighs back as he looked down at the junction of their bodies. "Look at how beautifully you take me."

Chris glanced down, and the sight of his penis buried to the hilt in her pussy made her tremble on the verge of orgasm. "Oh, God, I'm going to come."

"Yes, you are." He put his thumb to her clit, circling it

as he drew out, and then stroking it as he thrust back in. "Now you give it to me while I fuck you."

Chris shattered around him, her body arching up from the mattress as the night became a soundless, endless whirlwind of sensation. She could hear him whispering into her hair, his hands playing over her as he plunged in and out of her, pushing her through the agonizing satisfaction to more hunger, more need.

She saw the narrow splinter of his pupils and the sharp glitter of his fangs before he turned his face away. He needed more than sex from her, and it felt completely natural to reach up to pull him to her throat.

"Take it," she urged when he kept his mouth closed. "Show me how it feels. I want to know."

Jamys muttered something before his lips parted and he struck, his fangs piercing her flesh as his mind opened to hers. She exploded with him, feeling the dark thrill of his satisfaction as he drank from her and filled her over and over with the cool rush of his semen.

Chris came back to herself to find her arms and legs entwined around him. "I don't know about you, but I thought the grand tour of the stars was kind of unnecessary. I'd have been fine with orbiting the moon."

"I did not think to consult you," Jamys said gravely as he touched the curve of her throat. "We must try it again."

"Okay, but I'm only giving you sixty or seventy years to get it right." She tucked her chin in to see the two puncture wounds on the curve of her shoulder. "It doesn't hurt. I thought it would." She saw his frown, and added, "Oh, don't. Honestly, I loved my first bite."

"No Kyn has ever . . . ?" When she shook her head, he brought his thumb to his mouth, biting into it before pressing it to the marks he'd left on her. "We must take care, my beautiful girl. When I am inside you, I cannot think clearly. I cannot think at all."

"Technically that's my problem." She offered him a prim smile. "According to proper protocol, when a *tresora* consents to provide her lord with intimate pleasures, she must first provide him with a sufficient quantity of stored blood so that the temptation of thrall and rapture may be avoided."

He smiled a little. "That sounds like Burke."

"You would not believe how red his face got while he was saying it." She ran her hand down his arm, and linked her fingers with his. "So did I please you, my lord?"

"You know that you have already ruined me for all other females," he chided.

"I know, I'm the most amazing chick in the universe, and you are so, so lucky to have me, and maybe one day I'll even believe that." And get over her need for constant reassurance, which had to be annoying. "Just tell me anyway."

"I have no words for it. I have never felt such love." Jamys brought her hand up to his heart to press her palm over the slow, steady beat. "You please me with but one look, and arouse me with but a single touch. Tonight I felt you in my very soul." He bent his head to say the rest against her lips. "I love you, Christian."

As he kissed her, Chris looked up to see the koi swirling through the water overhead, their brilliant white and orange scales flashing with their movements. The blue water shimmered, darkening to a haunting emerald green as a shadow stretched across the ceiling, and the fish darted away.

Jamys stiffened, rolling away from her to grab his

head with his hands. Through clenched teeth he said, "No. You cannot. I *will* not."

"What is it? What's wrong?" Chris sat up and reached for him, only to feel him go limp under her hands. "Jamys?" He didn't move, not even when she shook him.

She grabbed her clothes, pulling them on as she tried to think of what could have caused this. It wasn't thrall; he hadn't taken enough blood from her for that. He wasn't injured, either.

"I don't know what to do," she told him, more terrified than she'd ever felt. "I'm going to see if there's a phone and call Burke."

A woman stepped into the bedroom. For a split second she looked like a frizzy-haired witch wearing a potato sack, and then she changed into Lucan.

She's some kind of shape-shifter. Chris smelled a strange, sharp honey scent that wasn't jasmine, and felt confused as she stepped backward. "Leave him alone."

"He is not our concern." Lucan smiled sadly as two men flanked him, both holding pistols and copper-clad knives. "We came to find you."

Chapter 17

Lucan opened his eyes to his own face, and slowly turned his head to see the mirror-world around him. His form and features appeared in glass walls fashioned to resemble the interior of his stronghold: a silent army of himself. The only difference between them appeared to be the fact they all wore gloves while his own hands lay bare.

A frigid breath of air and a tinkling sound made him glance up. Overhead silk threads held suspended a thousand jagged crystal blades, each sharp edge clad in a honed ribbon of copper.

The nightlands were ever an enigma, but for once the message they delivered was quite plain: If he made one wrong move, if he lost his temper, he would be cut to pieces.

"But I am so easily persuaded to violence," one of his images mentioned.

"Too many have died beneath my hand," another said.

"Or it may be that I am dead already," a third offered. "And this is my hell."

"Hell indeed," Lucan murmured, "if I must listen to myself prattle on for all eternity."

A fourth twin offered him a benign smile. "For all your icy wit, cunning schemes, and razor tongue, my lord, you are a simple soul." He gestured to one of the mirrors, where the image melted into Lucan as a boy, cowering before his mother, Gwynyth, in a rage. "Unwanted." Gwynyth's golden charms darkened into the remote beauty of Frances, the first mortal he had loved. "Unloved." Frances grew younger and tougher, her gown shrinking into one of Samantha's ugly suits. "Unworthy."

Lucan saw a flash of light in front of his nose, and glanced down as the falling crystal dagger smashed between his feet. "And now, unbelievably bored. Is this pathetic hothouse truly the best you can do?"

Another shimmering blade fell, but before it could bury itself in Lucan's arm, a towering figure dressed as a monk lifted a heavily scarred hand and caught it. "You will attend to me now, boy."

Lucan laughed, and the sound sent a shock wave through the crystal hanging over them. "I am neither a boy nor your attendant."

A dark-haired woman he had never before seen appeared in the mirror closest to him.

"You were my son." Grave dirt fell from her lips as she spoke, and ghosts danced in her gray eyes. "But I sent you away, and died alone and frightened."

At least this apparition had it wrong. "You are not my mother."

"The lady Blanche did give birth to you, my son." The priest held the woman's hand as she stepped out of the mirror. "For your safety and her own, she convinced her cousin Gwynyth to hide you at court while she used your existence to blackmail several lovers. Unfortunately she went too far by demanding marriage from a duke." The priest paused to brush some of the cobwebs from her shoulders. "He buried her alive in one of his family tombs."

One of the few things impossible to do in the night-lands was lie, and this impossible truth outraged Lucan. "Do you know what Gwynyth did to me? The hell she made of my boyhood?"

"Gwynyth saved your life by naming you *her* son," the priest told him. "Had she not, the duke would have seen to it that you joined your mother permanently."

Lucan watched the dark woman fade away. "I did well enough without a mother."

"So you did. You with your killing touch and your cold heart." The priest made the sign of the cross over him. "You who were to become Death. Darkness has no need, my son."

"I am a man," Lucan said, "not darkness or death, or your son."

"I would have been your father, but for your mother, who told me that you were Tremayne's get." His mirror image swelled and reshaped its form into a broader, older version of himself with glowing green eyes. "When he brought damnation to me, he denied being your sire, and told me you had been changed. On that night I lost the last remnant of my faith."

Lucan knew the nightlands made the priest's words the truth . . . or he believed what he said to be true.

"If by this tedious babbling you are attempting some manner of apology, you are seven centuries too late." Lucan ignored a sharp crack that shifted the glass floor beneath him. "I have no need for a father."

"Darkness has no need." The priest moved his gloved hand over the face of one of the standing mirrors, which darkened to show Samantha shackled inside a small cage. "Your woman has been taken prisoner by your nameless enemy." He reversed his hand, and Christian appeared, hurled to the deck before Samantha, who assumed a protective position over the girl. "So, too, the child she loves as a sister. Do you know what he does to women, your enemy?"

"Release me." When the priest said nothing, Lucan seized him by the throat, and a shower of crystal death rained down around them. "Goddamn you, let me out of here."

Dark metal oozed out of the older man's pores, covering his skin and robe until he became a copper statue of himself. Lucan held on, snarling as more crystal fell and sliced through his flesh, and the hand he had wrapped around the priest's throat became engulfed in flame and blackened.

"You are spellbound here by the one who means to take your kingdom from you," the priest said, his voice grinding over the words like rusted metal. "It is not within my power to free you."

"So you are as useless to me here as you were in life. How astonishing." Lucan flung the priest from him as his rage boiled over, pulverizing the crystal blades embedded in his flesh. His images on wall after wall exploded, filling the air with clouds of sparkling shards and stripping the copper facade from the priest.

Lucan destroyed the world around them, until the gray void descended, obliterating everything but him and the priest, their wounds erased, their garments restored.

"You believe I am useless, and perhaps I am," the priest said. "But this I can tell you, my son: I, too, have terrible powers, and for the love of a woman used them to destroy myself. You will come to a moment when you know these things, and only then will you understand me."

The priest vanished.

"If that preposterous idiot is punishment for my sins, then I salute your genius at torture." He was talking out loud to a God he no longer worshipped; surely madness had already begun to set in. Bespelled or not, he had to fight his way back to consciousness, find the women, and attend to his enemy.

Endless as the void seemed, Lucan knew it to be but a veil between worlds. He tempered his anger, gathering himself and focusing his thoughts on one objective: to awaken.

Centuries of self-discipline permitted him to move through that which was immovable, and gradually emerge from the clinging nothingness into a distant sense of his physical body. He could feel all around him his stronghold, his men, the club. With a final surge of will, he came to awareness, although he still remained outside his body, only hovering near it.

The enemy had taken him over, mind and body, and had draped him over an armchair sitting in the center of the dance floor. A bottle of bloodwine dangled from his right fist; in his left gleamed a copper-clad sword. Lucan recognized the weapon as Turner's finest work: a gift the weapons master had presented to him when he had joined the *jardin*. He swiped it through the air and drank from the bottle as twenty of his men stood in defensive positions around him.

Aldan glanced back at the impostor. "Someone has broken through the front line, my lord."

"It is the boy, I wager. Disarm him, but do not kill him," Lucan heard himself command. "He has knowledge I must have."

The doors to the club flung open, and Jamys Durand stepped inside, the daggers in his hands wet with fresh blood. The boy turned briefly to bar the door before he moved forward and inspected the interior of the club. He then leveled his gaze on the impostor.

"Where is she?"

When Thierry Durand had gone mad, Jamys had understood the reason for it. The hideous tortures inflicted on his father by the Brethren were nothing compared with the agony of believing Angelica was dead. The bond between Darkyn lord and *sygkenis* was absolute; severing it resulted in insanity. That his father in his deranged state had somehow bonded a second time, with Jema, had been a miracle, and the saving of him.

Jamys had known he was doomed from the moment the voice of the same Kyn he had contacted through Gifford had come into his head. *You will not interfere, boy.* He had struggled even as he felt his limbs growing numb and leaden. To his shame, he could do nothing but watch as Lucan dragged Christian out of the room.

Not even at the mercy of the Brethren inquisitors had he felt so helpless—or enraged.

It didn't matter to Jamys that Christian was mortal, and the bond between them imperfect. She was his woman, his wife, his love. And for taking her from him, Lucan would die.

The Kyn held Jamys captive in his own body until the

sound of the speedboat faded from the air, and then released him as suddenly as he had taken him over.

He takes her to his stronghold, his voice purred. *She belongs to Death now.*

She is mine. At the instant he regained control of his body, Jamys flung himself out of the bed and dragged on his garments. He ran from the house to the pier, searching the dark, empty waters. As he climbed onto the boat and cast off, he could smell her in the air, her scent permeated with love and terror.

He engaged the engine, and sailed from the island to the mainland, dropping anchor just beyond the shallows and diving from the deck into the chilly waters. He swam to the beach, emerging at a flat run for the nearest vehicle he saw, a sedan sitting at a traffic light.

The driver's eyes widened as Jamys wrenched open the locked door. "What do you think you're—" His voice cut off as soon as Jamys clamped a hand on his shoulder.

You want to give me the car and walk to your destination.

"Here, take it," the man said as he unfastened his seat belt and climbed out. "I'm going to walk home."

Jamys got in, slammed the door, and drove, swerving between two cars turning in front of him. As brakes screeched and angry voices shouted, he pressed the accelerator to the floor, speeding away.

Lights, cars, and buildings became a blur as Jamys drove north. Dimly he felt the seawater dripping from his clothes to soak the seat beneath him. He carried but two daggers, and as a mortal with an annoying voice crooned a holiday song from the dashboard, he clenched his fist and rammed it into the console, silencing the radio.

Lucan had a stronghold, a garrison, and the most dangerous weapon of all, his killing hands. Jamys had a car, two daggers, and a power that affected only mortals. He could almost hear his father's voice: *Be rational, my son. This is suicide.*

The voice was his father's, but not the sentiments. More than any other warrior, his father would understand this.

Should by some narrow chance you save the girl, she will never be yours, his mother whispered. *You are destined to live forever. She was born to die. Forget her. Save yourself.*

By betrayal his mother had saved herself when she had been captured by the Brethren. She'd won her freedom by becoming their agent and luring countless Kyn into the hands of the enemy. Knowing they would die slow, hideous deaths by torture, she'd done the same to her entire family. How easy it had been for her to tear apart the bonds of marriage and motherhood. . . .

The car slowed as Jamys recalled how his mother had changed after the trip to Italy. The separation from his *sygkenis* had driven Thierry to the brink of madness; being reunited with her had brought him back to sanity. Angelica had seemed equally relieved, and in the celebrations that followed, no one questioned what they might have under more ordinary circumstances.

Before the journey to Italy, Angelica had been cool and reserved; after returning, she had lavished her attentions on Thierry, often embarrassing the entire household with her wanton behavior. She began to berate the mortal servants she had always treated well, and took to punishing them for even the slightest mistakes—but never in front of Thierry.

Jamys had been alarmed by the changes in his mother's character, but when he spoke to his father about them, Thierry had dismissed them as temporary, the lingering effects of the separation.

Jamys remembered several chambermaids who had vanished; Angelica claimed they'd run off with their lovers, or had left to take better positions in other households. Yet none of them had ever been seen again, and now he suspected that his mother had killed them in one of her rages.

The Brethren hadn't simply turned Angelica into a traitor, he realized. They had broken her bond with Thierry, and had driven her mad in the process.

Everyone had assumed that, like Thierry, Angelica had recovered from being separated from her life companion as soon as they had been reunited. She had been clever enough to act the part of a *sygkenis* and prevent anyone from suspecting her insanity.

I knew I had gone mad long before I found Jema, his father had once said. *Had I been rational, I might have put an end to myself. But madness is its own purpose, and has its own beauties and desires.*

Years of guilt sifted away, their impossible weight turning to dust. The monster of Angelica's insanity had betrayed them to the Brethren. The mother Jamys had always loved, the beloved wife who had devoted herself to him and his father, had in fact never returned to them. She had died in Italy.

A memory of Angelica's face, now serene, drifted into his mind. As if she knew his thoughts, she nodded and smiled, and then she was gone.

Peace and determination entwined inside Jamys, eradicating his anger and fear as he drove the last miles to Fort Lauderdale. When he came to the barricades and detour signs directing traffic away from the stronghold, and saw the warriors who had taken discreet defensive positions, he turned off the road and parked in front of a crowded restaurant.

Inside the maître d' met him at the door. "I'm sorry, sir, but we don't offer valet parking."

Jamys touched his shoulder, issued his instructions, and then entered the restaurant. There were more than a hundred mortals dining, but the windows were closed and the ventilation minimal. Curious eyes turned drowsy, and voices fell silent as the scent of sandalwood spread through the dining room.

When the last mortal had stopped speaking, Jamys said, "My lady is in danger, and I need your help."

Once he had commanded them, he went back to the kitchens, and did the same with the waiters and all the staff except one teenage boy who had been washing dishes, from whom he borrowed his high-top sneakers.

"You will guard the premises until the others return," he instructed the boy as he finished tying the laces.

A final stop at the executive chef's station provided him with the last of his needs, and Jamys was ready. He walked through the now-empty dining room, plucking a napkin and a lighter from one of the tables as he passed.

Outside on the street the barricades lay on their sides, knocked over by a hundred bespelled mortals, who now filled the street in front of the stronghold. Lucan's warriors had left their positions to surround them and attempt to herd them away, only to find themselves being drawn into the mob of dancers.

Jamys chose an empty spot on the far side of the building as he stuffed the linen napkin in the neck of the bottle of brandy he had taken from the chef's station. He flicked the lighter, setting the brandy-soaked napkin aflame, and lobbed the bottle high over the heads of the mob. It smashed into the empty sidewalk, the spray immediately bursting into a large fireball and a plume of black smoke.

The secondary distraction of the fire drew away all but two of the warriors still standing guard at the entrance to the stronghold, and Jamys attacked them from their left flank, dropping beneath the thrust of their blades and coming up between them to bury his daggers in their sides. He struck to disable, not to kill, and one toppled to the ground while the other clutched his side and turned on him.

"Durand."

"Glenveagh." He countered his movements. "As you are, you cannot fight me. Stand down."

"The order is to kill anyone who attempts to intrude." He grimaced as he lifted his sword. "I must end you or die trying."

"So be it." Jamys feinted with one blade at Glenveagh's heart and, when the warrior parried, used his other fist to knock him into the street. As Glenveagh scrambled to his feet, Jamys entered and barred the door behind him.

Inside the nightclub twenty warriors stood in combat formation, their bodies surrounding a seated figure. The captain of the guard regarded him steadily, but he appeared pained, as if he was locked in dread.

Jamys advanced, stopping just out of range of the captain's blade. He stared past Aldan at Lucan, who lay sprawled atop an armchair that had been dragged out of his office, a bottle of bloodwine in one gloved fist and a long sword dangling from the other.

"Where is she?" Jamys demanded.

"The prodigal traitor returns." Lucan toasted him with the bottle before taking a swallow. He tossed the bloodwine aside, clambering to his feet with uncharacteristic clumsiness. "How biblical of you, boy."

"Give Christian to me," Jamys said, "and you need never lay eyes on either of us again."

"Finally bedded her, did you?" Lucan grinned. "Was she any good at it, or did she whine and flop about?" He shook his sword at Jamys. "There be the rub with fucking these mortal wenches. All tears, no stamina."

"Captain," Jamys said to Aldan, "Lord Alenfar has insulted me and Miss Lang."

The captain's expression turned grim. "So it would seem, my lord."

"You've no right to the Pearl Girl," Lucan snarled. "She is my property, as are these men, this stronghold, and all that surrounds us. They will all do my bidding now."

"No oath to you binds Christian," Jamys said. "Tonight she agreed to become my *kyara*, and gave herself to me." As Aldan stared at him, he nodded before he said to Lucan, "My scent is all over her. You had to know she was mine when you took her from the island."

"So I had her taken," Lucan sneered. "What of it? You can do nothing about it."

"Stand down and bear witness," the captain ordered, and the men moved to line the edge of the dance floor.

Outrage darkened Lucan's face. "What are you doing? Get back over here and defend me."

"Forgive us, my lord." Aldan sketched a bow so shallow it bordered insulting. "While the circumstances are yet unclear to me, by your own admission you have verified Lord Durand's claims against you. You have given him the right to challenge your rule." When Lucan's face remained blank, he added, "You have to fight him to the death, my lord."

"Oh, is that all?" Lucan dropped his blade and stripped off his gloves. "Come here, whelp. I will be merciful and make it quick."

"Using ability in a death challenge is not permitted, Suzerain." Aldan picked up his sword and thrust it at him. "You must fight by blade."

Jamys saw Lucan grasp the sword, and reach with his free hand to touch the golden medallion hanging around his throat. Ghost images of it echoed in his memory. He had seen the piece on Professor Gifford's Web site . . . and, before that, hanging from the bull neck of the Kyn Jamys had encountered on the night he had arrived.

The visiting warrior who had come to his suite to take Christian and use her for sex, what had he called her? *No need to play shy, Pearl Girl. I know how it is with ye household wenches.* He'd used the same sly nickname Lucan had just uttered— *You've no right to the Pearl Girl*—and had worn the same medallion.

Jamys had no more time to think, for Lucan came at him, his sword sweeping through the air toward his neck. Jamys dodged the blow meant to decapitate him and brought up his daggers to parry the vicious backhand thrust that followed.

Jamys ducked under his arm only to find himself pinned against one of the bars. As Lucan charged, he vaulted over the counter.

"Durand." A sword came flying at him, and Jamys reached up and caught the hilt. By then Lucan had reached him, and he barely eluded a blade thrust to his chest. The suzerain's sword cut through the flesh of his upper arm, causing his blood to spill in a wide swath.

Jamys dropped down, using his Kyn strength to leap over the bar behind the suzerain, who spun around to prevent the blow to his own neck. As their blades clashed, sparks burst from the metal, and Jamys used the split second of blinding light to fling his remaining dagger into the center of Lucan's neck.

With a roar the suzerain staggered backward, slashing at Jamys as he reached for him. He stumbled as Jamys yanked his dagger free, using the shorter blade to cut through the chain holding the medallion, which fell to the floor between them.

Lucan put a hand to the shallow wound at the base of his throat, and stared down at the glittering gold piece. When he looked up again, his eyes turned pure silver, and he threw his sword away from him in disgust. He then straightened and bowed his head. "The match is yours, Lord Durand."

Behind him Jamys could hear the murmurs of the men watching. By surrendering, Lucan had lost not only the fight but his rule over the *jardin*—and, if Jamys so chose, his head.

"So it is." Jamys lowered his blade and returned the bow. "But I did not challenge you, Suzerain. My quarrel is with the Kyn who held you bespelled."

"Bespelled. So that explains my madness." Lucan eyed Aldan, who had come to join them. "Captain, where is Mr. Vander?"

Aldan looked uncomfortable. "You permitted him to leave the stronghold unattended some hours ago, my lord."

"He has taken the women to a ship," Lucan told Ja-

mys. "I know not where it is moored, but we will find it."
His eyes shifted. "Herbert?"

"My lord." Burke appeared, his face battered and one
eye swelling shut. At his side he held a pistol, which he
returned to the holster inside his jacket. "I trust you are
yourself again?"

"Indeed. Lord Durand was kind enough to free me of
Vander's control." Lucan looked disgusted. "Did that
bastard use me to do that to you?"

"He did, my lord, but it was not an especially impressive beating." Burke sniffed. "I've actually suffered worse
at the hands of my chiropractor." He removed a device
from his pocket. "I also know where our ladies are being
held."

The *tresora* tapped the small screen, which zoomed
out to show a map of the South Florida coast. Two lights,
one blue and one red, clustered together a few miles off
the coast of Miami.

"Herbert." Lucan looked enormously pleased. "When
this is done, I believe I shall send you to my private retreat in the Bahamas with the lady of your choice for as
long as you desire."

"I thank you, my lord, but I already have a lady friend,
and we'd much rather prefer Marlins season tickets.
Shall I summon the fleet?" When Lucan nodded, Burke
bowed and hurried off.

Jamys regarded the suzerain. "You have a fleet?"

Lucan smiled. "Of sorts."

Aldan brought a cordless phone to Lucan. "There is a
call for you, my lord. It is from Vander."

Lucan's expression turned icy. "Put it on speaker."
When Aldan pressed a button, he said, "I do hope your

affairs are in order, Mr. Vander. You will find them quite impossible to manage when I reduce you to a heap of rotting flesh, which shall be the moment I find you."

A harsh laugh came over the speaker. "You may look, my lord, but you will not find. But I can be persuaded to give you back your slut. Give me your men and your stronghold, and she is yours."

"Good-bye, Mr. Vander." Lucan reached for the phone.

"Would you care to bid your whore the same?" The sound of a scuffle came over the speaker, and then Samantha's tight voice as she said, "Lucan, we're in trouble."

"I know," he replied, his voice as gentle as his eyes were murderous. "I'm coming, love, very soon now."

"Vander is Dutch, and he has barricaded hundreds of people inside his casino," she said. "He's had his men douse the entire place with gasoline. If you don't give him Alenfar, he's going to burn them alive."

Several bottles behind the bar exploded.

"Don't worry," Lucan said. "We know where you are, and we will give him what he wants."

"I love —," Samantha said before her voice was cut off and Vander spoke again. "Since you know where I am, you will come and surrender your territory and men to me at sunset tonight. Or I will set your women on fire and toss them in the casino."

Chapter 18

Chris had known something was wrong with Lucan from the moment they'd left the island. The men piloting the speedboat didn't belong to the *jardin*, while the suzerain sat down next to the cage he'd shoved her in and simply stared at the deck.

"Don't you think you should tell me what's going on?" she asked. "I mean, am I in trouble? Do I have to leave South Florida? What?"

Lucan's handsome face lifted, and then began to melt. "I suppose it does no harm," he muttered as he turned into a thin, snarled-haired woman with a dirty face.

"Oh, God." Chris shoved herself back into one corner of the cage. "Who are you?"

"My name is Werren." She tugged down the ragged hem of her tunic, which to Chris's eyes looked more like a burlap sack than something wearable. "You smell like Kyn, but you are mortal."

Chris wrapped her arms around her knees to keep them from knocking together. "Are you going to hurt me?"

"No." Werren nodded at the backs of the two men at the controls. "They will, if you resist."

"Resist what? Why did you take me?" She thought of Jamys, and shot across the cage. "Did you tranq him? Is that why he couldn't move?"

"If you mean the boy, no. His affliction was not my doing." Werren glanced back at the wake behind the boat. "When I came into the house, I felt the presence of another like us. An old one, like Dutch."

Chris heard the engine throttling down and looked over, squinting as bright lights blinded her momentarily. The men were guiding the speedboat alongside an old-fashioned wooden ship that seemed to be sitting on top of the water. A bump on the side of the speedboat drew her eyes to the side, where a shelf of coral reef appeared just beneath the water's surface. At the other end of the wooden ship were walkways attached to a bigger, more modern yacht, and ladders that dropped down to the decks of a half-dozen smaller boats.

One of the men caught something thrown down to him from the old ship, and came over to Werren. "He wants to see you on deck, Duchess." He reached up to the top of the cage and attached the cable before he let out a piercing whistle.

Chris was thrown to the bottom of the cage as it was jerked up into the air. She gripped the bars, looking down at Werren, who touched a finger to her lips before moving to climb off onto one of the ladders.

Chris felt her stomach roll as the cage swayed and jerked, but within minutes she was lowered down onto the deck of the ship, where more men came and removed the crane hook. They stepped aside as a blocky figure strode up and pulled open the door to the cage.

"My Pearl Girl." Vander bent to grab her by the hair

nd haul her to her feet. "Now you'll be servicing me
henever I want it."

Chris thought of the finger Werren had pressed to her
ps, bowed her head, and bit the inside of her cheek to
eep from telling him where he could go.

"You see?" Vander told the other men. "This is why
ou teach them proper while they're young and still
lortal." He gave her a shake. "You can use that tongue
n me later, girl." He shoved her at one of the men.
Take her below."

The man hustled her over to an opening above a tiny
aircase, and nearly pushed her down it. "Move your ass,
ut."

Chris took the steep steps two at a time until she
eached the deck below. The old, splintering planks
orming the floor had been patched over with sheets of
lywood, vinyl siding, and an assortment of scrap lum-
er, making the deck look like a quilt patched by a de-
lented carpenter. The guard pushed her again, this time
oward an adjoining space that held six empty cages and
ne occupied by Samantha, who appeared unconscious.

"What did you do to her?" Chris demanded without
hinking, and was slammed up against an empty cage.

"I thought you knew how to hold your tongue," the
uard said, jerking her back long enough to open the
oor to the cage and shove her inside. Once he'd locked
er in, he eyed Samantha, and grinned as he dragged
'hris's cage over alongside hers. "There. If she gets hun-
ry and wants a snack, you can stick your arm through
e bars." He laughed as he left the room.

"Chris." Samantha raised her head to look around
lem before she slowly pulled herself up into a sitting

position. Her right arm hung unmoving, and as she turned, Chris saw the odd bulge under her jacket.

"Who dislocated your shoulder?"

"The asshole that kicked me back down here when tried to run." She rested her head against the back of the cage. "You think you can help me pop it back in?"

Chris inspected the space between the bars and their positions before she nodded. "Scoot as close as you can. She reached for Sam's limp arm, and gently lifted i "Brace your feet against the bars. You know in the mov ies when they say this is gonna hurt like a fucking bitch?

"Yeah." Sam screamed as Chris snapped her arm ou and to the side.

"They lied." She reached in to feel the bone, whicl had slid back into place. "Try moving it now."

"You're right. Hurts like ten fucking bitches." Sam gingerly tested her arm, and glanced up. "Burke didn' teach you to do that."

"No, Dan did. Burke had me work with him for couple months in the infirmary." She glanced over a Werren entered, carrying a ring of keys. "This one is shifter."

"Yeah, I know." Samantha hauled herself to her fee "You leave the kid alone."

"The master has sent me to attend to your instruc tion." Werren unlocked both cages and opened th doors. "If you attempt another escape, he will kill th mortal and give you to the hull."

"Give me how?" Sam asked as she stepped out.

"It is an old punishment," Werren said. "You will b hung by a rope and dragged up and down against th hull until the barnacles strip the flesh from your back."

"Coburn," Sam muttered.

"I vote we don't try to escape," Chris said. "What instructions are we supposed to get?"

"I will explain," Werren said, "when we join the other women." She gestured for them to follow her.

As the raggedly dressed Kyn led them down another tight stairway, Sam quickly told her everything she knew. Chris didn't have much to add, other than what had happened between her and Jamys, which she kept to herself. If Vander killed them, it wouldn't matter that she had agreed to be his human wife.

Werren brought them down to a third level, and through a hatch in a bulkhead to the back of the deck.

She'd seen better living space in juvie, Chris decided as she looked around the empty area. All that decorated the wooden-planked walls was water stains and black streaks of tar or mildew; a sour, dank smell rose from the slatted floor, where the gaps showed them the shallow layer of brackish water beneath them. Dozens of women wearing pretty gowns watched them from where they lay or sat in an irregular spider's web of ropes hung from the upper beams; it took Chris a moment to realize they were crude hammocks.

Several guards came down the stairs, and one called out for the women to line up.

As Chris watched, each woman climbed down and formed a line in front of a guard. The first woman in line stripped out of her gown and shift, and handed it to the guard in exchange for a ragged sack like the one Werren wore. As the women slipped the ugly tunics over their heads, Chris saw how, like Werren's, they barely covered the women's naked bodies.

A guard carrying two more bundles of rags walked over to Chris and Sam. "Take off your clothes."

Sam stepped in front of Chris. "Not happening, pal." When he reached for the blade on his belt, she punched him in the face, sending him staggering backward until he landed on his ass. When a second guard came barreling at her, she sidestepped his hands and drove her knee into her abdomen. As he doubled over, she grabbed his collar and heaved him over toward the other men. He was unconscious before he hit the slats at their feet.

Chris watched the men shuffle back. "They weren't expecting a fight."

"Anyone else want me or my friend to take off our clothes?" Sam called out loud. The guards grabbed the man she had knocked out before they hurried up the stairs. The light from the upper deck vanished as they slammed shut the door. "I didn't think so."

Someone struck a match, and a glow appeared around Werren as she brought a candle in an old-fashioned brass holder over to Chris. "We can see in the dark," she said as she handed the light to her. "You cannot."

Now Chris could see some of the women climbing into the hammocks and covering themselves with thin blankets. "What is this, like, the punishment section?"

"This is where we live," Werren said. "The crew calls it the sluts' quarters."

"You mean, this is where he keeps you when you're not working on the casino ship?" Sam, who obviously knew a lot more about the women, demanded. "Down here? All of you?"

"Yes." Werren nodded to a pretty young brunette, who climbed up the stairs and sat on the step nearest to the door. "But it does not look like this all the time. Only when Dutch or the guards are here."

A blur of color and light encircled Chris, who found

herself standing in the middle of a beautiful garden of flowers. Overhead the sun glowed in a bright blue sky, and an orange butterfly fluttered right by her face. The women, all of whom were wearing gowns even more lovely than those they had removed earlier, reclined on cushioned chaises and armchairs. Some picked up books to read; others worked on needlepoint.

"Holy Toledo." Chris reached out to touch the curling petals of a tiger lily. "What is this?"

"It's what she does," Sam answered for Werren as she inspected their surroundings. "She can produce three-dimensional illusions. Very convincing ones. I speak from personal experience." She looked at the blonde. "So how long can you keep it up? An hour? Two?"

"It will last as long as I will it." Werren walked over to a pretty marble fountain, and sat down on its edge.

Sam caught Chris's arm as she started to go after her. "Hang on." She went to one of the other women, who smiled up at her. "When do they feed you?"

The woman looked bewildered. "We cannot stomach food. We are sustained by the water of the fount." She gestured at the water streaming from the tiered basins.

"Oh, you're living off imaginary water." Sam looked disgusted. "I should have guessed." She guided Chris over to the fountain. Once she leaned over and breathed in, she shook her head. "Jesus Christ."

Chris, who couldn't smell anything, frowned. "They can't live without feeding, can they?"

"Nope, but obviously they believe they do." Sam gave Werren a hard look. "I wonder why."

"Some illusions need not be seen," Werren said quietly as she looked up at Sam. "Please, Detective. It is a mercy."

Chris looked from one woman to the other. "Okay, I'm not getting the subtext here at all."

"Don't drink from the fountain, kiddo," Sam said to Chris as she bent over and dipped the end of one finger in the basin. When she drew it back and showed it to Chris, it was wet and red. "You won't like the taste."

Chris's throat tightened. "Guess I won't."

"Come with me." Werren rose and led them to a little gazebo shrouded in sweet pea vines. As soon as they stepped inside, the walls turned to bare wood and the vines faded from sight.

Werren closed the door to the women's quarters behind her, and lit a small glass storm lamp. Sitting atop a small table were stacks of envelopes and money bands. "Dutch sends me in here to count the money each night," she explained.

"What the hell have you done?" Sam gestured at the door. "Those women have no idea what they are."

"I told you, it was a mercy. They were brought on board as humans, like your friend." Werren sat down in the only chair in the room and rested her forehead against her hands. "Dutch kept them in his quarters until they were changed, and only then were they brought to me. Most of them were out of their minds with terror and pain and confusion. The few who understood always attempted to escape."

"So you've been keeping the truth from them for the last four hundred years." Sam shook her head.

"I kept them sane and alive." Werren dropped her hands. "Have you ever seen a woman being decapitated? I have, many times. That is what Dutch does to every woman who tries to flee him. Then he forces me to toss their bodies into the sea and clean their blood from deck."

"Why don't you just fight back?" Chris asked. "There are, what, at least fifty of you. He has maybe twenty guys at the most, and they're all still human."

"None of them have these." Werren curled her fingers around the medallion chained to her throat. "Dutch controls all of us through the gold. He can make us do whatever he wishes." She nodded at Sam. "Just as he made your lord do what he wished."

"That fucking medallion he gave him." Sam stomped around the room. "That's how he's been controlling him. He can channel his ability through the gold."

Chris recalled something Burke had told her about Kyn ability and its natural limitations, which included the number of humans which could be affected by it. Only a few Kyn like Richard Tremayne had talents powerful enough to affect large groups of people. "When does he do all of you?"

"I do not understand."

"When has he controlled all of you women at the same time?" Chris watched the other woman's expression. "He's never done it, has he?"

Werren cringed. "His power is absolute. He has simply never had occasion to—"

"Hang on." Chris held up her hands. "Have you ever watched Dutch take over a group of people at the same time?" Werren shook her head. "How about five at once?"

"No, never."

"Has he done three? No?" Chris braced her hands on the table and leaned in. "Have you ever once seen him control more than one person?"

"Not with my own eyes." Werren's expression turned resentful. "But he has done it. Dutch has often told the tale of how he took this ship and slaughtered the crew, without a single man at his back."

"Captured the ship all by himself, when no one else was around," Sam said. "Imagine that."

"Convenient as hell," Chris put in. "No witnesses."

"You don't know him. You are wrong." Werren shot to her feet and began shaking her head. "He would not say such things if they were not true."

"Wouldn't he, Werren?" Sam suggested. "You've just said that you've never seen him demonstrate this power over more than one person. Neither has anyone else. If he really had it, why wouldn't he show it off? It's not like the guy is modest."

Chris joined in. "For that matter, why does he need to keep guards watching over you and the other ladies? He should just be able to think you into doing whatever he wants, whenever he wants."

Werren shook her head. "You are mortal. You do not understand his power over us."

"Actually, I think I do." Something occurred to her. "If every woman on this ship is Darkyn, then they also have abilities like yours. What are they?"

Sam watched Werren, who remained silent. "Either you tell us now, or I go out and start asking."

"Analise can make herself appear as young as a girl, or as old as a crone," Werren said. "Naomi can erase small wounds from the flesh with a caress. Bethana summons unbearable longing in men and women. Sayda stills their minds so they may remember nothing."

As Werren continued describing her ladies' abilities, Chris's heart sank. From the way it sounded, none of the women on the ship had a violent or dangerous talent that might help them overpower the crew. Dutch had also spent the last four centuries terrorizing them, and had done such an excellent job that they were all as scared as a herd of bunnies caught in the middle of a biker run. It had never even occurred to them to remove the medallions that he used to keep them enslaved.

"You should go back to your ladies," Sam said once Werren had finished. "We'll join you in a minute."

Chris watched the woman leave. "We're really screwed."

"Vander wants Alenfar," Sam told her. "He thinks Lucan will trade his rule for me. If he doesn't, he's going to torch us and a couple hundred gamblers on the casino boat."

The thought of being burned alive made Chris shudder. "I could jump over the side, steal one of the boats."

Sam shook her head. "Too many guards with guns."

"I'm a fast swimmer, and it's my job. Besides, I owe you a life," she argued. "Let me save yours."

"You can do that by staying here and helping me spring all those people locked in the casino." Sam glanced at the door. "We have to get the women to work with us, too."

"How?" Chris asked. "They're so scared of Vander and the guards they're practically robots."

Her friend nodded. "Then it's high time we deprogram them."

Jamys took his leave of Lucan as the suzerain finished issuing orders to the garrison. "I will meet you and the men at the rendezvous once I have retrieved the gems."

"I hesitate to suggest you pursue a fool's errand," Lucan said, "but I doubt you will find anything of value in this secret cache. Samantha told me the extent to which Coburn was tortured before he was killed. Had the man truly been in possession of the emeralds, under such duress he surely would have revealed their location."

"Unless that memory was taken from him, as Gifford's were." Jamys bowed. "Until sunset, my lord."

Lucan clasped his hand to Jamys's forearm. "Come prepared to fight, my friend."

Ernesto Garcia stood outside the stronghold, and handed Jamys a pair of dark shades before he opened the door of the car waiting for them. "I have sent men ahead to secure the scene, but we will have to do this quickly to avoid drawing any attention from the surrounding merchants."

Jamys nodded and, once inside the car, picked up the courtesy phone. As Garcia drove to the jeweler's shop, he debated on how much to say before he dialed the number for his father's private chamber.

"The sun is still up, assassin," Thierry answered, his voice almost a snarl. "So unless you have found my son, or Florida has been invaded and has been put to the torch—"

"I am here, Father," Jamys said. "I have been at Alenfar since I left your house."

Silence answered him, and then Thierry said, "The very next time I see that damned Englishman, I will chop off his hands and stuff them down his gullet."

"I never told Lucan I had left Baucent without your permission." Jamys closed his eyes against the burning glare of the sun. "Father, when I was a small boy, and you were preparing to go into battle, do you remember what you would say to me?"

"Of course I do." Thierry's tone gentled. "I would say 'Protect the women, defend the household, and know that here or in heaven, I will see you again.' And never once did you shed a tear."

"Now it is your turn to be brave," he told his father. "For this night I go into battle."

For a long time Thierry said nothing. Then he sighed, and said, "You have always been a warrior in your heart, my son, and if now you must take up the sword, I know you will be the same in the field."

"Then if I may, I will ask you to protect my step-mother, and the men and women of the household," Jamys said slowly. "Please tell Jema that I love her as the mother of my heart."

"That will make her smile and weep," Thierry predicted. "Will you forgive me my harsh words, and my foolish fears?"

"I have, and pray you will do the same for mine," he assured him. "For everything in me that is good and strong and wise, I owe to you."

Thierry made a rough sound. "And will I see you again, Jamys?"

"Here or in heaven, Father. Farewell." He switched off the phone, and looked up to see Garcia driving into the alley behind a row of buildings.

"We have arrived, my lord." The *tresora* parked the car in front of a steel door marked COBURN FINE JEWELERS and retrieved a case from the floor.

At the door Jamys watched him pick the lock in seconds and, once inside, disarm the security system with a quick bypass circuit. "For a policeman, you have the skills of an accomplished thief."

"Often Lord Alenfar requires me to work on both sides of the law." Garcia nodded toward the interior.

"The shutters have been lowered so you will not be seen from the street. I will stand guard here."

Jamys went to the front of the shop, where the Persian rug Stryker had described had been laid out in front of the display cases. He knelt down and rolled it aside to reveal the large decorative tiles beneath, and ran the tip of his dagger along each one before he found a seam, and used the tip of his blade to dislodge the tile over the floor safe. A keypad set into the safe's door was the only access point, but he punched through it and gripped the side of the hole left behind to wrench open the steel lid.

A large black velvet case lay inside, and when Jamys removed it and opened the lid, he found it filled with trays of glittering emeralds in every shape imaginable. Yet when he came to the very bottom tray, which had three deep, fist-size impressions in the cloth, he found it empty.

Lucan had been correct; Coburn no longer possessed the Emeralds of Eternity. Jamys sat back on his heels and pushed the trays aside, eyeing the safe and the dull metal at the very bottom. He frowned and reached in, taking out the false bottom to expose a layer of bricks sealed in plastic, a thin electronic device, and coils of wire.

Like most Kyn, Jamys trained in the use of weapons of every era; he knew exactly what it was and how to employ it.

He reached for the trays of emeralds, and sorted through them until he found three round specimens that were only slightly smaller than the recesses in the empty tray. He glanced around the shop, rising to go to a display of golden jewelry cases, and chose one large enough to contain the black velvet tray. He then placed that and everything he needed in the bag, closed the safe, and re-covered it before joining Garcia at the back door.

"Did you find what you needed, my lord?" the *tresora* asked.

Will you die for her? the monk's voice mocked inside his head.

"Yes," he told them both.

Chapter 19

Chris followed Sam back into the garden, where Werren stood alone by the fountain. "Where are the other women?"

"It matters not." She bent to pluck a white rose and twirled it between her fingers. "If you wish to escape, I will not stop you. But you will not use any of us."

"I forgot, she has Kyn hearing," Samantha said as she walked up to the other women. "As long as you maintain whatever illusion is cloaking us right now, they won't see or hear us."

Werren smiled. "I will protect them from anything you do."

Samantha walked past her, turned, and brought her fist down on the other woman's nape. "Not if you're taking a nap." She caught Werren as she and the garden fell, and eased her down to the deck.

Chris glanced at the hostile faces of the other women surrounding them. "Your friend is okay; Sam just knocked her out. Werren wouldn't let us talk to the rest of you."

An old woman stepped forward. "Werren takes care

of us. We cannot have the garden without her. We are not interested in what you have to say."

"You want to rumble, Grandma?" Sam asked. "Bring it over here."

"Look, we're all in—on—the same boat," Chris said. "As long as you stay here, things will only get worse."

"The master is not always cruel," the pretty brunette said. "If we are obedient, he mostly ignores us."

"Every woman who has tried to escape Purgatory has been killed," the old woman said. "A dismal life here is better than burning forever in damnation. At least we have a chance to redeem ourselves in the eyes of God."

Sam approached her. "This isn't Purgatory. You're still alive in the real world; you've just been changed from mortal to immortal."

"What manner of immortal?"

"We heal spontaneously, have unique powers, and we don't age or die," Sam told her. "We're called the Darkyn."

Some of the women laughed; others appeared shocked; all of them looked frightened. The old woman went over to the covered barrel standing where the fountain had been and pried off the lid to look inside.

Chris went over to her. "Your name is Analise, isn't it?"

"Aye." She stared down at the dark contents of the barrel. "Werren would never let us drink until after she summoned the garden. She did not wish us to know we were drinking *blood*." She glanced up at Chris. "We are monsters. Vampires?"

"You're Darkyn," Chris corrected. "You're part of a superhuman race that is powerful and hard to kill, but that has also learned how to coexist peacefully with humans. Sam is Kyn, too."

Analise eyed her friend, who was talking to some of the other women. "There are others like us?"

"Thousands." Chris nodded. "All over the world. They live together in strongholds called *jardins*, and work together to live productive lives, and protect each other. They have many human friends and allies, like me, who help keep their existence secret."

"Why were we not permitted to live with them?" Analise asked. "Is it because we are women?"

"The other Darkyn out there don't even know about you, or that Dutch forced the change on you," Chris said. "I'm guessing he's been keeping you here because he's a sick bastard who hates women."

Analise had more questions, and Chris tried to answer them as honestly as she could. She could hear Sam doing the same for the rest of the women, until a low groan from Werren silenced all of them.

Analise went over and helped the blond woman to her feet. "Why did you never tell us the truth?"

"Learning what I was almost drove me mad." Werren rubbed the back of her neck. "I only wished to spare you."

"Spare us?" Analise slapped her, making Werren stagger backward. "We have been prisoners for centuries, made to whore for Dutch and the crew and any man who crooked a finger, when we might have escaped and found the others like us. You did not spare us. You damned us to hell."

"Do you remember Lonora? Estelle? Marielle?" Werren countered. "No, you would not. They were the first women he changed. The women I told the truth to. They all tried to escape, but Dutch stopped them with a thought. He beheaded each one of them in front of me.

That is why I did not tell you, Analise. Because I did not wish to toss your severed head to the waves, and swab your blood from the deck."

"You had no right," the old woman insisted.

"I did what I thought was best for you. For all of you." She turned to Sam. "Are you pleased with yourself, Detective? Now that they know, they will never again be content, and he will kill them, one by one, and start over."

"He can't turn any more women," Sam said gently. "Over time the process of the change has become lethal to humans, something else he kept from you. You and the others are all the immortal women he'll ever have."

Werren looked uncertain. "But Dutch intends to change the crew. That is why he brought the man here, and tortured him until he died. He had stolen the gems that made Dutch immortal. Once he has rule over the warriors and the stronghold on the mainland, he will send out those men to search until they find the treasure. With it Dutch will be able to change as many mortals as he pleases. Then he can build a fleet of ships manned by men who will never die, and go a-pirating forever."

"*That's* why he wants the emeralds?" Chris shook her head. "The jackass is starting to believe his own legend."

"Yeah, well, the Flying Dutchman is about to crash and burn." Sam looked around at the faces of the other women. "And we're going to be the ones who take him down."

"For the first time in its seventy-six-year history, Fort Lauderdale's annual Holiday on the Waves boat regatta has been rescheduled due to mechanical failures at four local bridges," WSVN weatherman Brent Cameron reported. "All of the affected bridges have been closed, and the hundreds of vessels registered to participate have been temporarily relocated out to sea while city engineers address the problems. City officials are confident that repairs will be made in time for the boat parade to take place on New Year's Eve."

Lucan switched off the television set and regarded Aldan and Burke. "*Four* bridges?"

"We considered shutting down five, my lord, but that would have caused serious traffic delays around the stadium," Burke said. "The Dolphins are hosting the Redskins tonight."

"Our friends in the Coast Guard report that they have successfully diverted all private and commercial vessels away from the strike zone, my lord," Aldan said. "The fleet is fully manned, heavily armed, and awaiting your orders."

"Excellent." Lucan went to his wall map of the Florida coast. "We will approach en masse and split into north and south divisions here." He indicated a spot a half mile from the strike coordinates. "The front line will disable any defensive weaponry first and then assume holding positions until I give the order to attack and board. The second lines are to move in to form a blockade. Nothing leaves Vander's vessel alive but Samantha, Christian, and the captive mortals."

"Yes, my lord." Aldan bowed and left the office.

Before he did the same, Burke took out a sheathed dagger, and offered it to Lucan. "If I may, my lord, I would ask that you take this into battle with you. I know you have no need of conventional weapons, but it belonged to my grandfather, and it always brought him luck."

Lucan drew out the old steel dagger. "I recall meeting a Burke in Berlin. He led the *tresori* resistance, and helped us free the Kyn captured by the Brethren among the Gestapo."

Burke nodded. "He considered you—and I will quote him—'the deadliest son of a bitch ever to walk the night.'" He smiled a little. "You also saved his life by intercepting a hail of Nazi bullets meant for him."

"I had forgotten that." Lucan clipped the sheath to his belt. "Is this why you volunteered to become my *tresora*, Herbert?"

"Choosing a lord to serve is a complex matter, but I would say that part of my motivation was the fact that my grandfather did not sire my father until *after* the war. Good hunting, my lord." The *tresora* bowed and departed.

Before he left the stronghold, Lucan went to the bar that had been smashed to hell during his brief battle with Jamys, and used Burke's dagger to pick up the golden medallion from the floor.

Although he was sorely tempted to fling the phony tribute into the sea, he carried it to Christian's office, where he draped it over one corner of the framed portrait of Darth Vader. He'd always known about her private nickname for him, of course, and had in fact secretly delighted in it.

"Tonight, my sweet girl," he murmured, "I believe I shall earn it."

After helping him with his final preparations, Garcia drove Jamys to the county's oceanside dock, where he gave him the keys to the newest of the DEA's speedboats, a sleek arrow of black and silver with four massive engines. "Are you certain you do not wish me to pilot for you, my lord?"

"Burke will have need of you at the stronghold." Jamys surveyed the horizon. "If I must use the gems, please relay my apologies to Lord Alenfar and his lady."

Garcia nodded. "And Miss Lang?"

He could think of a thousand things he wanted to tell Christian, but settled for the one he wanted her to remember most. "Tell my wife that I love her."

Garcia helped him launch, and from the boatyard Jamys headed out to sea. A bitter wind rose, flinging needling spray into his face as he opened up the throttle and pushed the powerful engines to full capacity. The hull sliced across the waves as the boat raced south, a shadow flying through the night.

As the miles passed and Jamys drew closer to the rendezvous point, he allowed himself to relive every moment he had experienced with Christian since returning to Alenfar. He could not regret a moment of it; he had lived more and better in the handful of nights they had spent together than he had in all the centuries since he had risen to walk the night. She had given him the gift of herself and her heart; he knew what it was to love and be loved by the other half of his soul. If he died tonight, and he suspected there was an excellent chance that he would, he would go with but one regret: that he had to leave her behind.

A half mile from the rendezvous point, Jamys switched off the boat's running lights, changed course, and headed east, guiding the speedboat between the fleet and the shoreline as he raced ahead of Lucan's front line. As he had hoped, the roar of the hundreds of engines heading toward Vander's ship masked the sound of his, and he was able to pull ahead of Lucan and the garrison without alerting them to his presence.

He spotted the bizarre silhouette of Vander's floating stronghold, which appeared to be cobbled together from an old pirate ship, an ultramodern yacht, and clusters of smaller boats tethered to them. No lights shone from any of the decks, but he detected the shapes of a dozen men standing watch on the old ship.

Once he shut down the engines, Jamys looped the strap of the waterproof bag Garcia had given him around his neck, and dived off the side of the speedboat.

Jamys took care not to resurface until he had reached the stern of the old ship. There he caught hold of the massive, rusted anchor chain and looked up at the remains of the letters that had long ago been carved into the rotted wood above his head: *OLDE OR E.*

He drew a dagger, clamping it between his teeth, and began to climb hand over hand up the chain. When he came within a foot of the railing, he jumped, catching hold of the edge of the upper deck and using it to pull himself up to eye level.

Women in ragged tunics stood behind each of the men standing guard, and in their hands held broken pieces of glass. Samantha and an old woman were walking across a makeshift bridge to the yacht; Christian stood with her back against the mainmast beside a fair-haired woman whose eyes were closed.

Even more astonishing, Vander's men walked past the pair without giving any sign that they noticed them.

The woman standing beside Chris opened her eyes and looked directly at Jamys, and then disappeared from sight, along with Chris, the other women, and Samantha.

Jamys knew of a few Kyn capable of creating illu-

sions—his mother had been one—but none so powerful
they could bespell an entire ship of mortals and Kyn
alike.

He released his grip on the deck, and plummeted
back into the water. He could hear the front line of the
fleet approaching now, and knew in a few minutes Lucan
would attack. He gauged the distance he would have to
swim to reach the yacht, where there were no guards, and
sank beneath the waves.

Sam broke the lock on the yacht's main cabin door, and
slipped inside as quietly as she could. The stink of gasoline made her hold her breath as she scanned the darkened casino, where hundreds of patrons huddled in
miserable clusters between several corpses that had
been executed with head shots, probably to intimidate
the rest of the hostages.

Knowing the smell of the gas and the ballroom di-
mensions of the cabin would make using *l'attrait* virtually impossible, Sam fell back on her knowledge of
movies and human nature.

"Ladies and gentlemen," she called out in a firm, clear
voice. "I'm with the Miami Bomb Squad. Several explo-
sive devices have been planted all over this casino to set
off the gasoline. My team and I can't defuse them until
we move you to a safe distance. I need you to be quiet
and follow my instructions exactly, because if you don't,
you will set off these bombs. Stay where you are until I
come to your group."

Sam went to the nearest bunch sitting around the rou-
lette wheel. "You, you, and you," she said, pointing to
obvious couples. "Hold hands and walk out onto the
deck. Wait at the railing and don't make a sound." As a

fat man lunged up from another group and tried to run past her, she caught him and shoved him back down. "Do that again, pal, and you'll be the last to go."

As she worked her way around the room, a few more jackasses tried similar tactics, which she countered easily, and one elderly man offered her a million dollars in exchange for letting him be first one off the ship.

Sam shook her head. "What happened to letting the women and children go first?"

"There aren't any kids," the old man told her, "and if you get a better offer from one of the women, I'll double it."

She took a moment to step close and shed enough scent to affect him. "You just volunteered to be the last one out of here. Also, if you do survive, you're going to donate that million dollars to Gamblers Anonymous."

"Last. Million. Gamblers." He nodded and sat back down.

Once the rest of the hostages had been sent out, Sam led the old man out onto the deck and moved to a spot where the breeze would help spread her scent. The night sky and cold air chased off the lingering fatigue of day, and she was able to bring the crowd under her command in a few minutes. She sorted them into lines according to how many she thought each of the smaller boats could carry, and issued her final instructions.

"Climb one at a time down the ladders. As soon as the last person is on board, start the boat engines and drive north away from the yacht to Biscayne Bay." She heard the sound of approaching engines and quickly finished with, "Dock your boats at the pier where the ferry picked you up, get into your cars, and go home."

The hostages began shuffling toward the ladders as

Sam ran to the starboard side of the yacht. Hundreds of small boats were closing in, each carrying warriors dressed in black and armed with rifles and swords. On the bow of the frontmost cruiser stood Lucan, his corn-silk mane tied back from his grim face, his hands empty and bare.

"No, no, not until we get them out of here." Sam took off at a flat run for the walkway between the casino and the old ship.

Chris pressed back against the mast as two more guards walked within inches of her and Werren. Although she knew they couldn't see or hear them, she still whispered. "How long do you think it'll take Sam to get the people out of the casino?"

"Not very long," Werren said. "Dutch ordered all the guards over to the *Horde*." She hesitated before she asked, "If we live through this, what will happen to us?"

"You won't be sex slaves anymore." Chris glanced at her. "Why?"

Her mouth tightened. "We have not lived in the world beyond this ship for centuries. When they were mortal, the other women were harlots. This is all we know, this life."

"I used to work in the sex trade," Chris told her. "I had no family, no education, no skills, and it was the only way I could survive. Walking away from that scared me, but not as much as what I knew I'd become if I kept doing it. That's the first step. You've got to want a better future for yourself."

"I have no future. Your master will kill me for abducting his lady." Werren looked miserable. "I deserve it."

"Maybe you do, but that's up to Sam," Chris reminded her. "And if she wanted to kill you, you'd already be dead." She saw a blur of movement overhead on the walkway to the casino. "Sam's coming back. Something must have gone wrong."

"Oh, no." Werren looked out at the boats approaching the ship. "Your master and his men—" Her eyes widened, and she made a choking sound before her expression blanked, and the illusion concealing them abruptly shifted away.

"How like women, to hide what whores they are." Dutch jumped down from the quarterdeck and seized Chris by the throat, holding the blade of his sword in front of her nose. "I had such plans for you, Pearl Girl. You were to be the first I changed once I had back my gems." He dragged her over to the side of the ship. "Now you'll feed me and the sharks."

A shard of glass slashed down in front of Chris's face and smashed against Dutch's fist. Analise threw away the fragments left in her hand. "You turn her loose, Dutchman."

"I never liked tupping you, you old bat, even when you made yourself pretty." He touched the medallion at his throat, and Analise became a statue. "I never want to see your ugly mug again."

The old woman made jerky movements as she clawed at her face, and as Chris shrieked for her to stop, she felt Dutch's breath on her throat and the agonizing stab of his fangs.

Blood poured down her chest when he lifted his mouth and made an obscene sucking sound. "Not as sweet as I thought you'd be." He turned his head as Analise collapsed to the deck, and Werren staggered over to him, dragging a struggling Sam along with her as she reached out and took the sword Dutch held out to her.

"Let her go," Chris choked out, but Werren pulled Sam away until they disappeared behind the mainmast.

"Lucan," he shouted, and Chris looked down to see her boss standing on the tower of a marlin boat. "Tell your men they and your territory are mine now, or my whore will behead yours."

"He's not here to surrender to you, you fool."

Chris looked over as the two *tresori* traitors appeared, both pointing guns at Dutch.

"What shit do you spew now?" Dutch demanded as he jerked Chris around and used her as a body shield. "You said if I took his woman that he would give me anything to get her back."

"We told you that so you would bring Alenfar here," one of the traitors sneered. "He will be the bait we use to draw out the smith, and find the jewels for our master. For that, we need to control him—with his woman."

"You used me for this?" Dutch sounded stunned. "But the jewels belong to me. Your master be damned."

"You will never have them." The *tresora* grinned, and then froze as a weapon fired. He glanced down with a puzzled expression at the front of his suit, and the gun he held pressed against the wet scarlet stain on his shirt.

"Anything gold touches is mine," Dutch said, his tone gloating. "Like the ring on your finger."

The *tresora* shot himself a second time and toppled over.

Dutch turned his head toward Werren, who was rushing toward him, and she stopped in her tracks. As the second *tresora* saw her lift the sword she still carried, he shot wildly at her. She neatly decapitated him before Sam lunged at her and kicked the sword out of her hand. They struggled for a moment before Sam slammed Werren into the mainmast. As the senseless woman fell against her, Sam hoisted her over her shoulder and started toward Dutch and Chris.

"The mortals lied to you, Hollander," a familiar voice said from behind them. "Coburn hid the jewels in a secret cache, which I found. I have brought them back to you."

Dutch dragged Chris around to face Jamys, who stood on the other side of the deck. Chris shook her head wildly, then screamed as the pirate struck a second time, tearing at her throat and drawing out her blood in huge swallows. When Jamys snarled, he raised his head. "You'll get no more use out of her, boy. She's done filled my belly proper. Drop your weapons."

Sam surged forward and nearly dropped Werren. "You bastard."

"All will be well, my lady." Jamys removed his daggers and dropped them onto the deck, kicking them away. To Dutch he said, "Release Lady Samantha and the other women, and I will give you the gems . . . and my head."

"Now, that is what I call a fair bargain." Dutch reached over and shoved Samantha and Werren over the side, and bellowed at the other women to jump.

Chris felt cold, but she was too tired to shiver. She looked into Jamys's eyes, and felt his thoughts entwine with hers. He meant to kill them both to stop Dutch and save the others, but he wasn't afraid. Neither was she, Chris realized, and her heart skipped a beat as she began to droop. She used the last of her strength to whisper her agreement: "Yes."

Jamys put a golden jeweler's case on the deck, and shoved it across to Dutch, who pushed Chris away as he bent down to grab it. Then Jamys was there, lifting her in his arms, his lips cold against her brow.

"Three hundred years I've waited to behold these beauties again," Dutch crooned as he fumbled with the latch on the case. "My pretty green rocks, what fortune we will know together."

Chris felt her lungs flatten, and the thud of her heart slowing, and turned her face into Jamys's chest.

"What is this?" Dutch growled. "These are not the emeralds that made me immortal."

"No." Jamys lifted a small device with a thumb switch. "They are not."

Chris closed her eyes as Jamys pressed the switch, and the world turned to fire.

Chapter 20

After the fire came the darkness, and the icy wind, and stars that filled up her burning eyes until she thought she would weep light. She put out her hand to touch them, and watched a small golden angel circle around it, kissing her fingertips.

Dying is like falling, Chris thought as she drifted down, Alice in the rabbit hole. *Jamys. Will you be there to catch me?*

I am here. Jamys reached for her from above. *Take my hands.*

But it's so lovely here. The terrible pain in her neck had gone, and so had the frightening gush of blood. She felt nothing but a drowsy peace now that she was dead. She wanted him to fall from earth with her, his arms around her as they danced with the angels.

Jamys kicked his way through the night to her, but when he took her in his arms, he tugged her back toward the light. *Come with me, love,* he murmured, holding her when she tried to pull away. *You promised you would take me with you. Let me show you the way to heaven.*

The light hurt her eyes, and so did the press of the

night as it tried to drag her back. She opened her mouth to tell him, and tasted the air, heavy and thick, like breathing in tears.

The night exploded into flames, shattered wood, icy slaps, and stinging hot wind. She writhed as Jamys turned her around, pressing his arm into her chest and forcing the tears from her mouth. The pain returned, huge and unbearable, bathing her inside and out with its merciless fires.

This was not heaven. He'd brought her to hell.

Jamys dragged her through the nightmare, slowly, steadily, until he lifted her and flung her onto an altar of icy metal. Chris rolled onto her back, her arms and legs clumsy, her hands clutching at nothing.

He lifted her again, carrying her through sloshing water to another hard place where she lay stunned and wretched as he pushed the dripping hair out of her face.

Stay with me, love, he whispered inside her head. *Stay with me, and I will take you back to Paradise.*

Chris closed her eyes. *Hurry, Jamys. Please hurry.*

Slowly the horrible pain faded, and the night returned for her, seducing her back to the comforting darkness. Yet each time she tried to lose herself in it, Jamys was there, his hands against her face, his mouth on hers, the sad poetry of his voice pouring into her heart.

Keep fighting for me.

My love.

You are stronger than you know.

My life.

Paradise awaits us.

My woman.

Never leave me.

My wife.

Chris slipped between the darkness and Jamys, floating to and fro until she thought she would never get off the languid carousel. Then something cool and wet touched her lips, and filled her with such sweetness that she thought the pleasure of it would swallow up her soul.

Drink of my love for you, Christian.

Instead of the night a dull grayness came over her, and dragged her away, taking Jamys along, too. How long they remained there, she didn't know, but he held on to her even then, and refused to be parted from her.

If you will not stay with me, then I will go with you.

When she lifted her head she was standing on the beach, her body draped in an old, soft man's shirt, her hair blowing in her eyes. When she lifted a hand to push it back, she realized there was so much more of it than she'd had before; the wind drew it out in long, gleaming dark curls.

It dismayed her until she recalled something she'd read once about death. *When you die, your hair keeps growing.*

The island was just as quiet as she remembered, and the dark waters surrounding it were just as empty. The shy half-moon slipped behind a streamer of dark cloud, and on the horizon, the first ribbon of dark amethyst stretched, wrapping the gift of the coming dawn.

Jamys came up behind her, and encircled her waist with his arms. *It's all right, love. Come back to bed.*

Is that where we were? She leaned back against him. *I can't remember. I don't know how I got here.*

I brought you. He turned her to face him, and his expression was so tight and drawn she lifted her fingers to stroke his cheek. *I thought I had lost you.*

I must have been sleepwalking. She reached up to touch her mouth to his, and felt the faintest stirring of a strange hunger. *I love Paradise. I never want to leave it again.*

Nor do I. He tugged her close, and tucked her head under his chin. *But we cannot stay here forever. It is time for us to go.*

She pulled back. *Go where?*

Sam stood at the boardwalk railing and surveyed the deserted beach. She'd never once seen it so empty. Always determined to enjoy their tropical vacation no matter what, the snowbirds and out-of-towners would brave anything from freezing temperatures to gale-force winds. But tonight no one occupied the golden sands or paddled in the blue-green ocean, and the only light came from the flames blazing along two rows of bronze braziers marching down to the water's edge.

Between each ivory pole stood a *jardin* warrior dressed in a dark suit. Each man wore a black armband, and held a sword across the gap between the braziers to form a canopy of steel.

Sam felt Lucan approaching a moment before the scent of night-blooming jasmine wrapped around her. "How did you get rid of the tourists?"

"Only with gentle persuasion." Night-blooming jasmine engulfed her as a velvet-gloved hand touched the small of her back. "You need not do this, love. I can see to it."

"No." She hated funerals almost as much as she despised death, and she was so tired. But Chris had been the sister that mortal life had never given her, and she had died with Jamys to save them all. Sam looked down at the wreath of red and white roses that Burke had given her. "I have to let her go."

Lucan turned his head as a group of dark-cloaked figures approached them. His gray eyes turned to chrome as they halted several feet away. "I granted you and your sisters freedom, Duchess. Now I suggest you use it to leave my territory."

The tallest stepped forward and politely pushed back her hood. "Forgive our intrusion, Suzerain, but we are not yours to command. We are hers." Werren's gaze shifted to Sam's face. "My lady. May we be allowed to pay our respects to your friends?"

She didn't want to do this now, either. "Yeah, sure." She gestured toward the braziers. "We'll join you in a minute."

Once the women had moved away, Lucan turned to her. "Yours to command, is it? That would mean they gave you their oath. Their blood oath."

"Things on the ship got a little crazy," she reminded him. "I didn't ask for it, but Werren insisted, because if they didn't, they couldn't help us, and with all the brainwashing Dutch did to them I thought . . . look, you had to be there, okay?"

He glanced down at the women. "What in God's name are you going to do with fifty-three immortal sex slaves?"

"I don't know," she admitted. "Buy them some decent clothes. Find them better jobs." She couldn't think of anything else.

His lips twitched. "Surprise me on my birthday?"

Sam didn't recognize the laugh that escaped her, nor could she end it. She laughed and laughed until the sound shriveled in her throat and wretchedness overtook her. She saw her fists hit her lover's jacket before they opened to clutch at it, and as Lucan's arms came around her to keep her upright, she felt something fall inside her.

I owe you a life. Chris's face came back to her in every detail: the lightning flash of her smile, the glow of laughter and love in her eyes. *Let me save yours.*

She swallowed until the sobbing retreated to her heart. "God, I miss her so much."

Lucan held her until she calmed, and kept one arm around her as he reached down to pick up the wreath that had fallen at her feet. He produced a silk handkerchief and gently dried the tears from her face before he tucked her against his side. "Come now. We'll say goodbye to them together."

As they walked down between the torches to the water, the men bowed their heads, and Werren and the other women curtsied. Lucan stopped, turning around with her as he surveyed the other Kyn.

"We all of us know loss," he said, his voice deep and soft. "Families and friends, loving and beloved. Those who walked with us in life, who were taken from us in peace and in battle. Tonight we count among them our warrior brother Lord Jamys Durand, and our mortal sister Christian Lang. I know they wished only to be together." He glanced down at the wreath of flowers. "They sacrificed their love, and their lives, so that all of the Dutchman's other victims might escape. I will never forget their courage or their generosity."

Sam reached into her pocket and took out the heart-shaped crystal Chris had left behind on her desk. "One day you were a tough little street kid, and the next you'd become this strong, smart woman. You were more than a friend to me. You became my sister. I didn't realize it was happening. Before you I never had a family. I don't know why I never told you that. I should have." Sam tucked the crystal into the heart of one of the red roses, closing its petals over it before she looked out at the sea. "Take care of her for me, Jamie."

Sam placed the wreath on the edge of the next wave that rolled in, and straightened to watch the sea carry it out with the tide. It floated for a long time, whirling in a slow circle before a long curl of foam swept over it and it disappeared from sight.

Werren and the other women came to stand beside Sam and Lucan. As the courtesan murmured something in an old language, each woman tossed a coin into the water. Sam thought it was some Kyn variety on a wishing well before she realized the coins they were giving to the sea were actually Dutch's golden medallions.

"You're going to make some guy with a metal detector very rich tomorrow," Sam said to Werren.

"'Tis fitting," the courtesan said. "Dutch loved his gold as deeply as he hated mortals. Your lord has made it clear that we are unwelcome here, my lady. Do you wish us to go away now?"

"Is that what you and the girls want to do?"

Werren glanced at Lucan before she answered. "We have been a long time kept away from the world. None of us know how to properly conduct ourselves. But we have seen that you have very few Kyn females among your *jardin*, and men cannot properly attend to you and your ladies." Werren nodded at the men of the garrison. "In exchange for sanctuary and instruction on how to live in this world, we will make ourselves your maidservants."

"You were slaves. You don't have to be maids or serve anyone for any reason, ever again." The sound of a boat motor penetrated Sam's misery, and she looked down the length of the pier to see the vague shape of a speedboat running slow and without lights. To Lucan, she said, "I think your gentle persuasion just wore off."

Sam followed Lucan as he headed for the pier. "Don't bother chasing them away," she said, peering at the pair who had stepped off the boat. "We're pretty much done here."

Lucan stopped in his tracks. "On this I fear I must disagree with you, love."

"What's this? You're arguing with me, instead of treating me like ... an ... invalid." The scent carried on the breeze reminded Sam of sandalwood and orange blossoms, and hit her like a sap to the skull. *"Jamie?"*

It couldn't be them, of course. The tall boy barely had an inch of dark hair covering his head, while the girl beside him had long, luxurious curls that fell to her waist. But as they drew closer, Sam saw their faces and grabbed Lucan's hand. "You can disagree with me any time you like, my man."

"My lord, my lady." Jamys bowed and surveyed the Kyn staring at them from the beach. "Forgive the intrusion, which I hope is welcome."

"You're forgiven." Sam launched herself at him, hugging him before she turned to grab Chris. "You exploded with the ship. We just did the funeral thing for you." She kissed her friend, hugged her, and then shook her. "Where the hell have you been? Why didn't you call us? Were you in a hospital? You blew up. I *saw* you blow up."

"Yeah, we did kind of blow up. After that, I was really

lost in space," Chris said, and made a pained face. "And sort of dead for a week."

Lucan took hold of her chin and studied her face. "She is no longer mortal." He eyed Jamys. "You changed her. How?"

"Wait," Sam said, looking over at the other Kyn. "Let's go say hello to everyone who was just mourning you, and head back to the stronghold where we can have this discussion in private."

It took some time to do that, as all the warriors and the women from the ship gathered around them to express their surprise and happiness. Lucan finally dismissed the men, and sent Aldan to take the women to one of their hotels. Once they reached the penthouse, however, Jamys had little in the way of answers to offer.

"The explosion sent us both into the water on the far side of the ship. At first I was separated from Christian, but after an hour of searching I found her, and brought her to the surface. By that time the fleet had left, but I was able to swim with her to where I left my boat anchored. From there I took her to a house on a nearby private island, where she remained with hardly a spark of life in her for the next week. I waited for as long as I dared to see if she would make the change. I was preparing to bring her back to the mainland when she awoke as she is."

Lucan frowned at Chris. "What is that mark on her neck?"

"This?" Chris tugged down the collar of her T-shirt to display a cross-shaped burn scar. "The blast drove my mom's crucifix into my skin. Jamys said he had to dig it out of me, and then things really got weird."

"When I removed the cross, the open wound glowed with a green light," Jamys said. "A few moments later, it healed itself from the inside out."

"Did you use your blood to heal it?" Sam asked.

"No, but when Chris began to slip away, I fed her from my veins. It was a foolish act of pure desperation." He glanced at Lucan. "I mean no offense, my lord."

"I am only too well acquainted with those feelings, Jamys." He regarded Chris. "You survived a lethal explosion and an hour under the water, so whatever changed you happened before the bomb went off."

"Nothing happened. Well, besides Dutch practically draining me dry." Chris reached up and touched the scar on her neck. "This sounds crazy, I know, but I think it might have been my mom's cross. Like maybe God decided to give me and Jamys another chance."

Sam had seen too many murders to believe in that kind of God, but she was so happy to have Chris back she didn't care what had done the dirty work. "How do you feel about being one of the fang gang?"

"Still trying to get used to it." She laced her fingers through Jamys's. "When I first came to, I thought I was in the afterlife. A really great afterlife. When Jamys told me that I'd changed, and we could finally be together, well . . ." She smiled at Lucan. "I love you both, and I loved being an almost-*tresora*, but I quit."

Epilogue

Durand Stronghold
Freeport, Bahamas

"How long is that boy going to pace the floor out there?" Dr. Alexandra Keller asked as she finished checking Chris Durand's pupil reactions.

"Until you let me change out of this paper towel and I can go reassure him I'm okay." Chris fluttered her lashes. "So tell me I'm okay, Doc."

"You're more than okay. You've made a beautiful, complete transition and all of the wounds you sustained in the explosion have healed cleanly." She clicked off her penlight. "All you have to do is give me some more blood, tell me what superpower you got stuck with, and I'm outta here."

"I don't know the name for my ability," Chris admitted. "I could show you how it works, though." She eyed the door, and a low sound came from the other side. "I can touch another Kyn without actually touching them. I haven't tried it on mortals yet, but it probably works on them, too."

"Psychic touchy-feely." Alex made a note in the chart. "Now, that's a new one."

Chris grinned. "My range is pretty good, too. I can be a mile away and give him a kiss." She blew one at the door, which resulted in a soft groan. "Anywhere on his body."

"Let's keep it PG-rated while I'm here." Alex closed the chart and sat down on the chair next to the bed. "Chris, the fact is you're too young to be Kyndred, so you weren't changed because you already had vampire DNA. Just to be sure, I double-checked the blood work the *jardin* doc did on you when you started working at the stronghold. You went from ordinary human to Kyn without any help, except maybe this." She tapped the top of the cross-shaped scar. "I think your cross might have had similar properties to one that may have recently turned a Frenchwoman from mortal to Kyn."

"Does it matter?"

"It might." Alex hesitated before she said, "I compared your old blood tests to hers to see what genes you might share, and I discovered you have quite a lot in common. Your profiles indicate that you and Simone have the same parent. She's your half sister."

"But I'm an only child." She went still as she recalled what Frankie had told her. "My father was some guy my mother met while she was on vacation in France. Is he still . . . ?"

Alex made a face. "Sorry, sweetheart. He died of leukemia ten years ago." She touched Chris's shoulder. "But hey, you've got a sister over there, and she's made the change, too. If it's okay, I'd like to let her know about you."

"Let me talk to Jamys about it first. We don't want any

more new drama." When Alex gave her a blank look, Chris added, "For saving Sam's life, Lucan convinced your guy to give Jamys rule over the Caribbean islands. The *tresoran* council believes I was killed in the explosion on the *Golden Horde*, and so do the traitors. The few people who know different aren't going to expose me. We're safe here, and we're happy. End of drama."

"What about the emeralds Richard wants?" Alex asked. "You and Jamys have any ideas where they are?"

"We traced them to a jeweler in Fort Lauderdale, but they were stolen from him and have vanished again." She shrugged. "Not like we need them anymore."

"If Richard finds out you were changed, you're going to have plenty of drama on your hands," the doctor warned her. "So just keep a low profile for now, and we'll let you know what happens with this idiot gem quest." She went to the door and opened it suddenly, startling Jamys. "She's all yours."

"Yes." Jamys smiled at Chris. "She is."

After Dr. Keller had left, Jamys and Chris went for a walk on the beach, where some of the women were sitting and watching the waves.

"My lord, my lady." Werren got to her feet and dusted off her hands. "Did all go as expected with the leech?"

"We call them doctors now," Chris said, and nodded. "I'm doing fine. How about you and the ladies?"

"Very well, thank you."

When Jamys had offered to bring the women from the *Golden Horde* down to the islands with them, Sam had been grateful, Lucan annoyed, and Chris uncertain. But since arriving, the women had worked tirelessly to help set up their household and keep things running smoothly, and were now talking about opening some gift and clothing shops to bring in some additional income for the *jardin*.

"A courier brought a package from Lord Alenfar while you were being examined," Werren said. "I left it on the night table by your bed."

Chris looped her arm through Jamys's as they walked back up to the main house. "Do you think it's the emeralds, and he wants us to hide them from Richard?"

He kissed the top of her head. "I am too busy hiding *you* from Richard."

In the bedchamber Chris opened the small package, which contained a folded note and Father Bartley's journal. "Someone's been borrowing things from museums without permission." She opened the note to read it out loud. "'Burn this, bury it, but do not let it fall into the hands of another mortal fool. L.'" She tried to hand the note and the journal to Jamys, but the binding split suddenly and the pages from the journal dropped to the floor. "Terrific, I broke it."

Jamys crouched down and picked up the pages, but when he tried to replace them in the binding, he stopped and lifted one of the inner flaps. "There is something under here." He took out a yellowed, folded piece of parchment and opened it to reveal an old map of Florida.

"There are some roads or trails marked." She peered at what had been written in the faded ink in one corner. "This looks like directions to somewhere in central Florida." She pointed to three gem-shaped symbols drawn next to a circled area. "This could be the first mate's map." She looked up at Jamys. "What if the pirate who confessed to Bartley stole it before he jumped ship?"

"We can no longer pursue this quest without exposing you to the high lord." Jamys took the map from her, folded it up, and placed it in a plain envelope. "We should send it to the Kyn lord who rules over the territory marked on the map, and let him decide what to do with it."

"Her," Chris corrected. "The suzeraina of Orlando is Jayr mac Byrne." She took a pen and jotted the address of Jayr's stronghold on the envelope before she put it and the journal aside. "Do you think the emeralds are somewhere in her territory?"

"I do not care where they are," Jamys said as he drew her down to the bed. "I have the only treasure I want right here."

Continue reading for a special preview
of the next Lords of the Darkyn novel,

Nightbound

Coming from Signet Select in May 2013

Beaumaris knew some humans were born with the natural ability to resist *l'attrait*, the scent produced by the Kyn that allowed them to influence and control mortals. A few were even immune to it, but those mortals were so rare that he had never before personally encountered one.

Until now.

He watched Alys as she retreated into the lobby, her limbs easy in her loose khaki garments, a thick bunch of her fiery hair bobbing from where she'd pulled it through the back of her cap. She intercepted a porter to speak with him before moving on to the elevators. Not once did she glance back at him.

To her I am nothing more than a human male in a bar.

Beau had not bothered with mortal females for so long that the annoyance he now felt with this one gave him pause. Like all Kyn, he had indulged himself with human women from time to time, enjoying their welcoming warmth and the fragile sweetness of their passions. None had ever touched his heart, however, and over the centuries the lovers he had taken had become an endless procession of willing lips and caressing hands, the blur of their features fading from his memory even as he slipped out of their beds.

Alys. Even her name intrigued him.

This cheeky wench had been neither willing nor welcoming; perhaps that was what rendered her so singular. Her taste in clothing was nothing short of appalling, but even her wretchedly fitted garments could not disguise her charms. Tall and slender as a yearling filly, Alys had been graced with skin like sunlit snow, the eyes of a fawn, and the mouth of an enchantress.

Save for that startled look she had given him when he'd first spoken to her, she'd also shown as much interest in him as she might a potted plant.

Testing the depth of her resistance would please him to no end, but Beau had to find Stuart. Once Alys had disappeared from view, he began making his way along the bar. None of the men answered to the name or knew the man he sought. Exasperated, Beau went to the reception desk and compelled the clerk to give him a key card to Stuart's room on the seventh floor.

From outside the door to Stuart's room he heard the sound of the shower and let himself in. He didn't interrupt the mortal's bath, but used the time to inspect the man's cases. He carried no weapons but had filled one case with electronic gadgetry and a second with large old books. He opened one volume to read the title page, but the words were beyond his understanding.

He tossed the book back into the case, infuriated by his own anger. As a mortal he had been taught to fight, not read; as an immortal shame had compelled him to hide his ignorance from the other Kyn. When the Realm had nearly fallen to Byrne's bastard half brother and his

Saracen conspirators, Beau had realized that his own, long-kept secrets could be revealed someday. A week after Jayr had been named suzeraina, Beau had gone into the city to seek a solution.

He'd soon learned that anyone could enroll in a literacy class at one of the public libraries; the mortals who taught them were volunteers who required no payment in return. Even better, most classes were held after sunset to benefit those who were obligated to work during the day.

His first teacher, a retired librarian with seemingly endless patience, had prevented him from giving up several times that first month. "Reading is like learning another language," Mrs. Decker would say. "You can't expect to be fluent from the start. You must learn, and practice what you learn."

As a Darkyn, Beau knew himself to be superior to mortals in almost every way; as a reader, he discovered he was painfully slow and made many mistakes. Mrs. Decker began asking him to stay behind after class was dismissed to work with her for another half hour.

"You're fighting this too much, my dear," she'd told him after he'd struggled through a line from his primer. "Words are not bombs, ready to explode if you fumble them. Think of them as more like gifts under the Christmas tree, waiting to be unwrapped." Her finger went to the line he'd mangled. "*Sally*. You know that's the name for the little girl in the story. *Blue* is the color of the sky on a summer day. *Ball* is her brother's favorite toy."

Beau nodded and sounded out the word in the middle of the line. "*Kicks*." He thought for a moment. "What Sally wants to do to her brother's . . . toy."

Mrs. Decker had chuckled. "Exactly."

Beau heard the shower shut off, and replaced the book in the case. Once he used *l'attrait* to bring the professor under his control, he would interrogate him and learn how much he knew about the renegades and how best to lure their leader into Beau's hands.

The bathroom door opened and Alys walked out, her hands busy tucking a towel around her damp body. Beau was so astonished to see her that at first all he did was stare. She stopped as soon as she saw him, turned, and ran for the door.

Beau reached it before she did and slapped a hand against it to keep it closed. She spun around him, and without thinking, Beau clamped an arm around her waist. "You needn't—"

She kicked at him, knocking them both off-balance. As they fell forward, Beau brought up his free arm so that it would land on the carpet before her face, then used it to kept most of his weight off her.

"Be still," he said into her arm as she wriggled under him. Her warm, damp body smelled of almond-scented soap and her own fiery scent. She was not afraid, he realized, but furious, and the scent he was shedding was not affecting her in the slightest. "I am not here to hurt you."

Beau lifted up enough to roll her onto her back, but when she struck at his face he pinned her wrists to the carpet. He glanced down and saw that her towel now lay wadded under her. That was what burned through his garments against his cool skin—the bare front of her body.

"I'll fight you," she promised, "and whatever you do to me, I *will* hurt you."

"This is a mistake." Beau started to lift himself from her, then stopped. "I did not come here to assault you or see you naked, or whatever you are thinking."

"You're on top of me," she pointed out. "I'm naked. You have an erection. What am I supposed to think?"

"I do not . . ." Bloody hell, he was as hard as a club. Softening his voice, he said, "I apologize."

"I'll press charges," she promised. "After I hurt you."

Beau released her wrists and pushed himself up, turning away as quickly as he could. "Cover yourself now, girl." He could hear her crawling backward and wrapping the towel around herself. "I came to see—"

She tried to get at the door again, and he was obliged to trap her against it.

"This didn't work for you the last time," Beau told her. "We can roll about on the floor again or you can listen to me and stop trying to run out of here screaming." She instantly opened her mouth and took in a deep breath, forcing him to clamp his hand over her lips. "That was not a suggestion."

She made an angry, muffled sound.

"Listen to me. I can stuff something in your mouth"— Christ Jesus, why had he said that?—"or you can promise me you will not scream by nodding. What's it to be, then?"

Over the edge of his hand, her eyes narrowed, and then she gave a single nod. As soon as he took his hand away she said, "Would you please get off me?" As soon as he shifted his body away from hers she ducked under his arm and retreated a safe distance. "Now get out of here or I'll call security."

"I can't. I have business with Dr. Stuart." When she moved toward the phone, he added, "I did check with the front desk. The clerk said that his room number was seven-fourteen, and unless they've changed the numbers in the last three minutes, *this* is room seven-fourteen."

She picked up the receiver, placing it on her shoulder before she hitched up the front of the towel. "How did you get in here?"

"You left the door ajar." She wore no ring on her wedding finger, and she didn't behave like a wife. Beau's lust darkened as he imagined her long, graceful body spread beneath some rutting, gray-haired scholar—but surely she was too young for that. "Forgive me, but who are you? The professor's daughter?"

"I didn't leave the door open." Doubt flickered over her features, and her confusion made her seem even younger. "At least I don't think I did." She slowly replaced the receiver. "I'm Dr. Stuart. The *only* Dr. Stuart."

"You can't be." He studied her. "I'm looking for Dr. *Al* Stuart."

"That's me," she insisted. "A. L. Stuart. I use my initials for professional purposes."

Beau dragged a hand through his hair. "You're a woman, and hardly more than a child."

"I'm twenty-six, and I earned my first PhD when I was twenty-one. Excuse me, but I'm uncomfortable talking to you like this." She unzipped a backpack and bent over to rummage through it. "Why did you assume I was a man?"

Beau caught himself admiring the long, elegant lines of her bare legs. "Tremayne told me your name was *Al* Stuart. When we spoke in the bar, you knew I was looking for a man."

"I didn't know who you were or what you wanted, so I was simply being careful." She straightened. "You should have mentioned that you were from the Hylord Foundation."

He inclined his head. "I also happen to be cautious with strangers."

"You mean when you're not tackling them?" She scooped up a robe from the end of the bed. "I have the preliminary excavation schedule prepared. I was going to fax it to Ireland in the morning." She shrugged into the robe, turning her back to him as she let the towel drop to the floor and tied the belt. "I also plan to file progress reports twice a week, if that's acceptable." She faced him, her features completely composed, but her scent was still hot with anger and something more. "Are you with Hylord's local office? Should I e-mail a copy to you?"

Obviously the girl was immune to *l'attrait*, which meant he would have to rely on persuasion. "I have been sent by the—by Hylord to oversee your project."

That startled a laugh out of her. "*You're* an archaeologist?" When he shook his head, her gaze went from his face to his chest and toes, and then flashed up again. "What other digs have you worked on?"

He couldn't deceive her on that score. "This would be my first."

Her jaw set. "I'm sorry, but I can't have this."

"It's done," he assured her. "I'm yours."

Her scent abruptly cooled. "This project is very problematical. I have a great deal of work to do in a very short amount of time." As even as her tone was, her eyes filled with some strange emotion, as if she regretted the words she spoke. "I can't afford to be distracted by someone like you."

She had no choice in the matter, but still her rejection rankled. "Why do you believe that I would be a hindrance?" He gestured at the carpet. "Other than the unfortunate tackling incident, which I promise will not be repeated."

"In order to make accurate reports to the foundation on my progress, you'll have to shadow me constantly." Her lips twisted. "That is the real reason they sent you, isn't it, Mr. . . . ah . . . ?"

"Beauregard York." He offered the Americanized name that he used when among mortals. "Do call me Beau." He offered her his most fetching smile as he lied to her. "I was not sent here to spy on you, Dr. Stuart."

"Logic dictates no other alternative," she informed him. "Your foundation has been very generous, but they've also made several stipulations to ensure secrecy. This is the first major project I've conducted, making me unproven in the field. My peers already consider my theories to be everything from unfounded to ludicrous."

Beau was surprised she could speak so calmly about it. "What would make them believe that?"

"When the Order of the Knights Templar was disbanded by the Pope, some were able to escape. According to my research, at least one of them fled Europe for the Spanish Main, and then sailed from there to Florida. I believe he came here with a group of Spanish priests and with them founded a mission to convert the Timucua natives." She hesitated, tugging at the belt of her robe. "My colleagues think that is nonsensical, but what they flatly refuse to accept is my theory as to the Templars' other motive for coming here."

"You have a second theory?"

She nodded. "Before he left the mission, the Templar concealed something very old and valuable there. I've never been able to precisely identify the artifact he left behind, but I have a very good idea of what it is. I've also published several articles in trade magazines about it, which is why my colleagues think I'm crazy."

Beau wondered what she would say if she knew a former Templar was standing right in front of her. "Your colleagues sound small-minded."

"They're limited by ego and fear. I'm not, although I do understand the risk I'm taking. Failure on my part will put an end to my career, and a connection to me has the potential to damage the foundation's reputation." Alys watched his face. "So, Mr. York. If you're not here to monitor me, then why would they give someone with no archaeological experience this assignment?"

He grinned. "Oh, to manage things."

"And that." She shook a finger at his face. "*That* is the other problem I have with you. You're far too attractive. Half of my interns are young, impressionable girls. I don't want them distracted from their work, especially if you decide to tackle one of them."

So she thinks me handsome. Beau had never been especially vain, but her compliment pleased him. "You seem to think I can do nothing but roll about on the floor with women."

She gave him a tight smile. "I can go only by experience."

"Well, Doctor, I don't. And if your young interns are hoping to impress me, perhaps they'll work harder." Someone knocked on the door behind him, and he glanced through the peephole. "There's an Asian lad standing in the hall. He's carrying a very large case."

"One of my interns. I have some equipment to check." She offered him her hand, and when he took it, she gave him a brisk handshake. "Thank you for stopping in to meet me, Mr. York, but I really can't use you on the project. Please give my regrets and my regards to Mr. Tremayne."